not my fault

A NOVEL

S B FRASCA

Print ISBN: 978-1-66789-677-9

eBook ISBN: 978-1-66789-678-6

Printed in the United States of America on SFI Certified paper.

First Edition

1

NOT MY FAULT. *Non mea culpa.* Funny how it sounds more official in Latin. I guess the two weeks I spent trying to teach myself a dead language wasn't a complete waste of time after all. I really want to stand on the desk and shout it like Julius Caesar but that would be dumb because I'm in the library. The words will have to speak for me.

It's not my fault I'm invisible. I take a quick look around to see if anyone notices me but as usual *I am furniture if not for the breathing.* I read that somewhere and right now I'm grateful. Other times I'm not so grateful.

Before I know it my right hand starts to carve. It slashes at the straight lines of the N with confidence. *Oh yeah* I'm stealth. N is for ninja. Then slowly it drags the knife around the curve of the O. And I'm good too. I have eyes and they don't lie to me. Except maybe when I look in the mirror.

Shhh. I freeze. But there's only silence. To be safe I retract the silver blade and slide it into the secret pocket under the flap of my jacket. I'm not finished but I'll have to move away quick if somebody is coming. But nobody's coming. *Let's be real* nobody is ever coming. My only friends here are books. Big books with big faces of presidents and gods and emperors. They surround me like a fan club and look over my shoulder as I get back to work. They're watching in awe and anticipation. I have to finish *non mea culpa* for them.

"Hy?" I almost fall off my chair at the sound of my name. I know it's my name because it's said like a question.

Yes I call myself Hy. It's shortened from the stupid name my mom gave me and I don't have to change my initials or student ID or anything. And I figured people were gonna make fun of the name she gave me anyway because *I* would if I were them so why not make them say *Hi Hy* or *Hey Hy*? It's funny to watch people try out different combinations because they're the ones who end up sounding awkward no matter what.

Turns out nobody really says much to me anyway except to bother me or call on me in class so at least it sounds like people are saying my name all the time to each other and I can imagine I have lots of friends. When I hear a kid say *let's go get high* I hear *let's go get Hy* and I'm part of the conversation. So maybe I did that on purpose. I don't know.

The only drag is I always have to wait and make sure someone is talking right *to* me and not just saying *Hi* to someone else behind me so I don't look stupid for answering. I also kinda wish my last name was Jinx or Perbole. That would make everyone laugh at roll call and that kind of laughing is okay because I'd be in on the joke. And if I'm in on the joke I'm not *the* joke.

But right now I'm smiling because I know this person is not going to make fun of me. Come to think of it she was probably where the *shhh* came from. This person is the librarian Mrs. Nardo. She's nice enough but she kind of smells like old people. I'm not sure why old people smell like old people. Like it's a perfume they make you buy when you're over seventy or something. I'll have to ask Gram later. I don't think she'll mind me asking because she's pretty cool for old people.

"Hey Mrs. Nardo DaVinci." We have this joke. She doesn't mind because we both have funny names.

"We will be closing in fifteen minutes, Hy." She smiles her old people smile at me and I can tell those aren't her own teeth. It looks like she's wearing one of those mouthguards with teeth drawn on it. But I would never tell her that. My mom taught me to be polite.

"Okay thank you." I feel bad but I want her to leave so she doesn't see what I'm doing.

I can't believe it's almost six. I finished my homework pretty fast so I must've spent buttloads of time on *non mea culpa*. I watch Mrs. Nardo stoop over Ryan Malloy at one of the front tables to tell him she is closing up soon. I think he has earbuds in and didn't hear her the first time. At least I hope so because I don't want to think of Ryan Malloy as being rude. He stacks all his books and shoves them into his badass backpack with surf stickers all over it.

One of the popular girls appears from nowhere with her flock of sheep and puts her hand on his shoulder and he turns around and even from here I can tell she's making those eyes at him. I can't really see her eyes from here but I know. And I can't see his eyes either but I know he's probably making those same eyes at her. Or *eye* actually because there's a hunk of blond hair covering one of them. It gives me a weird feeling. I'm not really sure if it gives me a good weird feeling or a bad weird feeling. I think it's just a feeling I both want and don't want at the same time. If that makes sense.

Anyway how come Mrs. Nardo didn't see *non mea culpa*? I must've been trying to surprise my fan club when she came over and had my arm over it or something. I don't think her eyes are that good

3

anyway. I push my chemistry book away and trace the grooves with my finger because I don't really remember doing it and half of me is hoping it was a dream. My fans are starting to cheer and this time I *shhh* them. Nobody can know it's me. Now I'm sweating bullets so I stand up and head to the door wearing my jacket by the hood like the cool kids do.

Good they're gone. I bet they went to make those eyes at each other somewhere else. Like maybe the dark hallway by the janitor's closet. I know because sometimes I watch. Sometimes I watch from the inside of the janitor's closet and even touch myself the way they touch each other. I lick my lips and hug myself and sometimes I push up against the mop handle if Mr. Mayfield hasn't taken it out yet.

I want to feel what they're feeling. I mean I can *feel* it but I can't feel it the way *they* must be feeling it because there's two of them and only one of me. They do a lot of *yeah*ing and *mmm*ing and then all I really feel is frustrated because now I'm stuck in the janitor's closet till they're done.

It's suppertime and I'm hungry even though I forgot what hungry is supposed to feel like. I usually just put food in my mouth and keep going until there's nothing left in front of me. I never feel full but sometimes I feel sick and then I know I've gone past full. Mom says I'm *emotionally* feeding myself. She says I'm overweight but she loves me. So does she love me the way I am *even though* I'm overweight? Or does she love me and really want me *not to be* overweight?

I know she's not happy to take me clothes shopping. And not just because of my size but because of what I pick out. It's not what she would pick out for me but she tries. She tries to let me choose. Except when I pick something that looks like a costume in a dystopian fairy-tale. We can laugh together about stuff like that but I think deep down we both want to cry.

I start walking the six blocks to my house. On the way I pop into F Mart for a snack. I've asked Mr. Fadikar why he named his store that and he says F is the first letter of his last name and Mart is for market. But I told him it's kinda weird because F *anything* is funny to kids. It's like cursing without saying the F word. He looked confused but he's old people and English isn't his first language. The kids in the neighborhood call his store the F bomb and F You. Also last year someone took a can of spray paint and blacked out the M on the sign so it just said Fart until I helped him clean it off with paint thinner. I have all that paint stuff in my garage and he gave me some free snacks so that was good.

I'm in a chocolate mood today so I grab a bag of the mini peanut butter cups and my mouth starts watering like a dog. At the counter I dig in the right front pocket of my jeans for the five bucks I know is in there from yesterday. Gram gave it to me for helping her with some chores like changing lightbulbs and emptying her cat's litter box.

"Why are your pants so tall Hy?" Mr. Fadikar's eyes crinkle up.

I could call him F Man or Fart Man like the other kids to be funny but I like Mr. Fadikar and don't want to make him feel bad. To me he's not a joke. To me he's a man who worked hard and started a business and that's cool. It's not his fault his English isn't perfect. The other kids don't get it. They make fun of his accent and mixed up words. It's a shame their parents didn't teach them respect or anything.

I know he meant *long* and I shrug because I like my pants long and draggy and I don't know why. But I know they must look weird and dirty at the bottom to Mr. Fadikar because he's always dressed nice and his pants end right above his polished shoes.

"Ah you kids with your fashions!"

He gives me back my change and comes around the counter to put a hand on my shoulder like a friend. Or maybe a dad. I smile at him because Mr. Fadikar never makes me feel bad for buying snacks with my chore money. I feel like he gets me.

"See you Mr. Fadikar."

I stuff the bag of peanut butter cups in my backpack because I know my mom won't want to see it. On the way home I think about showing Mr. Fadikar some of my artwork and then I have a better idea. I go right to the garage and start throwing some sprays into my old canvas tote.

"Hy? Is that you?" Mom's coming into the garage now so I shove the tote under the bench. She hugs me and I smell flowers but also a meaty smell in her hair because she's probably been cooking supper. She does that thing moms do pushing my hair behind my ears because it's hanging in my face. "You need a haircut honey."

I want to ask why because nobody cares anyway and I'm okay with it. Instead I tell her I don't want it super short because it hides my face when I want it to and she said I could grow it long and tie it back with a rubber band. But I don't want it super long either. I tell her this and she rolls her eyes like she's done a million times before but not in a mean way. I wish I could look the way she wants me to look so she'd be happier.

"How's roasted chicken and potatoes and…green beans? My mouth waters a little but not like a dog this time.

"Good thanks." I grab my backpack off the floor and head up to my room.

"We'll eat in half an hour!" She yells up the stairs.

Speaking of dogs Rufus jingle jangles into my room with his tail all waggy. I keep telling Mom he's got too many tags on his collar for such a little guy but she says she likes hearing where he is at all times. She says the day she doesn't hear the jingle jangle will be a sad day. I think that's dramatic but whatever. I fall onto my beanbag and he tries to lick my face but I push him away. I don't want to push Rufus away because he digs me and he wants me to pet him but today I don't want his bad breath stinking up my face. It's not his fault because a couple of his teeth stick out and his tongue never really goes back into his mouth all the way. He keeps trying to lick me so I get up and sit on my bed. Then I get an idea.

I grab a sketchbook from the pile on the nightstand and open to a new page. I grab my colored pencils and I draw and draw. I color and shade and forget all about the peanut butter cups in my backpack. When Mom calls me for supper I drop my pencils and shoot both hands in the air like it was some big timed art competition. My fans hold their breath from their positions above me as the judges circle like sharks. They suddenly stop in front of me and their faces screw up into big joker grins.

"THE WINNER!" One judge shouts and holds up my sketch and everyone goes crazy. In the crowd I see Leonardo DaVinci *the real one not the librarian* and Zeus and my favorite band Punk Immortal. They all cheer and give me the thumbs up. Now I just have to figure out how to reduce it to the size of a nickel for Rufus's collar. I hop off my bed and give a little bow and I think I may actually be hungry for real.

2

I LIKE SATURDAYS because I don't have to talk to anyone if I don't want to. I can spend pretty much the whole day watching movies or working on some new idea. Today I want to work on the idea for Mr. Fadikar. I looked up *not my fault* in Hindi and it's this really cool pattern of lines and curves. I know exactly where I'm gonna do it too.

There's an old cement bandshell at the edge of the park. I'd never go there at night because it's where all the shady kids hang out and I've heard crazy stuff about drugs and some kind of fight club. But in the day nobody's there because the blacktop's all cracked and messed up and no good for skate boarding or anything. Plus it's kind of raining today but it won't matter to me because the bandshell is a curved shape so it's sheltered from the rain.

"I'm going out!" I yell to my mom but then I see a note on the fridge saying she had to cover for someone at work.

She's a nurse so sometimes they need her in a hurry on her day off. She works so hard and I try not to think about my dad too much at times like this because it makes me mad. It makes me mad that he left us. It makes me mad that she has to do everything for me because my dad is such an A-hole. That's what she calls him when she's had too much beer and I don't blame her. That's what I call him too when my birthday goes by without hearing from him. But usually she doesn't complain and even says we're better off without someone like that hanging around to make us feel *not good enough.*

Apparently he found someone *good enough* in another state and they have two *good enough* kids that aren't fat and a *good enough* golden retriever whose breath doesn't stink because he can close his mouth all the way. I don't blame Mom for my dad leaving us even though we have to pretend he doesn't exist because *he* pretends *we* don't exist. I don't blame her because she's a good person and I know it's not her fault. And just like that I have an idea for a badass birthday present for her. And I know one thing for sure. I know that if I ever have a kid I won't pretend my kid doesn't exist. Ever.

The bandshell is gray and ugly because nobody cares. I'm trying to imagine when there were real musicians playing here back in the old days and it makes me feel blues and reds and purples so I just grab my sprays and start. I brought a picture of *not my fault* in Hindi and now I'm following the lines and loops and curves. I hope it's accurate because it's for Mr. Fadikar and I care what he thinks.

After a while I'm sweating so I stop to take off my hoodie and I see someone sitting there in the far corner. I freeze because I know what I'm doing isn't really legal even though nobody should care if all I'm doing is making it look better.

"Hi." She speaks first. I say *she* because of her voice. But I shouldn't jump to conclusions.

"That's my name don't wear it out." It's my best line.

"*What's* your name?" She's confused naturally.

"No *Hy.* That's my name." This part cracks me up because it's like an old black and white comedy skit my mom showed me a long time ago. They're at a baseball game talking about players named *who what* and *I don't know.* It's so funny.

"Um. Okay. Hi *Hi*." She gets it. I'm moving closer because she's sitting and I'm standing. Maybe I'll look more imposing but I'm only five seven with my kicks on.

"That's H *Y*." Up close she looks kinda pretty.

"Dunno. You tell me." And she's smart. Now I'm starting to buzz a little.

I push my hair behind my ears because mom says my face is nice and I should let people see it. She smiles and I can see a glint of something like a gold tooth. Really? Oh right. I remember reading that fashion recycles every couple of decades or whatever. So technically if you don't change anything then eventually you'll be back in style. Ha. I'll let my mom know because she's been rockin' the same hairstyle since middle school. *But wait* what I'd really like to know is how my English teacher Mr. Burnett justifies the Sherlock Holmes get-up. It's not like he ever lived through that era.

"What's your name?" I'm feeling unusually confident. Maybe it's the mural behind me. It's like my own giant bodyguard.

"Belinda. But you can call me *Buh*."

"Really?" I'm thinking this is a strange coincidence.

"No not really." She laughs.

She's messing with me but not in the way Jordan Costa messes with me. Jordan Costa put a post-it on my back that said *WHAT AM I* and he followed me all the way to the chemistry lab to watch everyone laughing until Mr. Solomon took it off. I knew he was doing it but I didn't take it off in front of anyone because I didn't want them to think I care. Even though I do care. I want to take the post-it and cram it down his throat. I want to write *A-hole* on his forehead in permanent marker. Jordan Costa acts all cool but somebody told me they found his mom and the gym teacher behind the bleachers at the school dance so maybe Jordan messes with me because he's angry. My mom calls it *misplaced anger*. I have misplaced anger sometimes but I don't think I hurt anyone's feelings on purpose.

I must've been thinking about Jordon too long because Belinda is right in front of me now. Her skin is an awesome color. It's like a caramel milkshake. I automatically think about which colored pencils I'd use to get the right blend. Her eyes look like racoon eyes and I can't tell if they're all smudged because of the rain or if she was crying. She looks like she might be older than me but that could be the makeup too.

"What is it?" She's using her chin to point at the half-finished mural behind me because her hands are stuffed into her pockets. Now I see her mouth up close and it's not a gold tooth. It's a retainer like the kind you wear after braces. Duh. And now I think she's *not* older than me. I feel kinda dumb thinking she had a gold tooth.

"Just a design." I don't want to tell her about *not my fault* because I don't know her yet. She could be a spy for the FBI. Even I know this is crazy but I can't take that chance. She nods and makes that face that says she might be impressed. I'm suddenly aware of needing to finish so I turn around and pick up my purple spray. But now I'm inspired by her retainer so I put it down and grab the metallic one.

Man it looks good. Belinda's been watching me finish and I think I may have showed off a little. The gold makes the whole thing pop and it reminds me of when I was doing my Hindi research I saw all these pictures of brides wearing fancy jewelry. So that makes sense.

We're walking back through the park now and the rain's let up enough so we don't get soaked but I put my hood up anyway. Her hair's in these kind of slick braids so she won't look like a drowned rat but I will for sure. We're not talking much which is cool with me. I feel like

I have a new friend and I don't want to ruin it by saying something stupid. But then I have to.

"Maybe don't tell anyone you've seen me do this?"

"Who would I tell?" She's kicking a water bottle in front of her and her shoes look brand new. "I don't even go to West Glade." Huh. I guess it must be obvious that I do.

She tells me she goes to a private girls' school in the next town over. Her family must have money so I'm wondering what brought her to this neighborhood and this park and this bandshell all by herself. She tells me her boyfriend lives nearby and they had a fight so she left. Maybe that explains the racoon eyes. And then it makes me feel jealous because at least she has someone to have a fight *with*.

Then I ask her how she's going to get home and she says she'll call her dad. I wonder how a dad lets his daughter with a retainer wear all that makeup and have a boyfriend that she's allowed to see by herself in another neighborhood but I don't ask that. I wouldn't really know how a normal dad should act. Instead I ask if maybe she wants to come to my house for a soda first. It just comes out and surprises me. I'm not really that brave. Or at least I wasn't until now.

Rufus jingle jangles over all excited and jumps up on Belinda but she doesn't seem annoyed. She crouches down and scratches his ears and even lets him lick her face. This makes me like her even more. I grab some cheesy crackers and two cans of diet soda. *Diet* because mom won't keep regular soda in the house. I'm not sure I want anyone to see my bedroom because I'm kinda private so we just sit at the table in the kitchen and talk about our favorite music. Turns out we like a bunch of the same stuff and that's cool.

"I better go." She's standing now and typing into her phone.

"You want the address here?" I'm assuming she's asking her dad to come get her.

"Nah, I'm gonna head back to the public library and get picked up there."

I'm not sure why but I just met her and I don't even know if she's telling me the truth about anything so I just say *cool* and walk with her back through the park so I can get another look at the bandshell. When we get up to it there are two kids I've never seen before hanging out in it and one kid's saying to the other *whoa this is rad* and the other kid's agreeing and I feel my body tingle all over. Belinda gives me the side-eye and smiles and says nothing and I know she'll keep my secret.

3

"YOU LOOK DIFFERENT today." Mom's staring at me while I'm trying to eat my cereal.

I can tell she's trying to figure it out. I shrug and I can't help but smile. I mean I did pick out a clean shirt with no paint on the front and I brushed my hair until it was smooth. But I don't think it's those things she's noticing because she knows me pretty well. Maybe she can tell I just feel a little different inside since I met Belinda. Because I do. It's funny I thought only art could give me that feeling.

"I made a new friend." Mom's eyebrows shoot up and she takes a sip of her coffee. "Saturday while you were at work. I was just over in the park and this girl was there by herself." I'm careful not to mention the bandshell.

Mom's eyes do something like squinting for a second like she's trying to figure out where this is going. I can read her pretty well by now. But I don't want her making up all kinds of stuff in her head so I keep talking. "She was just cool you know? It looked like she'd been crying and needed someone to talk to so we talked about music and stuff."

"Is she in any of your classes?" Mom didn't really know what to say because what really was there to say?

"She doesn't go to West Glade. She goes to a private school. And we came back here for snacks. Is that okay?"

Mom puts her hand on mine and says *of course*. She says she trusts me. I can tell she's thinking it over in her head because she doesn't know this person but she also wants me to have friends. Or even *a* friend. She's probably happy I'm trying.

I don't tell her I went back yesterday and waited by the bandshell for a long time to see if Belinda would come back because we never exchanged numbers or anything. But she never showed up and I finally got grossed out by the cigarette butts and little plastic bags everywhere so I added some more highlights to the mural and went home. I added more gold because I thought that in the sun it would look amazing. I was right. I can't wait to show Mr. Fadikar.

People bitch about Mondays but I'm good with Mondays. I've got Art first period and it kinda gives purpose to my day. Plus I dig Mr. Sanchez. It's like if all teachers had an ON/OFF switch his would always be ON. When he talks he takes me all over the world and back in time with some of the best artists and my head feels like it's gonna explode by the time the bell rings. Mr. Sanchez says the stuff I do in class is *inspired*. When he gives us an assignment for homework I spend hours and hours on it just to impress him.

I walk through the gross beige-colored halls to my next class and imagine them lined with Monets and Warhols instead of dirty smudges and gum wads. Sometimes I wonder if I didn't have Mr. Sanchez for Art whether *not my fault* would exist. I guess that's what he means by inspired. The rumor is Mr. Sanchez has a boyfriend even though no one's ever seen him. I don't care and it pisses me off that anyone still cares at this point. I mean what year is it? I have to get out of this podunk town. I'm suffocating under the weight of a million small minds. I can't imagine what Mr. Sanchez is feeling. Or maybe I can.

The rest of the morning is okay because I'm pretty good at math and science and teachers like the good students who don't talk back or fool around. I feel like I've dodged a bullet because I haven't seen Jordan Costa yet. There are other kids like Lucas who pick up the slack though. And there's always the *bitch brigade*. Speaking of which when I get my lunch tray I make sure to find the farthest table away from them. But today they must be extra bored because Tara Lowe spots me sitting by myself and I can *feel* it before she says it. Like the calm before the storm.

"What do you call a bear sitting alone at lunch?" It's so loud the whole lunchroom gets quiet and looks at me. I'm holding my breath.

"Hy-bernating!"

She says it like a witch and the wicked laughs fill the room like thunder. It's so bad it makes me miss Jordan Costa. But she's dating Jordan Costa. I actually think I might cry right at the table. But I can't. I just can't. I let my hair fall in front of my face and curse ever thinking I was clever to give myself the nickname. Why couldn't my mom have named me a something normal like Alex or Jamie so I wouldn't be caught in this trap?

I push the taters into my mouth one at a time without moving a muscle. Then it sounds like they've forgotten about me so I finish everything on my plate but I'm gagging on the grease and focusing on not vomiting. I should tell Ms. Sinclair my guidance counselor about Tara and Jordan but I know it'll be worse for me if they get in trouble. The whole *No Room for Bullies* campaign isn't really working here at West Glade. I just have to wait it out and focus on my own project. Then I get an idea. A really good one.

I get through the rest of the day without more drama and decide to visit Gram before going home. She only lives three blocks in the opposite direction and maybe I can do more chores for snack money.

Gram isn't even my mom's mom she's my dad's mom which is pretty weird since we don't even see my dad. Turns out she doesn't see Dad either. I overheard Mom and her talking one day about him and how he *disowned his family* and was *ashamed of his roots.* I guess his other wife had more money or something and made him start over like we never happened.

Gram smokes a lot and the whole house smells like an ashtray so I hold my breath when I have to go inside. But we usually just hang on her porch. Today I sit on her beat-up porch swing that creaks really loud when I swing on it and it acts like a doorbell. She comes to the screen door in a pinkish housecoat thing which I think had flowers on it at some point but it's so faded I can't tell. Her orangey hair is sticking up all over and with her wrinkly tan face she looks like a troll doll and I almost laugh out loud but I catch myself.

"Hey Gram." I think I woke her up because *well for one* the hair but also because she's squinting at me like she's trying to remember who I am. I feel sad for her that her own son doesn't come see her and she has other grandkids she doesn't even know but then I feel good because at least she has me.

"Oh." That's all she says when she finally recognizes me and pushes open the pointless screen door that has big holes in it. I wish I could help her fix it but I'm not really handy that way. I get mad for a second about her son *my dad* not being around to help her. "I don't have any money today." She doesn't sound kind like a grandma should and I feel my face get hot because it's not like I only visit to get money from her but I'm embarrassed because maybe it was *part* of the reason.

I thought Gram and I were cool and before I can even help it I'm crying. I think it's probably more from just the whole lunchroom incident I had to keep inside all day but her face changes and she comes over and sits next to me and puts a skinny arm around my shoulder. We just sit there for a while neither one of us saying anything and I wipe my nose with my sleeve. I don't blame Gram for not being kind or not having any money because it's not her fault her life isn't so fun.

And just like that I decide to include her in my art project. I ask Gram if she has anything she needs done for no money and she says *not today*. On my way out of her tiny yard I check out the busted picket fence and smile to myself. I think we're still cool.

It's only Monday and I think about how I have to wait all week to do more *not my fault* projects but then I remember I can make the tag for Rufus's collar. It's gonna be a challenge to do one that small but I'm excited. I start running just for the hell of it but get out of breath so I slow down to a fast walk instead. My backpack weighs a ton and I wish I had money to buy a new one because one of the straps is breaking and it hurts my shoulder. I decide I have to ask Mom for a new backpack even though she might want to know what I spent all my birthday money on and I don't want to tell her it was on spray paint. Mom knows I'm into art supplies and stuff but she doesn't know about the tags and murals. She doesn't need more things to worry about like me getting in trouble.

I never really thought about what our house looks like until Belinda came over. She didn't make faces or anything but I saw her eyes get wide and then look around quick without turning her head. Maybe the fact that none of the furniture matches or that the sink is all stained brown from the dripping faucet is weird to her. I look around now and try to see through her eyes because she probably lives in a nice house with matching furniture or even a badass mansion with marble floors and servants. I see the blanket covering the hole in the sofa and the broken floor tiles and there's nothing I can do about it. Mom does the best she can and the house is clean*ish* except for the ants. *Ping.* Lightbulb moment.

I think about Mr. Sanchez and how he tells me to *follow my inspiration.* Rufus's bling will have to wait because I have so much inspiration happening at once it's hard to stay on track. He's been jingle jangling around my ankles since I came home and I bend down to scratch his ears. He's just happy with any attention and I think that a dog's life must be much easier because it's not screwed up by all the complicated feelings humans have.

My mom's not home and my homework will have to wait too so I can follow my inspiration. I follow it to the corner of my room behind my dresser. As much as I'm into color this *not my fault* will be just black and white so I dig a black marker out of my desk drawer and get started.

Horizontal. Vertical. Diagonal. Parallel. The words are like tiny rows of ants crossing each other. In some places it's taking the shape of a giant tic tac toe board or a math equation or a chemistry formula and it's looking awesome. I get lost in it until I hear Mom come home and I have to push my dresser against the wall quick to cover it up. But I'm still buzzing because I know it's there and it'll wait for me like a friend who wants to hang out.

I dump my books on my bed to make it look like I've been doing homework in case Mom comes in. But she doesn't. And now I hear two voices. So after a few minutes I head downstairs. Rufus comes too because he's got that internal clock thing that knows exactly when he gets fed.

"There's my sunshine!" I almost laugh out loud because *one* she's never called me that and *two* she's never called *anyone* that. And she says it in a girlier voice which makes it worse but also makes more sense when I see the dude leaning against the counter with a beer in his hand and I remember she's still dating.

"Then what're you Mother Nature?" I'm being silly but she laughs so that's good.

"This is Earl." Of course it is. Seriously he's straight from central casting with his bushy moustache and leather vest. I would not be surprised to see his face on a vintage cigarette billboard off Route 66. He even looks dusty *if that's possible* like he's been out dodging tumbleweeds.

I say hello and try and make eye contact because Mom's always reminding me to but his eyes are busy looking me up and down. I've seen the look before and it makes me uncomfortable. It's not a nice look. I need to get away quick so I reach into the cabinet and open a can of dog food. I spoon some into Rufus's bowl and put the rest in the fridge.

"I've got a lot of homework." Mom gives me a hug and says she'll call me for dinner. I think she saw Earl's face and it makes me sad because I want her to have someone and don't want to be the reason she doesn't. In my room I dig the bag of peanut butter cups out of my underwear drawer and tear it open. I eat one after the other until they're all gone and then I stare at the big heap of wrappers like they just appeared out of nowhere. It's like I go into a trance or something. My stomach feels sick but now my heart doesn't hurt as much.

Earl doesn't stay for dinner. She must've told him to get lost.

"I'm sorry Mom." We're washing the dishes after our spaghetti and she doesn't even ask what I mean because she knows and she says I have nothing to be sorry for and she loves me. Her eyes fill up and she says anyone who wants to love her is going to have to love me too. She says we're a package deal. We hug for a long time and my eyes fill up for the second time in one day but this time it feels good.

4

DREAMS SUCK PRETTY much. They're either so bad they scare the crap out of me for days or they're so good I'm depressed when I wake up and realize they were only dreams. Last night my dream was so good I wanted to stay in it forever. I wonder if anyone's tried to freeze themselves during an awesome dream. I wonder if the soul or neurons or whatever would just live in the dream uninterrupted if the body was unplugged. I mean I'm into science and I know there's a lot of question marks between this plane of existence and the next one but it's a cool idea. There are probably some sci-fi movies that dig into it.

I'm lying in bed and I lift up the sheet to see if I somehow still magically have the body from my dream. Nope. I didn't really expect to but it doesn't hurt to check. I grab the roll around my stomach and wonder how old you have to be for that fat-sucking procedure. Not that I could afford it or anything. Maybe I should get a grip and start eating better and ride my bike. *Yes* I admit I have a bike and I don't ride it. Maybe it's because I outgrew it four years ago or maybe that's just an excuse. I've seen grown men in our neighborhood riding little kid bikes and they don't seem to care what people think. But maybe they *should* care because it looks creepy.

I remember it's Friday and roll out of bed to get dressed for school. I hear other kids complaining all the time but I like school. The learning part that is. The kids not so much. Some kids are okay and leave me alone but no one's invited me over or anything. Then I see the ants on the wall behind my dresser and I'm excited. I had to stop in that corner so it wouldn't show yet but over the past few days I was able to do some behind the closet door and in the bottom corner behind my beanbag. My room's pretty small so it shouldn't take that long to finish.

This whole *not my fault* thing's getting bigger and more complicated so maybe I should make a list to keep track of all the separate pieces and installations. I'm curating my first big show and there needs to be organization. *Believe in yourself and others will follow.* I saw that on a giant mug in the thrift store window. I guess that's true even when you're some A-hole cult leader or dictator unfortunately. My thing's just art but it's getting a life of its own and I'm just here to help. Like it already exists and I happen to be the one uncovering it and giving it meaning. Anyway I know it's giving *me* meaning and now I can't imagine what I would do without it.

Maybe I should pay more attention to what I look like if I'm representing this project. My jeans are all pretty much shredded on the bottom from dragging so I dig deeper in the drawer and find a pair of cords that look decent. There are a few shirts hanging in my closet that are better fitting than the T-shirts I usually wear so I grab a blue one. I can't do much about the busted kicks and I don't want to wear flip flips or dress shoes to school. Oh well.

In the bathroom I brush my teeth and check myself out in the mirror. It's a work in progress. I can't do much different with my hair so I just brush it. At least it's clean. Then I remember tomorrow is Saturday and maybe *just maybe* Belinda will go to the bandshell again. Now I'm wondering if that's really why I'm looking at myself in the mirror.

"Honey you're going to be late!" She's right. My timing's off with this new *caring what I look like* thing.

"Coming!" Even though I can walk to school Mom drives me when she can.

"Wow. You clean up nicely." She's smiling big and I think to myself it's going to be an okay day. She knows not to say anything else and I'm grateful for that.

The anti-bullying campaign posters are still up in the halls and I look at the date. The assembly is today and I bet we'll hear a lot of pep talks and bullshit about not bullying. But I'm prepared. A couple days ago I made a drawing of a superhero punching a real bull in the face and the speech bubble above him says *not my fault*. I think it's pretty good because I have a lot of old comic books to compare it to. All I have to do now is make copies so I go to the library at the end of second period before the assembly and make thirty copies on the copy machine.

Mrs. Nardo isn't there and I don't think the student librarian will care what I'm doing because he doesn't know me. He doesn't even notice me which is good because nobody can know what I'm doing. Not yet. I shove the copies in my bag and take a second to pay a visit to *non mea culpa*. The library's a ghost town so I go back to the table in the biography section and there it is right where I left it. That's a joke because it's obviously not going anywhere. It's not small but it's pretty subtle because the wood is dark and the letters are carved thin. But after today if someone points it out they might translate it and tie it together. I think I should've thought a bit more about this one because it's school property and I can't wash it off. Ugh.

I head to the assembly and take a seat in the back row against the wall so no one can launch spitballs at my head or anything. Not that someone would be dumb enough to bully me in an anti-bullying assembly but you never know. It might be more of a challenge. There could be a whole bully hierarchy where they try and outdo each other for a higher rank.

So *blah blah blah* they go on and on with their self-righteous cheerleading and I know for a fact none of these goodie two-shoes have ever been bullied. It's like we're the animals at the shelter that need saving but none of the owners that mistreated us feel bad about the way they treated us so what's the point? It's like telling a room full of people who would never be criminals not to be criminals *duh* and the few criminals in the room that already *are* criminals just ignore them because they'll keep doing it until they get caught and even after they get caught. I'm picturing Jordan Costa and Tara Lowe in prison stripes bullying the other inmates all slapstick style like in an old silent movie. Since there's no sound they can't use words so they have to do things like hide around a corner and stick a foot out to trip them and then make big doubled over laughing gestures while the screen flashes *Ha Ha Ha!* text in a black box.

I'm actually entertaining myself in my head so much I don't notice the assembly's over until someone's trying to get past me in the aisle. I grab my backpack and rush to the side door where kids are filing out and stand on the other side of where one of the goodie two-shoes is handing out the lame *No Room for Bullies* flyers. With my head down I hand out my copies of *not my fault.* I know for a fact no one will even look at it until later. And of the thirty copies I handed out maybe half will get thrown away. So that leaves fifteen possible views to get people talking. And so my audience grows a little. Then I panic because if one of the copies makes it back to Mr. Sanchez he might recognize my drawing style and tell the principal. But Mr. Sanchez is pretty cool with me so he'd probably ask me first and maybe he'd even think it was a rad artist move and keep my secret. I feel a little less panicked but more than that I notice I feel more *alive*. It's scary for sure because I've spent so long trying to be invisible but this art thing is giving me courage too so I have to risk being more visible. Not enough courage for the cafeteria though. I decide to skip lunch.

Good thing I shoved a banana and a bag of pretzels in my backpack before I left my house. I don't usually do that but maybe my subconscious was preparing me for this moment. It's cool to think like that. Like we're connected to the universe in ways we're not always aware of at the time. It's warm and sunny out which is normal for where we live so I pick an empty bench outside the science building and pull out my sketchbook. West Glade doesn't really have a nice lawn like some other schools or I would sit in the grass instead.

I think maybe I should get started on Mom's idea because her birthday is coming up. Looking around at all the other kids on the benches and the blacktop I realize that ninety percent of them have their faces glued to their phones. All this time I've been jealous that I only have my mom's super old crappy phone that basically just makes calls and suddenly I'm ok with it. Suddenly I feel different in maybe a *good* way.

Anyway I start to sketch a mother and child image I've seen in religious paintings a lot. Not that we're religious but the symbol works with my idea that she's a good mom even though it's just the two of us and it's not her fault we don't have more and I don't have a dad. Over her head I start to make a halo and I'm happy with how it's turning out when a shadow covers the page. It's crazy but I feel immediately like an animal in danger and my instinct is to bolt as fast as I can. And my instinct is right only it's not Jordan or Tara. It's Lucas.

"What'cha drawing Hy-brid?" *Gee* like I haven't heard this one before. But Lucas is too brain dead to worry about being original. I just squint up at him because the sun is in my eyes and I can see that naturally he's got two followers because bullies need an audience. What happens next is a blur because I don't know what comes over me.

"Your gorgeous face." His followers laugh like they're impressed with the sarcastic comeback and before I can stop him Lucas rips my sketch out of the sketchbook and tears it into a million pieces. His followers look uncomfortable for a second. Then Lucas spins and pushes through them without saying anything. I can't believe he got so mad and I think I must've struck a nerve. I mean he's not a handsome kid with his hooked nose and acne and big overbite so maybe he's sensitive about being ugly. So why is he picking on *me*? Guess he didn't expect me to stand up to him and now I feel empowered so it was worth it. I can make another sketch no problem. And this is gonna sound crazy but I also feel bad that *I* hurt *his* feelings.

The bell rings and everyone starts heading back into the buildings. I'll have to redo my mom's sketch later. The rest of the day is uneventful and that's okay by me. I've had my share of drama for one day. On the way home I debate stopping at Gram's house to see if she's in a better mood but decide not to risk it. I'll go to F Mart instead. Maybe I could even sweep up or something in exchange for some cheese curls.

"Hey Mr. Fadikar." But when I pull open the door it's not Mr. Fadikar behind the counter. It's Mrs. Fadikar. "Oh hey Mrs. Fadikar." She gives me a tired smile and I wait until the man in front of me finishes paying for his beef jerky. "Is Mr. Fadikar here?" She's usually so happy and I'm getting the feeling something is wrong.

"He's in hospital." My eyes must look wide because she bows her head. "He's not feeling well."

I just stand there because I don't know what to say. He's always here and now he's not and I wanted to show him the mural in Hindi. I don't know Mrs. Fadikar that well and I'm not sure I should tell her about it so I guess I have to wait for him to get better. I say *okay* and *I'm sorry to hear that* and head home.

5

IS THAT SINGING? It *is* singing. And not one but two voices singing in harmony. *What the?* I open my door. It's coming from the kitchen. I head downstairs and when I turn the corner I stop short because I don't understand what I'm seeing. My mom is at the stove flipping pancakes and that's weird enough but sitting at the kitchen table *and I can't believe this* is Belinda. I blink and rub my eyes and am suddenly ashamed to be wearing ratty old pajamas. I must be dreaming.

"Hy honey your friend's here." So I'm not dreaming and my mom's being super embarrassing. They were just singing. Together. I could die right now.

"Hi Hy. Your mom told me your full name." I shoot Mom daggers for doing that. "I think it's a cool name. But I won't use it if you don't want me to." Belinda sounds kinda sincere.

"Excuse me." It's all I say so I can run upstairs to brush my teeth and put on some real clothes. I mean I was hoping to see Belinda but not like this. I was caught off guard but maybe I should focus on the fact that she came to see me. I wonder how many times you have to hang out with someone to be considered friends. Even better now I don't have to go wait under the bandshell all day to see if she shows up. But I do want to go take a picture of the bandshell for Mr. Fadikar because he's not around to see it for himself.

I try to act casual and help myself to some pancakes because I see Belinda's already had some. My mom's actually pretty cool to let her in and feed her and entertain her. She could've just said I wasn't awake and to come back but I know she wants me to have a friend pretty bad. I catch her eye and give her a *thanks* smile. We have that kind of communication between us.

Walking across the park I ask Belinda how she remembered where I lived and she says she took a picture of the corner street signs and used GPS. My phone is so ancient I don't think I've even tried to do that.

"Are you going to see your boyfriend today?" I ask because I remember her telling me this is why she was even in the neighborhood last Saturday.

"Nah. We broke up." I can't say exactly what I feel when she says that but it's not disappointment that's for sure.

"Oh. Sorry." It was all I thought of to say.

She says *no biggie* and shrugs. I get the feeling it isn't no biggie and of course I'm curious and want to ask all sorts of questions like *why did you break up* and *did you go all the way* and nosy stuff like that because I've never had that kind of relationship. But I figured she'd tell me more if she wanted to. Today she doesn't have braids but she has these big puffy mouse ears. In the sunlight I can see her diamond-shaped eyes are a really light brown with gold flecks and she has on a yellow tank top over baggy black joggers with white stripes down the sides. I really like her style but I know her clothes are expensive. Not only that but her body is so thin and perfect she could wear a garbage bag and it would look good. I wonder if I had money and a different body whether I could be mad stylish too.

her window. For a second I think she said she has a *nanny* but then I remember her saying the driver's name.

"What about your mom?" I'm guzzling the soda now like someone's going to snatch it away from me.

"She's dead." She says it so matter of fact I nearly choke. The bubbles are stuck halfway down my throat so it's either a burp or a hurl. Neither one is ideal so I burp and quickly apologize.

"Geez. That's tough. Sorry." She elbows me like a sister would and tells me it's okay because it was a long time ago and she was a little girl when her mom got sick.

We sit in silence for a while and I try to picture her life at home with no mom and a dad who apparently isn't there much. Then I'm so curious about her caramel milkshake skin and fluffy mouse ears and diamond-shaped eyes. I want to be really brave and ask her what ethnicity her parents are, but I'm not sure about what's rude or too personal. Also I'm not used to talking this much to anyone except maybe my mom. So I just put my arm next to hers and tell her I'd take a caramel milkshake over a vanilla one any day. It's true and it makes my face hot right after because she gives me a really sweet smile.

The palm trees sail by out the window and we finally pull up to the entrance of the Blue Horizon. I've never seen this beach before and it has a gate so I'm guessing it's not a public beach. Manny rolls down his window and shows the guard a badge thing and the gate raises. Yup.

The sand feels really good between my toes and we find two beach chairs or *chaise lounges* like my mom said once in a mock British accent when she was trying to be fancy. Speaking of fancy this place is off the charts. A guy in a white uniform comes running over with four towels and two tall glasses of ice water with lime slices on the edges. His name tag says Gerard. I'm wondering why we need four towels for two of us and then he starts wrapping one around the chair like a bathrobe. I don't even think we have four towels at home *period*. And I definitely don't think chairs need bathrobes.

Speaking of bathrobes Gerard leaves and comes back with two actual bathrobes. Seriously? I'm so fascinated with the whole towel slash bathrobe thing I didn't notice Belinda went down to the ocean. Her joggers are pushed up to her knees and she's standing ankle deep waving at me. I roll my jeans up as much as I can and walk towards her really aware of how pale I am. There aren't tons of people around and only one or two in the water. It's not a hot day *thank god* because *one* I don't want to sweat in front of Belinda and *two* I don't want to wear a bathing suit in front of Belinda even though she said the Cabana could give me one. She kicks the water at me and runs away and I chase her and we splash each other and this goes on for a while. I'm laughing and having fun and I keep looking up at the shiny black car thinking any minute now it's gonna turn into a pumpkin.

We stuff our faces with hamburgers and fries and ice cream all brought to us with a big smile by Gerard. I feel something else besides pleasure though. I feel funny about a guy old enough to be my dad or even granddad jumping through hoops for two kids. I guess it's weird to be on *this side* for once. Before my mom went back to nursing school she was Gerard ten times over. As a little kid I sat in plenty of booths and lobbies and watched people order her around and call her by anything but her name. I ask Belinda how long Gerard has been working here and she says *who?* Exactly. I can't blame Belinda though because I'm guessing her family's never been on the other side of the nametag.

"Thanks. I had a great time." I mean it too. Not like when I say it to the mom at a birthday party she forced her kid to invite me to out of pity and the whole time I sit by myself eating potato chips.

Manny opens my door and gives me a wink. I thank him too and make sure to use his name. Mom isn't home because her shift ends at nine so she doesn't see me get dropped off like a celebrity. I'll tell her later. Belinda and I exchange numbers and she says we can get together next Saturday because tomorrow she's with her dad. I'm over the moon about my new friend. Between Belinda and my art project my life is feeling pretty good right now.

Speaking of my art project I need to bust ass if I want to get my *ants* installation done while Mom is out. According to my calculations I've got about four hours. So I toss Rufus a treat which hits him in the face as usual and I feel bad. I guess I'm just hoping one day he'll actually catch it. I pat him as kind of a *sorry* and head upstairs.

6

"YOU NEED A new backpack honey." No duh Mom. I don't say that because it would be disrespectful but I'm glad she noticed without me saying anything. "In fact I think you could use some new clothes too."

She gives a big smile and hands me the milk. It seems like we do most of our talking at the breakfast table which is nice because she tries to set my day up with a little confidence. I think about what *color* confidence is and it's either red or orange. I guess I'm probably more like blue and gray at this point. But I'd like to try on some purple because it's halfway between blue and red.

"Sure that would be great. Thanks." I don't ask her where she's getting the money but I know she has a credit card. Maybe it's not maxed out this month. I feel a new wave of love for my mom. I told her all about Belinda taking me to the fancy beach in a car with a driver like some celebrity and she listened with her eyes lit up like stars. Maybe that's why she wants me to have some new things and maybe some new confidence. If only you could buy confidence in a store. Can't hurt to try.

We head to the mall in Mom's old car and now I'm noticing the stains on the seats and the clanging sound it makes when she starts it up. She keeps telling me she's going to teach me how to drive but she never gets around to it. I think I can take Drivers Ed in school soon but I really wish we had money for lessons from a real driving school. I decide I definitely need to get a summer job to save up. As long as I can remember I've pictured myself driving out of here one day and never looking back.

Inside the ancient department store that looks like it's always going out of business there are rows of T-shirts in a rainbow of colors and I make a beeline for a purple one with a picture of a lion wearing headphones. Mom raises her eyebrows but I love it and she nods. We go through the racks and settle on some plain V-necks and a soft red hoodie with gray arms that looks like one of those varsity team jackets. We both actually agree that I look pretty cool in cargo style joggers that bunch at the ankles and I wonder why it took me so long to figure that out. It'll take some getting used to not having my pants drag on the ground. I grab a plain black backpack because it won't show dirt and on our way out I get a pair of white Hi-tops. This I'm so amped about. To me they are two blank canvases just waiting to be filled in. I mentally add it to my growing list of art projects. Speaking of which I really need to use the rest of this day to work on one of them because tomorrow I go back to school. Mom and I share a footlong sub and I thank her for all the new stuff.

"I'm going to visit Nana. You coming with me?" She's talking about my other grandma the one I call Nana who is in a place for people with diseases like Alzheimer's and Dementia. I think she has the first one. It's sad because she doesn't always remember us and sometimes doesn't even know we're there.

"Can I skip it this time?"

I don't want to disappoint my mom after all she just got me but I really need to *follow my inspiration* like Mr. Sanchez says. And I'm not used to having so many things to do on the weekend. Plus the facility Nana's in isn't like the ones in the movies with the caring people all around making her comfortable and playing games with her. Her room is small and depressing and every time we visit she's sitting by herself just staring at the wall. Mom spends half the time yelling at the staff about her *quality of life* and that they're *neglectful*. Most of the time they roll their eyes and ignore her but once when I was about ten I heard a male nurse say *you get what you pay for* under his breath. I remember feeling hot all over which now I know was humiliation because we were poor.

Thankfully she doesn't make me go see Nana and just drops me off at home. I run up to my room and try on all my new gear. Since no one's watching I try different poses and faces in her full-length mirror and I know this is weird but I can feel myself changing. I mess around with my hair and wonder *for the first time ever* if I could pull off a cool color. I wonder if I've gotten it wrong this whole time by trying to be invisible. I guess I was thinking if I didn't stand out no one would notice me or make fun of me. But they make fun of me anyway so it didn't work. It's like they can tell I'm trying so hard *not* to be noticed that it makes them notice me even more. Kind of like when you see celebrities supposedly caught on camera walking through an airport with a hat and sunglasses and overcoat and you think how dumb of them because that disguise actually calls *more* attention than if they would've just dressed normal.

I stand there for a few minutes daydreaming about my new look. Then Rufus farts and it stinks so bad it snaps me out of it. Thanks dude. I change back into some ratty clothes that can get paint on them and go over my list of possible projects for today. *What's that Leonardo?* Right. Gram's fence it is.

In the garage I think about the colors and calculate how much paint I'll need and throw it all in my canvas bag. Then I do something crazy. I dig my yellow bike out from behind the Christmas decorations and wipe all the cobwebs off. This bike was already second hand when I got it so it's really a dinosaur now. I find the helmet but it's too small so I ditch it.

I'm kind of wobbly and my knees are hitting my chest but they always say *it's like riding a bike* about everything else so *actually* riding a bike must be something that's hard to forget. I steer *way* around people and dogs just to be careful and maybe only get one funny look. I get to Gram's in about ten minutes and ditch the bike on the sad patch of yellow grass in front of her mailbox. My guess is it's yellow from all the neighbors' dogs peeing because people aren't so considerate around here. And my bike happens to be a brighter shade of yellow so in my head it looks intentional lying on top of it. Like art.

I unload my paint bag and think about how this old slash new mode of transportation will sure be a time saver between all my installations. Gram's house is in even worse shape than ours but I can't blame her because she's old and has no money and no help to fix it up. She's not really even that old but Mom told me once she doesn't take care of herself and sometimes it seems like she just gave up on life.

The fence was white at some point but most of the paint has peeled off and there are some broken and leaning pickets. The second picket at the left corner is loose and actually leaning on the first so that it looks like the letter N already. Cool. I take this as a huge sign and feel the inspiration coming on. I kneel down and realize my butt is sticking out into the road but it's Sunday and not a lot of people are around. Closing my eyes I can see Gram's faded pink flowered nightie and orange troll hair. She's got a gray cat so I'll work that in also. I remember a long time ago she had a little vegetable garden with tomatoes and beans. So I'll need red green pink orange and gray paint but first white spray for the pickets. I'm pretty sure Gram is passed out somewhere inside because she drinks but after a quick peek to make sure she's not on the porch or in the window I get started.

Over the next couple hours I'm Picasso and Monet and Banksy combined and *not my fault* is hiding but emerging all twisted up in green vines and pink flowers. The outline of a gray cat in the shape of an F chases an asymmetrical orange butterfly across three pickets in a dotted line. You get the idea. I'm in the zone and sweating and I can feel people behind me now. I stop and turn around slowly but this time the audience isn't imaginary. There's a lady holding the hand of a little boy and an older man with a fedora type hat. And they're smiling. At me.

The perspective from across the street is so different. Up close it's a lot of color but the words come more into focus when you step farther back. I'm in that *after* haze again where I look at my creation and try to remember being a part of it. In the background Gram's house now has an *intentional* busted vibe like vintage chic instead of just plain neglect. The fence art actually transforms its surroundings if that makes sense. Like the rich guy who wears a diamond watch with holey T-shirts and ratty kicks. Without the diamond watch he just looks busted but when he puts it on he's saying he *meant* to look busted.

Part of me wants to get Gram out here to show her *not my fault* and the smarter part of me says to let her discover it on her own and see if she digs it. This way I can always deny it was me if she hates it. I pull out my phone and take a few pictures.

On the way home I decide to stop at F Mart and see if Mr. Fadikar is back from the hospital. He's not. Mrs. Fadikar isn't there either. I want to say *who are you* to the guy behind the counter but that would be rude. Then I wonder if this could be their son because he kind of looks like them and he's probably around twenty-five or something.

"Hello. Can I help you with something?" He has no accent and his English is good.

"I was looking for Mr. Fadikar. Is he still sick?" I immediately feel like I shouldn't have said that. He looks at me kinda sad and nods like it hurts him. Now I'm nodding and it hurts me too because his face doesn't look like the face of someone hopeful.

"I'm Arjun. He's my father." He puts his hand out to me and I shake it.

"I'm Hy." I don't feel like playing the usual games with my name and the strange thing is he has no questions. He just says *nice to meet you Hy*. Then his face lights up a little and asks if I want a soda on the house. I say *sure* and he tells me to go grab one from the case. I wonder if it's because he can tell I have no money or because he can tell his dad is my friend. Either way the grape soda tastes so good I almost forget to be sad about Mr. Fadikar.

But then I have a scary thought. What if Mr. Fadikar doesn't get to see the mural I made for him? I'm almost panicking now. I need to at least show him the picture. "Can I visit him in the hospital?" My face must show the panic because Arjun looks surprised. He says he'll ask him and for me to come back day after tomorrow. I thank Arjun and jump on my bike. Maybe everything will be alright.

1

THERE'S A CROWD around the art room door and Mr. Sanchez is in the center with his arm going up and down. When I get closer I can see he's scrubbing the door with a wet sponge and his face looks like stone. The kids aren't talking or backing away or even helping. They're just all standing there like dummies. I push between Ellie who's really smart but quiet and some other girl with pink dipped hair *very cool* and see what Mr. Sanchez is trying to scrub off. My stomach hurts for him like I've been punched. In big capital letters three times across the whole door is *FAG*. In red spray. And all he's doing is blurring it a little. I take a chance and elbow through more so I'm right next to him.

"I'll help you Mr. Sanchez. But it won't come off like that." Mr. Sanchez drops his arm and looks at me with the saddest eyes. I'd think an art teacher would know this. But it's not like he's a tagger or anything. "Acetone might work but it could take off the door paint. Same with turpentine. Do you have that stuff in the art room? We can try." There's a spark of what I think is *thanks* in his eyes now.

"They don't let me keep those flammable solvents here. But thank you Hy." He sighs and opens the door wide. "Inside everyone. Show's over. Take your seats."

I can barely concentrate during class because my mind is racing about helping Mr. Sanchez erase that nasty word. Besides the obvious hate that stupid kids need to spew to make themselves feel bigger is the bad rap it gives graffiti. My head is hot and I want to scream. What if it doesn't come off and Mr. Sanchez has to wait for the school to repaint the door? Good luck with that one. And then just like all the other times I get an idea.

Art happens to be second to last period on Wednesdays so I don't have to wait long. I bolt out the side door to where I now leave my sad-ass bike. There's no way I'm going to put it in the bike rack because it'll either get stolen *as a joke because no one would seriously steal it* or give one of my personal bullies another reason to make fun of me. So I leave it behind the dumpster in back of the cafeteria. No one goes back there because it stinks like garbage. And sure enough there it is right where I left it. Only now there's a banana peel on the seat. The hair on the back of my neck stands up. A banana peel on the banana seat of my banana yellow bike. Someone's either being funny or mean but hopefully doesn't know who the bike belongs to. Actually, now that I look closer I see it's not a banana *peel* but a whole banana.

I look around to see if anyone is watching me and I freeze when I see the back door of the cafeteria half open and one of the lunch ladies *Dixie according to her name tag* is wedged in the door with her hand holding a cigarette outside. She's super big and the door is resting on her belly. I want to tell her not to smoke but that's her business so I don't.

"That yours?" Dixie lets out a cackly laugh and points at the banana with a ridiculously long painted fingernail. Then she scratches at her scalp through her hairnet with the same fingernail. Five bucks says she doesn't wash her hands before handling our food but then I remember they have to wear plastic gloves. Now if I find a two-inch fingernail in my mashed potatoes at least I'll know who it belongs to. I bet I'd be skinny as a rail if I just spent one day watching them prepare our lunches. I'm feeling queasy just thinking about it.

Again with the big cackly laugh but she doesn't say anything else so I don't know if she put it there or what. So weird. I get on my bike and wave my hand in a combined *thanks* and *goodbye* gesture but I really feel like flipping her the bird. I guess I'm just getting fed up. When I'm out of sight I toss the banana into the bushes and try to stay focused on my plan.

My plan is to get some acetone and thinner and rags *just for show* because I'm going to try and convince Mr. Sanchez to let me paint the door for a class grade. So I throw in all my best acrylic colors and brushes because I don't think he'll let me use sprays. Then on second thought I throw in a couple mini sprays and a sketch pad and pen and scissors because I'll have to be super quick. I want Mr. Sanchez to come to school tomorrow and look at that door and be proud and not feel ashamed or mad because of some ignorant douchebags. Why does anyone care who he wants to be with? I mean I'm curious but only because I'm curious who makes him happy and it's such crap that there are kids my age who still aren't getting with the program.

When I make it back to West Glade the halls are almost empty. Mr. Sanchez isn't in his room and the door is locked. There are taped sheets of cardboard over most of the door but the red letters are still visible around the edges. I put my bag down and take off the tape and cardboard piece by piece and it's still there. Three times. Not that I expected it to be gone but it's just as ugly and angry as it was the first time I saw it and makes me feel sick all over again. I'm taking a big risk but I decide if anyone passes by and asks I'll say that Mr. Sanchez asked me to paint it over as an assignment. Most people know I'm sort of teacher's pet in Art. I think Mr. Sanchez of all people would understand me following my inspiration. Plus they have to paint over it anyway so I think of it as a temporary installation.

Sitting on my butt I'm just staring and thinking about the best way to silence this anger in red. Whoever did this doesn't think it's okay for a man to be with a man so I close my eyes and picture the door. Then I picture other kinds of doors and their symbols. Enter. Exit. Welcome. Open. Closed. Restroom. *Restroom.* I feel a jolt and my eyes open. I can see it now clear as day. Got to act quick before I get shut down. I grab the sketch pad and draw a two-inch symbol for *men* and another one for *women.* Then I draw a hybrid version with half a skirt. The word *hybrid* makes me think of Lucas and how I haven't seen him since he called me that. Which is a good thing.

Cutting out the symbols I take the stencil and start. No one has come into the hallway yet. One by one side by side row after row my symbols hold hands like a chain of paper dolls. All in gray. The pattern may *look* random but they are telling me who wants to be with who and I am listening. I didn't paint the background first on purpose so that the angry red words could still be partially visible. The symbols are a reaction to the hate and it's like they're standing in front of it. I think it makes more of a statement that way. When all the symbols are in place I stand back. It's still missing something and then I remember the most important part. A small brush and a squeeze of acrylic and in ten minutes I'm done. I throw all my stuff into my bag and take a quick picture with my phone.

"You there. What are you doin'?" I nearly jump out of my skin. Mr. Mayfield is standing there with his mop and bucket and for a second I lock eyes with him and wonder if he knows I use his closet sometimes to spy on kids making out. I don't see any recognition in his eyes but maybe he's a better spy than I give him credit for.

"Uh…I…you scared me." I put my hand to my chest to take attention away from the fact that I stuttered. Everyone knows stuttering is a sure sign of guilt. "I was admiring this art someone did on Mr. Sanchez's door." He stares at me blankly. "To cover the vandalism." I don't think Mr. Mayfield even knew about it judging by the look on his face. He comes closer to check it out dragging his wheelie bucket. He squints at the spray paper dolls then back at me. "Cool right?" I smile and he leans in to take a closer look and I check out his wrinkly face in profile. Honestly I don't know how many art installations Mr. Mayfield's been to. I don't want to assume but an educated guess would be zero. Well I'm about to get shamed.

"I like the way the artist made the symbols only one color and not all different colors because race ain't the issue here." His voice has a slow twang and my mouth hangs open. He sneaks a peek at my open bag on the floor and then winks at me.

"I agree." It's all I can manage because that *was* a deliberate decision I made and he nailed it. And no you definitely can't judge a book by its cover. Mr. Mayfield starts whistling a tune and wheels his bucket back the way he came before stopping and turning back to me.

"You better go on now. No one's supposed to be here this late." And then he's gone.

I almost expect the end credits to roll and the theme music to fade in because the whole scene was like a movie. I make a mental note to search out Mr. Mayfield again sometime and see what else he knows about art.

It's going on suppertime so I ride my bike home fast and don't stop at F Mart even though Mr. Fadikar's son told me to come back yesterday. I'll just have to go tomorrow. Mom's car isn't in the driveway but I can smell pizza from the front door and Rufus doesn't even acknowledge me because he's sitting right under the box on the counter in case something falls into his mouth. At least his mouth is already half open. I crack myself up.

"Mom?" No answer. I put my hand on the box and it's still warm. "Mom?" I call again and then I just open it and pull a big stringy slice out and shove it in my mouth. The grease drips down my chin and I tilt my head up till I can grab a paper towel. Mom pulls up in her noisy car. She could never sneak up on anyone or be a getaway driver for bank robbers with that car.

"Guess where I've been?" Her eyebrows are raised in a *you're in trouble* way and my brain tries to compute what she could possibly mean. I've been kind of going rogue lately with my project so it could mean anything.

"I've been at your grandma's." She says it with her hands on her hips like that's all she needs to say and I'm just going to confess. Well I'm not.

"And?" *Sorry Mom.* Nope. She looks at me for a long time and I keep munching on my slice. Rufus paws at my shin so I throw him a crust. He takes off with it like I might chase him down to get it back. Silly little dude.

"Well *somebody* painted her fence without her permission." Mom says *somebody* with ridiculous drama.

"Oh. How cool. Well it sure needed it so *somebody* must've wanted to do something nice for her even though she's not always so nice." I'm glaring at my mom now. "Does it look good?"

She drops her arms in what I think is surrender and loses the drama eyebrows. She's no good at being mad. Not at me anyway. "It's actually… really beautiful." She comes over and grabs a slice out of the box and bites into it.

We just stand there at the counter side by side eating our pizza. Enough said about that I guess. I got the message I probably should've asked and she got the message I'm expressing myself and no one gives a rat's ass about Gram's fence including Gram herself. It took her days to notice because she doesn't even leave the house and she probably only noticed because people were stopping to stare.

After one more slice it occurs to me that all this bike riding might actually be doing me some good and I stop at two slices. I notice my energy is more amped lately and I like the feeling. I think Mom notices too because she smiles at me when I close the box and wipe my hands. Also I wipe my hands on a paper towel and not my pants which is kind of a new thing.

In my room it's hard to focus on my homework because my walls are seventy-five percent covered with *not my fault* ants just begging to be finished. Mom hasn't said anything but she must've seen it by now because there is clean laundry on my bed. I really have to give her credit for being a cool mom. My art is growing and it's true I only do it if it improves instead of defaces with the exception maybe of *non mea culpa* but still. I'm not getting permission for any of it. I guess the whole anonymous thing is exciting to me too.

I finally just grab my books and go down to the living room so I can work on my homework. I really need a computer to do some research for my essay on human rights but we don't have internet service right now so I'll have to use lunch period tomorrow at the library. I should've done it after school but there are sacrifices for following your inspiration.

The next few hours are a blur as I stand on my bed and my dresser to fill in all the white places near the ceiling. I make the words march around in circles and cut back on a diagonal. When I was little I'd put drops of sugar water on the kitchen countertop and watch the tiny black ants form a pattern of straight lines to the drops and circles once they found them. I remember watching them up close for hours imagining myself as one of them. They had what I wanted. They had friends and teamwork and purpose. I can't even remember going to bed but the next thing I know my mom is pinching my toe to wake me up.

8

"WHAT DOES IT mean?"

"It's obvious dumbass. The little bathroom dudes and dudettes are all mixed together holding hands. Like it doesn't matter who's with who."

"I know *that* pendejo. I'm talking about the letters in their heads."

I walk up and take my place in the crowd. It's déjà vu except Mr. Sanchez isn't here and the art room is dark.

"Dunno. Just looks like random letters to me."

"Yeah I guess." I can't take this ignorance so I chime in.

"Wait maybe the letters connect to make words or something." Come *on* people. The two kids stare at me like the walls just spoke or something. Then they look at it again. More kids are walking up and staring. I must say I really like seeing the reactions as a spectator.

"Whoa." Lucy Lisbon says. "Very cool."

I like her. And I don't think she's a lesbian even though everyone calls her Lesbo. She wears so much make-up and seems so ultra girly to me but maybe that's my bad because it's a stereotype. Maybe it's like calling a bald guy *Curly* or a short guy *Stretch*. Or maybe she *is* a lesbian and is owning the nickname. I want to ask her what's her secret because she's so confident and name calling doesn't seem to get to her.

I think I'm getting good at this *I'm just part of the curious crowd* thing because some teacher shows up and eyeballs all of us. He moves us back and unlocks the door. Those of us who have Art this period head in and take our stations. He flicks on all the lights and tells us to just work independently on something.

About half an hour later Mr. Sanchez shows up with Mr. Lockheed. I'm not sure if he's the Principal or the Vice Principal but I always see him at assemblies in a suit. My station isn't near the door so I get up and pretend to sort through the colored pencils to get closer. They're talking so quiet I can't hear what they're saying but Mr. Sanchez is clenching his hands into fists and he looks pissed off. *Wait.* I thought he would be happy or impressed or proud that one of his students was *inspired.* Especially using art to make a statement and cover up hate. He catches me looking at him. I look away fast and hope he didn't make any connection.

"Hy can I have a word please?" Mr. Sanchez calls to me as I'm packing up. I walk over to his desk and my heart starts doing flips in my chest. He's still pretty handsome but he looks tired and different today and it makes me sad. "Do you know anything about the overnight pop-up piece on the door?" But now he's smiling a little around his eyes and I feel better. I shrug and hope I'm better at acting than I feel.

"I think it's pretty cool." I'm not so secretly asking for approval but trying to act nonchalant anyway. Mr. Sanchez nods.

"I think it's *brilliant.*" My breath sucks in a little and I curse myself for reacting. "And I wish I could thank the artist personally for such an inspired reaction to a hate message directed at me." I'm blushing. I know it. "In fact I want to leave it but Principal Lockheed doesn't think it belongs on a classroom door." He rolls his eyes in a dramatic way.

"Even the *ART* room door?" I can't help myself and Mr. Sanchez lets out a little laugh.

"Funny right? He didn't react this quickly with the offensive graffiti underneath." Then he gets a mock serious tone. "He wants it *quote* removed immediately and there will be no further investigation or punishment for the *vandal*." At this word I flinch because it's just ridiculous. I wonder if by doing this I somehow took the attention away from finding out who the real vandal is. I hang my head and my hair falls into my face. "So do you still want to help me with it after school? I brought in some acetone." He smiles and the bell rings at that exact second. I nod and run to my next class.

I spend my lunch period in the library because like I said I need to use the computer to research my essay. Kids are everywhere with their shiny laptops and tablets and I'm jealous because they can just do their homework at home. My stomach is growling and I'm racing against the clock to print out as much info as possible.

I dig around in my bag for the new granola bar my mom got for me and eat it in two bites. It's pretty good. The wrapper says *oatmeal fig bar* and it actually feels healthier than what I usually eat. I guzzle from my water bottle and when I go to grab the pages from the printer I freeze. There's a stack of *not my fault* cartoon flyers next to the printer. But I only printed thirty on Monday and handed them out on the down low at the assembly. So who printed these? I quickly look around and can't really identify anyone that might have done it or why so I just head off to Chemistry.

We get assigned lab partners and mine is *oh shit* Kaitlyn. Kaitlyn is one of Tara's followers who had a good laugh at me in the cafeteria the other day. She has a high ponytail and lip gloss and is trying really hard to look like a Barbie doll. She doesn't come close but I'm not a bully so I'd never point it out.

We get started and I'm feeling sick to my stomach because I'm just waiting for her to make a joke or call me names but she doesn't. I mix our compounds and she records the reactions and we don't talk much at first but it's okay. Kaitlyn's actually okay when she's not with Tara. She even smiles at me a couple of times and I'm thinking that maybe Tara's the rotten apple who spoils the bunch.

"I like your shirt." I'm shocked to hear this and then I look down and see I'm wearing the purple one with the lion wearing headphones and I'm less shocked.

"Thanks. I thought it was pretty cool." She nods and looks away quick and for the first time I think she might be as shy as I am and that's why she hangs out with someone like Tara. "I like your hair. It's so shiny." God I'm so bad at this but I think she deserves a compliment for being so brave with me.

I'm no genius but I think it takes more guts to be nice to someone than to be mean. Especially from someone like me that people make fun of. When you're nice you're putting yourself out there for rejection but being mean is easy because you're just pushing people away. Credit goes to Mom for that nugget of wisdom.

The bell rings and we turn in our lab work and put away the test tubes and other stuff. I take a chance and tell Kaitlyn *thanks* for being a cool lab partner and for being nice. She smiles and looks kind of sorry but I feel good. I wonder if my new friendship with Belinda has made me stronger. Or my art project. Or both.

The clock *tick tick ticks* away in History class because I know I have to meet Mr. Sanchez after to help erase my installment. I'm kind of sad about this but not sure what I expected anyway. Like the

Smithsonian was going to rush in and put up police tape and declare it a national treasure? Yeah right. But I think it made the right impression on Mr. Sanchez so that's enough. And maybe just maybe some of the other people who saw it got something from it too.

"Hy?" Uh-oh I was daydreaming again.

"Can you please repeat the question Mrs. Wyatt?"

"I said please give us an example of human rights." Oh this is easy because it's already in the front of my brain.

"Freedom of expression." I'm sitting taller now and trying to speak up even though my cheeks are burning.

"Good. Can you expand a bit?" Mrs. Wyatt is close to me now and she's smiling with her crooked teeth. I take a deep breath.

"I think people should be able to express themselves but not if it hurts other people." There are some snickers around me and I know it's because they're thinking I'm talking about me personally but I'm not. I go on before I lose my nerve. "Art is a form of expression and it can be inspiring or provoking. But just like words it shouldn't be used to hate or encourage hatred." Mrs. Wyatt is staring at me now. We lock eyes and even through her glasses I can tell hers are getting kind of teary. Whoa. That's weird. Must've struck a nerve or something. I've been doing that lately.

"Thank you Hy. That's a good point." She clears her throat and is walking back up to the front when the bell rings. I grab my bag and jet.

I have to pee really bad so I hit the bathroom first and pray none of my bullies have to pee too. Bathrooms are the worst because I can't escape and there are no teachers around. But I get lucky and get to pee in peace this time. On my way down to the art room I see Mr. Mayfield the janitor at the end of the hall and give him a little wave. He waves back and it makes me happy. Some seniors whose names I don't know catch this and make confused faces. *Like a student can't be cool with the janitor? I don't care at this point. We're buds now. Kindred spirits.*

"Don't worry. I documented the piece before I started." Mr. Sanchez is already at it.

He's crouched in front of the door with rags and a bottle of acetone. *It's as if he can tell what I'm thinking and wants to make me feel better about erasing it. Technically I never said I did it but I guess he saw right through me.*

"It's actually coming off." *I'm pretty surprised.*

"Slowly but surely." He tosses me a rag. We scrub and scrub. I take over the bottom half and he does the top because he's taller. Actually the *FAG* is harder to scrub off which is annoying. It's probably a cheaper spray. And it's like blood red which makes it worse. An hour later it's almost gone but still all smeary looking so they'll have to repaint anyway. Mr. Sanchez gives me a high five. "Thanks Hy. See you Friday." *I think again how lucky I am to have Mr. Sanchez as a teacher.*

My tires need air already. *Maybe the bike actually needs new tires at this point because they're kind of bald. So it's a struggle pedaling home and I'm sweating.* I stop at F Mart but the door is locked. The *closed* sign makes it pretty clear. *Nobody's there but it's only five in the afternoon. I know Mr. Fadikar's in the hospital so maybe his family couldn't cover the shifts.* I get back on my bike and ride the rest of the way home.

It's been a long day and I kind of want to talk to my Mom about some of it but when I get home she's not there. I settle onto the couch with a bag of potato chips and turn on the TV. *My head is so full with all the stuff that happened today I just sit and watch some TV judge solve other people's problems for a while.*

About an hour later I get a text from my mom saying she's going on a date right after her shift and for me to wish her luck. She also says there's leftover chicken in the fridge and I can zap a rice pouch in the microwave. I text *ok good luck* even though I'm not sure what luck has to do with anything. She's pretty and kind but I wonder for a second where she's meeting guys like Earl because she just works at the hospital and comes home. Then I guess she's probably meeting them at the hospital because it's a big place with lots of employees. Or the guys could even be patients. Yikes. Well I do hope she finds someone nice because she's dated a few losers over the years and it's hard on both of us. Mom deserves better. In fact I suddenly remember the sketch I was making when Lucas snatched it and tore it up. I grab my sketchbook from my bag and feed Rufus. My heated-up dinner gets cold again at the kitchen table because I'm focusing on redrawing Mom's halo.

9

NOW I LOVE Fridays even more because I get to see Belinda Saturdays. So like yesterday I pretty much lie low and sail through the day because the top of the week was hectic. The good news is Lucas hasn't even come near me since I told him off. I'm hoping he'll leave me alone for good.

The bell rings for lunch period and instead of heading to the cafeteria like a lamb to slaughter I find a bench outside the math building and wolf down the PB&J Mom made me. She also gave me a chocolate milk but I decide to save it for later. I've been eating different and I notice my clothes are feeling looser. I even noticed this morning my face is thinner and not so bad looking which is funny because I used to avoid the mirror at all costs.

I've still got thirty minutes left so I look around but all the other kids are in groups already. I decide to see if Mr. Mayfield the janitor is around for an art chat. The hallway by the janitor room is in the basement and it's pretty dark. I knock on the door and call out for Mr. Mayfield but he's not around. Then I hear some breathing right behind me. I spin around thinking it's him but it's not. Holy crap. If a teenager can have a heart attack I just had one.

Even though it's dark I can see the unmistakable outline of Jordan Costa's face with the swoop of dark hair. For a second I feel something other than fear which is what I usually feel when I see him. But he's moving closer to me and not saying anything and I can hear his breathing and it's heavy. I close my eyes and brace myself for a sucker punch or a lugie landing on my face and wish he'd just get it over with. But what comes next is so mind blowing I can't even comprehend it.

Jordan Costa kisses me. At least I think that's what happened because I've never been kissed before. It's soft and kinda sweet like he just drank an orange soda or something. I open my eyes slowly because I don't want to interrupt what's happening and his huge brown eyes are looking right into mine. The only way I can describe what I'm feeling is *the most*. I'm feeling *the most* hate and *the most* love and *the most* repulsion and *the most* lust all wrapped into one. Just last week this guy was making sure I felt ugly and embarrassed. Now he's making me feel wanted and special and I don't get it. He probably doesn't get it either.

I lean in quick and kiss him back because I want to feel the good the bad and the ugly again. This time I open my mouth a little because that's what I've seen people do and I've practiced on my hand. We tilt our heads to opposite sides and he holds my face with both hands and I think I'm going to faint. My heart is beating a million miles a minute and I wonder if he can taste my PB&J. I'm so grateful I didn't have tuna for lunch.

"Don't tell *anyone*. I mean it." We're both breathing heavy and he looks so intense and it sounds like a threat but I don't care because everything's different now. I feel what a superhero must feel like getting powers for the first time. But Jordan should know I could never say anything. *One* no one would believe me because Jordan Costa is one of the popular kids and he makes fun of me in front of everyone and *two* I wouldn't want to share this anyway. I'm afraid if I share it with anyone it won't be mine anymore. I could just die happy right now. How pathetic is that?

"I won't tell anyone." I promise but Jordan doesn't look happy. He looks confused. And after a second he just turns around and jogs off down the hall. Not exactly the fairytale ending but who cares. The whole rest of the day I walk around looking for signs it's just a dream and I'm gonna wake up any second and be pissed off. I look for chocolate water fountains and two headed teachers with gills or *anything* out of the ordinary. But everything still seems normal and boring.

Spanish class is a little challenging for me because we have to talk out loud a lot in another language and I'm not that comfortable talking out loud in my *own* language. My mom says it's good to learn because we have a lot of Spanish speaking people where we live but the most Spanish I'm learning is the curse words the kids use to insult each other. I'm barely paying attention to *Maria esta caminando a la tienda* when the fire alarm goes off. It's so loud and we have to drop everything and file out of the building.

Kaitlyn is also in my Spanish class and since we were lab partners together we're kind of cool now. So we're heading outside and talking about music and when we get onto the black top she looks over my shoulder and she drops the friendly face. I don't even have to turn around to know why. She backs away from me slowly and looks the other way and I brace myself for something embarrassing. But then I remember the janitor's hallway and the kiss and I feel like I'm a different person now. There's no going back. Even if it was a dare or a sick joke or whatever I *know* it was real and we both felt it. For the first time I am a part of something that happens between two people that feels *good* and nobody can take that away. But it doesn't mean they won't try.

"Oh look! Kaitlyn's earning her community service today!" There are some giggles behind Tara but not so many this time. "Hello 911? There's been an attempted Hy-jacking." A couple more giggles and then Tara gets serious. "Stay *away* Kaitlyn." I look at Kaitlyn and her face is all screwed up and I feel bad for her because she shouldn't have to take orders from Tara.

"She'd rather be Hy than *Lowe.*" It just comes out of my mouth and there are some *oohs* and *oh snaps* and I think I just said something clever. Tara's face looks all red like she can't believe that I would dare to talk back to her and for a second I'm nervous because I don't know what she'll do. But then I see Jordan coming over quick from the left.

"Leave it Tara. It's not worth it." His eyes flick at me for just a millisecond and he puts his arm around Tara and steers her in the other direction.

They walk toward the basketball hoops and Kaitlyn follows them and I don't feel so brave anymore. I'm the one standing alone again and I wonder why life has to be so cruel. Suddenly I have this memory of being on the huge rollercoaster at a theme park and I close my eyes. My stomach's flipping with each up and down just like now. Well I made it without barfing then and I can make it without crying now.

Seems like an hour before we can go back inside but that's probably just me. I'm probably the only one who actually *wants* to go back to class. The rest of the day I just feel numb and I think it's because my brain is just protecting my body from pixelating into a million little dots. Whoa what a cool image. I'm getting another idea for my project.

Finally the school day is over and on my way out I pass the bulletin board in the main hallway and freeze. Someone has pinned up five of my *not my fault* flyers in a row and they're colored in like pages from a kid's coloring book. But I look closer and that's not the only thing that's different. In one of them the superhero has glasses and a dress with a big W on it. Anyone who has Mrs. Wyatt will recognize her. Especially since the bull has big crooked teeth. In another one the bull has massive balls hanging down colored red and a big penis sticking out. That's just typical. In the third one the superhero is the principal I'm guessing with a letter P and he's punching out a student. That one isn't so good because you can still see the bull underneath. In the last one the superhero's been made into a priest or the pope or something which was easy because they both have capes. And I think the bull's supposed to be Jesus but it really just looks like a bull with a beard and sandals.

I don't know how long I've been standing there but now I'm aware of other kids looking and pointing. There's lots and lots of laughing and I feel torn between pride because my art *inspired* other art in a way and shame because the new art is making fun of people which is defeating the whole purpose of the original flyer.

Finally one of the ladies from the principal's office marches up with her arms swinging all dramatic and after looking to see what's causing the laughing she takes them all down. I swear I see her lips pressing together in the way you do when you're trying not to laugh. I mean they *are* kind of funny. And maybe Mrs. Wyatt would think so too. Or maybe she wouldn't now that I think about it. But a lot of comedy involves roasting people in general. I guess it's hard to know where the line of hurt feelings is until you cross it. And then if you *keep* crossing it you're clearly the A-hole. Well Tara's clearly an A-hole. Lucas is clearly an A-hole too and Jordan *well* Jordan's complicated now.

I think I need new underwear. It never bothered me before but now they feel all bunchy and annoying. Maybe it's the bike seat or maybe they're just old and losing shape or whatever. I'm riding home trying to keep my butt up off the seat and I decide to ride past Gram's house to check out the fence as an observer. I haven't seen Gram since and I'm kind of nervous to run into her. But as I get close I see the colors poking out against the faded houses on the street and it makes my heart happy. I coast by slowly and notice there's no dog poop or litter I usually see in front. It actually looks like someone cares and I'm thinking it can't be a coincidence.

"Hy! Yoo-hoo!" Uh-oh. There's Gram sitting up on her porch swing waving a skinny old bird wing at me. I hit the brakes too hard and dust flies up into my face and I cough a little. "Come here you." Well I can't *not* go there. I don't think it's ever cool to ignore your grandma unless she's being a total d-bag that is. And even then.

"Hey Gram." I'm aware I'm trying to act all sunny like I didn't paint her property without her permission and take off like a coward. I'm glad she grinds out her cigarette in the gross ashtray next to her with a hundred other cigarette butts in it. I sit too hard next to her on the porch swing and the thing groans and tilts and I'm afraid she's going to end up in my lap. I mean she weighs nothing. But she doesn't end up in my lap and she even lets out a weird *whoop* like she's on an amusement park ride or something. She smells a little like booze but her hair is combed and her eyes are actually twinkly today and it makes me smile for real. "What have you done with my grandma?!" I take a chance at being funny. She slaps me on the arm and giggles.

"What have you done with my fence?!" Now she's funny right back. And it suddenly feels like we don't have to say anything else. Like in just two minutes and two funny sentences we said all we need to between us. I guess that's kind of what love is. Love is when you don't need to say much or explain yourself to be understood. This time it's *me* who puts my arm around *her*.

10

MY PHONE PINGS. I wake up confused because *let's be real* my phone never pings. I grab it off the floor where it still sits in the back pocket of my joggers and remember it's Saturday. And Saturday means Belinda. I look at my phone screen and *yup* it's her.

hey meet me @ the bandshell

k gimme 15

I jump out of bed and into the shower without even waiting for it to get hot. Fastest shower ever. I'm happy Mom got me new clothes last Sunday because now I don't feel like such a shlub. I throw on a black V-neck and the joggers and my new kicks. I check out my face in the mirror and try to see the face Jordan Costa saw before he kissed me. I don't have any zits so my skin is okay. I smile wide and check out my teeth and they're pretty straight and clean. Mom says I got my green eyes from my dad because hers are brown. I run my fingers through my hair to get some of the water out and then head downstairs. I hope Belinda sees the same face Jordan sees.

When I get to the bandshell Belinda is more like the person from two Saturdays ago. She's not the *happy jumping in the water Belinda* but more like the *definitely been crying* Belinda. It's not raining but she's all tucked in the corner of the bandshell with her hoodie up like it is.

I'm out of breath because I hightailed it here so I put my hands on my knees for a second.

"What's up?" I say meaning *what's wrong*. She sniffles and wipes her nose with the back of her sleeve so I guess she's not done crying. She takes a long time to answer and I'm thinking we don't know each other that well so I don't want to be nosy but then I think why else would she have asked me to come here if she didn't want to tell me. I go closer to her and sit on the edge of the bandshell. She looks up at me with a sad smile. Ha. I love a good oxymoron.

"I'm preggo." Well of all the things she could've said I wouldn't have guessed that in a million years. Not that I have any experience with any of this stuff outside of health class so I'm just floored. She's so young and how does that even happen. I mean I know *how* it happens but how could she *let* it happen.

"Um. Whoa." It's the most intelligent answer I can manage and I kick myself for sounding so stupid and unsophisticated. But she's in a whole nother league of teenager.

"I know right?" She doesn't sound much more sophisticated than I do so I'm a little relieved.

"But how?" Really this is going to be a painful conversation if she doesn't just take the lead and spare me from asking all the details. I'm way too embarrassed for this.

"Remember a couple weeks ago I told you I had a fight with my boyfriend?" I nod. "Well I broke up with him because I told him I thought I was preggo and he said *no way I want nothin' to do with that mess*." She says his part with a sneery face and it makes him sound like a dumbass. Maybe he *is* a dumbass. "And it turns out I am. According to the stick with the two lines on it. And I thought he'd come around but he didn't." I just let out a big breath because I don't know what else to say and then I think about it some.

"But what part doesn't he want to do with?" I wonder if it's clear what I'm asking without me having to ask it. She looks at me with squinty eyes like she's deciphering my question. Guess not.

"The baby. He doesn't want the baby." Now she's bug-eyed like *duh* and I just swallow. Belinda wants to keep the baby. Jesus. I can't say I blame her boyfriend if he's her age. And if he's older well that's a different kind of problem. I suddenly feel like I'm in over my head with this new friend. Like our fun beach days are over already and I wonder if it's selfish to feel disappointed.

"But what about your dad?" Seriously I can't imagine he's okay with it.

"I haven't told him." She laughs a mean laugh and shakes her head. "Like he even knows *anything* about me."

And this breaks my heart because I know she lost her mom and her dad's not around much. But she probably should've told him she had a boyfriend because Manny *has* to know. He's driving her to another neighborhood and waiting for her and apparently not telling her dad. But I guess not everyone has a close relationship with a parent like I do. And come to think of it I don't tell my mom about the bullying much because I know she'd go to the school and make a stink and it'd make everything worse. But pregnant is way up there as far as secrets go.

Belinda starts to cry again and I move next to her and let her lean on me. She's literally crying on my shoulder. It's weird but I see everything lately inside a *not my fault* bubble. I'm like a psychic waving my hands over a crystal ball and in it I see Belinda with a huge belly. There's a black bar over her eyes like a censorship thing with *not my fault* in white chalk like it's a chalkboard. I know it's kind of old school because there aren't really chalkboards so much now in classrooms but that's okay. Then I think it's funny that old school actually means *old school* in this case. But is it her fault? I mean I guess physically she should've known better but mentally maybe she's messed up and looking for attention if all she's really got is her driver Manny to know what she's up to.

"Why not *not* have the baby?" I just blurt it out because I think it has to be an option right? "I mean you're so young and that's a huge deal." She pulls away from my shoulder and looks at me through smudgy eyes. I realize I don't know about her religion or beliefs or anything like that and maybe it's not an option for her after all. She gives me a real smile and I notice this close up she isn't wearing a retainer and her teeth are super straight and white. As if she could be any prettier.

"Thanks for being cool Hy." She's not crying anymore and stands up. "I know I shouldn't have a baby this young. And I don't really want to." She walks to the other side of the bandshell and I look again at her belly but there's no bump or anything. She must see me looking at her trying to find evidence of a baby somewhere because she wraps her arms around herself. "And it's super early." Then she picks up a rock and throws it into the bushes. "But I guess I just wanted *him* to want it. To want *me.*"

I nod because I do understand what she's saying. And I feel bad for her. Even with all her money and clothes and driver. I'm no psychologist but it sounds to me like she's trying to make a new family because she doesn't have much of one now. We sit a while looking at the mural and it makes me think of Mr. Fadikar. "So what are you going to do?" I finally say. I don't know how I can help her but I'll try.

"Well I know what I'm *not* going to do. I'm *not* going to tell my dad." This surprises me. But then I remember she's used to *not* telling him anything so it would be a pretty tough thing to start with. "Yeah he'll send me to a convent or something." Belinda isn't smiling so I guess she's serious. "Or I'll have to make an appointment at one of those places." And I guess *one of those places* is a clinic where they'll help her have a baby if she wants one or help her *not* have a baby if she doesn't.

We've had whole assemblies and health classes on this very subject in my school. Everything from the nuts and bolts of it to the choices you have after it happens. I know there are laws in some places and people who follow religions that would give someone like Belinda no choice in the matter. I mean I can respect people having different views on it for themselves and all but I don't really get how someone unrelated to you can tell you what to do with your own body. If it was another kind of operation like to remove your appendix or something nobody could force you not to do it. I know it's not really the same thing but I just also think there are so many babies made from not great circumstances that weren't wanted in the first place and it's sad. I guess I'm not religious because I lean more towards the science of it all. As far as me using the *not my fault* halo for Mom I'm just using religious symbolism. A lot of the great artists do.

"So what should we do today?" I'm changing the subject because I want to get her mind off this stuff for a second. She blows a big breath out and pops her eyes wide like she's clearing her thoughts.

"Yeah. Sorry I'm such a downer." *What?* No. I don't want her to feel bad.

"Let's do something fun. Did Manny bring you today?" Then I'm immediately embarrassed because I don't want her to have to always drive me somewhere and treat me because I have no money. But she nods and her face lights up quick.

"We passed a dinky carnival back in Rosedale." Rosedale's a nicer area and I think she lives near there.

"Sure." Now's the hard part. "Belinda I…"

"Don't have any money." She finishes for me. "It's okay. I have too much." She's grinning those white teeth at me now and I want to tell her how generous she is and how grateful I am but all I manage is *thanks*.

Manny's parked at the same intersection as last week and I wonder what it looks like to the people who live right there. It must look like a Hollywood movie or something where the princess is trying to be a normal girl so she's slumming it in the bad neighborhood. And here I come her poor raggedy little friend who's living a fairytale dream as her sidekick. Maybe we're even getting ready to switch places and see if anyone notices. Ha. If they only knew the whole story that would change the G rating. I give a little wave in the air to anyone who might be looking at us and get into the back seat.

The rest of the day is fun like last Saturday minus the towel servants plus the weight of Belinda's confession. We ride the Tilt-o-Wheel and try not to vomit. We eat chili dogs and funnel cakes and try not to vomit. The carny folk scare the crap out of me and I'm *used* to people looking and smelling homeless. Not to be mean but a lot of my neighbors would fit right in here. The problem is I wouldn't trust Mr. McCabe to operate the rides or run the safety inspections any more than I would these guys. I get that teeth are optional in this line of work but way too many sets of eyes are *all* pupils and no irises. In other words from what I've heard that means they're high as kites. And that's not a comforting thought when I'm twenty feet in the air.

Manny drops me off at home in one piece and I get out of the car with my goldfish in a plastic bag and giant stuffed elephant. "Thanks Manny." We're buds now and he gives me a fist bump through the window. "And thanks a million Belinda. That was super fun. Let me know what's up." She gives me a half-mouth smile and leans her head back on the seat. We don't have to say anything else.

The car pulls away and I feel someone watching me. Little Brian Wolk is standing in his driveway holding a beat-up soccer ball. He's only about five and I'm wondering where his mom is. Then I realize he's not staring at me he's staring at the giant elephant of course. And without thinking I walk up to him and hold out the elephant that's as big as he is.

"You want him?" His eyes bug out and he drops the soccer ball like a hot potato and grabs the elephant out of my arms and runs into his house so fast it makes me laugh. I'm too old for stuffed animals anyway and I'm pretty sure whatever Belinda whispered to the carny guy had something to do with me winning it in the first place. Plus I've still got my goldfish. I hold the bag up in front of my eyes and watch it swim in circles for a minute. "What's your name?" No answer. But I notice there's a white spot on the tip of one fin. "Okay how about Michael?" A nod to a certain musical legend of course. No answer again but no objection either so I'll take that as a *yes*.

11

I WAKE UP in a sweat. I'm pretty sure it's Sunday but I check my calendar anyway. It must be early because the sky still looks kind of dark. Why am I not surprised I had totally weird-ass dreams about carny folk stealing babies? I head to the bathroom and fumble for the light switch.

"AAHH!" I don't mean to yell but there's a strange man standing there *peeing* into my toilet. He jumps too.

"Oh my God sorry!" He donkey-kicks the door shut and I run back to my room. Mom comes right in after me.

"Sorry honey." She's laughing though. "Well you just met Ray." She sits on the edge of my bed. "Not exactly how I wanted you to but..." She's smiling big and I'm aware of the *reason* she's smiling big because I'm not stupid.

"How long've you known him Mom?" I don't mean to sound like the parent but *geez*.

"Over a year honey. We work together at the hospital." She looks at me with her eyebrows raised challenging me to say something.

"How come I never met him?" Then I lower my voice to a whisper. "And how come then you had the Earl of d-bags over the other day?" She laughs out loud and that makes me laugh too.

"Until recently there was no reason for you to meet him. He was with someone else so we were just friends." There's some stumbling and banging around and I think Ray must be hustling to get dressed.

"I saw his *butt* Mom." She stares at me for a second and then we both crack up again. Mom's wiping tears from her eyes and I'm shoving her with my shoulder. Her robe is soft and warm and I feel safe.

"Get dressed and come down for pancakes."

"Whoa. Two weekends in a row?" I'm teasing but seriously psyched about it.

It's only 6:42 AM and I'm sitting across the kitchen table from a man in a white button-down shirt and blue jeans. He's going bald and has more hair on the sides of his head than the top but his face looks nice. I mean he's not looking at me in an *unkind* way like the others. And Mom's just beaming.

"It's really nice to meet you. Your mom's told me so much about you." Now I'm embarrassed. "She says you're a great artist. I'd love to see some of your work." Is this guy for real?

"Sure." It's all I can say because I'm not really good at this conversation thing with new people and plus Mom's just put a stack of blueberry pancakes on the table between us. For the next half hour or so the three of us make small talk and eat pancakes. Then Ray leaves and I watch him drive away. "Wow Mom." I'm looking out the window and she's scraping the plates into the garbage. "He's pretty cool." And I mean it. And not because he drives a new silver car but that's not such a bad thing either.

"He makes me happy honey. But it's really new so I don't want to get my hopes up too high." She gives me a shrug and I realize that grown-ups don't have all the answers. They're just like us kids dealing with insecurities and figuring things out. Well I sure hope this guy works out for Mom because I like him too.

So before I do anything else I have to see if Mr. Fadikar is back from the hospital. Or if he's not whether I can go visit him in the hospital to show him the picture of the mural. I actually *miss* Mr. Fadikar. I miss talking to him even though I've been a lot busier and distracted lately.

My tires still need air and I have to spend way too much time digging around in the garage for the pump. I know we had one and Mom never throws anything out so I just keep searching through old lawn chairs and tools and *seriously?* a baby stroller and crib. I'm about to give up when I see the black handle of the pump sticking out underneath a FOR SALE sign. Wait a second. I just got a wicked idea on how to make some money. I'm going to have a garage sale. I'm going to clean out the garage and sell any decent stuff that nobody's used in years and make some cash. Everybody wins. And maybe I can even sell some artwork. Oh man I am so pumped. And now my tires are pumped too so I hop on my bike and take off for the F Mart.

When I lean my bike up against the wall near the entrance I'm happy to see someone coming out so I know it's open. But Mr. Fadikar isn't behind the counter. I recognize his son though and I'm mad at myself because I can't remember his name.

"Hello. My name is Hy." I'm hoping he says his name too without me having to ask it. "Remember we met last week?" He looks at me for a second and then smiles and comes from behind the counter. He sticks out his hand and I shake it.

"Arjun." Good he said it. "You were friends with my father, right?" Okay call me crazy but I think he just said you *were* friends with my father. Then I get a hot feeling up my spine and it's like I just know. "I'm sorry. My father passed away on Thursday." *Boom.* The hot feeling just exploded in my head and I feel dizzy. Arjun must see this because he grabs the chair from behind the counter and eases me into it. And then he's handing me a tissue so I must need one. *Yup* I know I'm crying now because I can taste it. But I'm too sad to be embarrassed because all I can think about is Mr. Fadikar is gone and I didn't get to show him the mural.

"But *not my fault…*" I hear my own voice and it sounds like it's coming from someone else.

"What? Of course it's not your fault." Arjun doesn't get it. But why would he? I have to stop this crying and explain what I mean.

"No the mural. I made it for Mr. Fadikar…I mean I made it for your father." He looks confused so I get up from the chair *slowly.* "Can I show you?" He nods and puts the closed sign in the window and locks up behind us.

We walk in silence the few blocks with him half next to me half following me. When we get close to the bandshell Arjun stops in his tracks. I look back and now *he's* the one crying. It's always weird seeing someone cry. It's not like smiling or frowning or laughing or shouting in anger. It's such a private thing. I keep walking toward the bandshell to give him more privacy.

Eventually he walks up to join me and we sit on the edge next to each other.

"Thank you my friend. This is…unexpected." I manage a nod. "Can you tell me about what inspired it?" There's that word again.

So I tell Arjun about the other kids and how they made fun of his father's English and the F Mart and how *I* respected him for coming to a new country and starting a business and all that. And then I tell him about the whole *not my fault* project and how the mural fits in.

He just sits and listens and wipes his nose with a tissue. Then I have one more idea.

"You know this mural could take on another meaning now. It could mean it's *not my fault* I got sick and had to leave my family behind." I stop for a second because I'm feeling like I might cry again. And then I go on and tell Arjun about how maybe he was even like a dad to me too because my own dad doesn't want to know me. Then quickly I tell him I hope I don't offend him because Mr. Fadikar's his real dad but Arjun just shakes his head and says he would've been so happy to hear that.

"Mind if I take a picture?" He's standing now and getting his phone out. Arjun's phone is new like Belinda's and not ancient like mine. I bet the camera is awesome.

"Sure. I mean *no* I don't mind." He snaps a few from different angles and we head back without saying much else. "Will you run the F Mart now?" It dawns on me the F Mart might not be there one day.

"We're not sure yet exactly what will become of the store but for now my mother and I will keep it open." I nod and take the three bucks out of my pocket and grab a big bag of cheese curls. Arjun takes one of the singles out of my hand and winks at me because it costs more than that and I shove the other two back in my pocket. I give him a wave and a *see ya* and head home on my bike.

My mom is out thankfully because my self-sabotage should neither be witnessed nor interrupted. I crawl under my covers and tear open the bag of cheese curls and start the train rolling. Hand to mouth to hand to mouth to hand to mouth. Repeat until all trace of orange powdery residue is gone. But it's like trying to douse a beach bonfire with a few grains of sand. At least that's what I saw them do in a movie once. The fire in my belly is being doused one cheese curl at a time while Rufus whines outside my door.

It's just so huge. Mr. Fadikar is gone. Gone as in never coming back. As in never going to smile or listen to me or give me words of encouragement or free snacks ever again. And poor Mrs. Fadikar. She must be *so* sad. And his son Arjun. For a minute I try to imagine what it would be like to lose my dad and I feel nothing. Then I try to imagine what it would be like to lose my mom and I start crying so hard I don't even hear her come home until she's in my room and pulling back my covers.

"What's wrong honey??" Her face is all screwed up with worry and then she sees the empty bag of cheese curls with the orange stains on the sheets. She sighs a big sigh and plops down on my bed.

"This is just too much." It's so weird to think that only a few hours ago we were both *laughing* right here on my bed. I tell her about Mr. Fadikar and she says a lot of *oh honey* and *I'm so sorry* and rocks me in her arms. I know I should tell her about the mural but I'm scared she'll get really mad and put an end to my project. Gram's fence is one thing and she cut me a break because it actually made Gram's property look better but the bandshell is public property and I could get in serious trouble.

"You want to tell me about these walls?" We're lying back on the pillows and she doesn't sound mad so I risk a side-eye to try and read her expression. Her expression actually looks more like awe than pissed off and she's tilting her head to follow the *not my faults* around in circles. I tell her about the ants and my memory of the sugar water. She laughs and says she remembers it too. Then I find myself telling her about the meaning of the project and how the same three words defend each subject in a different way. She's smiling so I take another chance. I dig through my backpack and find the original sketch of the superhero and the bull and tell her about the copies I made and handed out at the assembly. Her eyebrows shoot up as she checks out the sketch.

"They didn't catch you?"

"Nope."

"I think I'm more impressed with the fact you put yourself out there. You took a big risk of being discovered." Mom grins. "You must be really feeling this art thing." I hope she means what she says because she doesn't know the half of it.

12

MOM HAS THE late shift which means she starts after dinner and gets home when I'm leaving for school in the morning. So after she takes off for the hospital I just bum around the house for a while. I watch some stupid show on house decorating and realize I could care less about that stuff and then just head upstairs. But I'm still feeling pretty low about Mr. Fadikar and I don't even want to draw or anything.

I head into the bathroom to take a shower and take all my clothes off. I take a good look at myself in the bathroom mirror and think that for someone who is so amped on art and color I have the most boring brown hair ever. It's not even a shiny dark chocolate color like Belinda's. It's a watery mud puddle brown and I'm sick of it. So I rummage around under the sink because I know my mom stocks up on hair dye trying to stay blond. I pull out a crushed looking box from the back of the cabinet and it looks pretty old like it's abandoned so I open it. I mean why not? Most of my music idols have crazy color hair.

I take a deep breath and follow the instructions step by step. *Oh my god* it stinks so bad. No more than spray paint but I'm not usually spraying my own head. So I have to sit and wait for thirty minutes except after about twenty I panic and throw my head under the bathtub faucet. But it's too late. When I pull the towel away the color underneath is not the same brown or even a cool blond because I stopped short of the time it said. Instead the color is more like *pumpkin* and I'm mortified. But you know what? The hell with it. I can't call myself an artist if I don't allow myself the freedom of expression. Even if it means screwing up. Hey wait a minute. Gram and I could go on tour together. Troll one and troll two. I laugh out loud and think I must be okay if I can still crack myself up. But *uh-oh* Mom. I grab my phone.

Mom don't be mad

What did you do

I used a box of your hair dye

Oh honey

I'm all set for Halloween

Lol are you ok?

Yup I'm cool

Ok see you in the AM

xo

Seriously though. She's being cool but what have I done? I actually have to go to school and see people tomorrow. And I was thinking that nobody would notice or better still think it looks badass and shower me with compliments? I dig around in my closet for a hat. I find a dirty gray baseball hat with a dolphin on it and I wonder where I even got it because I don't remember. I slap it on and tuck the new orangey hair behind my ears. Okay I can relax a little. It's not that obvious with the hat.

I'm so tired. I grab an old comic book and get into bed. Hey the guy on the cover's got orange hair. Twinning with my cartoon brother. But I can't keep my eyes open and finally I turn out the light and think about Jordan Costa. I have been thinking about him every night since the *incident*. I replay it over and over and relive the same awesome tingly feelings. Sometimes I even help myself to some more tingly feelings because why not? But I mean what was he even thinking. If anyone found out about me his reputation would be absolutely shattered. My reputation wouldn't suffer in the least. In fact it would probably get a boost because I assume nobody has expectations of me in the first place. But for Jordan it would be pretty scandalous if you go by the fact that Tara is his girlfriend. It makes me smile just thinking about it and even though he didn't defend me in front of her I still know something scandalous about her boyfriend that *she* does not.

The next thing I know my alarm is stabbing through my skull with a *beep beep beep*. I check my hair in the mirror to make sure it wasn't a dream and *nope* it wasn't and *yup* I'm still a ginger clown. I think it's important to wear some good clothes today because someone might notice me more than before. I'm eating my cereal when Mom comes home and she looks tired but still happy. She freezes when she sees me.

"That bad?" I haven't put the hat on yet but I've brushed my hair off my face.

"Actually it's dyn-o-mite." What trip is she on with the Seventies sit-com words.

"Wait you *like* it?" I'm shocked.

"It's like you're wearing the sun as a hat. It brightens your face. Honestly I was expecting cheese curls but it's more melon." I grimace at the mention of cheese curls. "Thank Jesus." She puts a hand on my head like Jesus with a disciple. Speaking of Jesus I really need to figure out how I'm going to do Mom's *not my fault*. I don't have big poster board or anything so I might ask Mr. Sanchez. But then I remember something.

"Oh Mom? Can I do a garage sale?" She thinks about it.

"Is there enough stuff?"

"Geez Mom have you been out in the garage lately? You're a bonafide hoarder." She laughs. "Seriously I think I could really make some money. And maybe even sell some artwork." She shrugs at this.

"Okay. If you want to do all the work of cleaning and tagging and making posters. And you'll have to advertise you know."

"Yup. Thanks Mom."

It's raining so she drives me to school and drops me out front swearing to me that I don't look like Bozo. I wear the baseball cap anyway. But I know we're not allowed to wear hats in class so if I ever needed strength I need it today. *If anyone makes any comments just smile back* Mom says. She says it'll confuse them. Maybe she's had some experience with teasing. I never really asked her about her own childhood that much.

We don't have assigned seats so I can hide at the back of History class and take off my cap after everyone's seated. Mrs. Wyatt notices me and does a double take but thankfully doesn't call on me for the whole class. I think she gets me and I feel bad about the drawing someone did of her on my flyer. I hope she didn't see it before it got taken down.

I'm leaving History and before I get I chance to put my cap back on I see Jordan and Tara walking toward me. If I could describe how he's looking at me I would say *laser beams.* Seriously I feel hot like his eyes are burning right through me. Tara doesn't notice me at first but then she asks Jordan something and I guess he doesn't answer so she looks at him and follows his eyes right to me. And she looks back at Jordan and then back at me. It's like time is standing still and everyone else in the hallway freezes while the three of us exist in our own little vortex. Jordan can't seem to take his eyes off me and Tara looks really spooked like she's seen a ghost or something. Then I hear my mom's voice in my head and I smile. That's all. I just smile at Jordan and he turns and takes off like a scared rabbit. And Tara takes off after him. Well whaddya know. Thanks Mom.

I'm in the hallway still trying to decipher what that look from Jordan meant when someone grabs my arm and pulls me into the stairwell. Before I can even see or react there's a mouth on mine and it's urgent and soft and familiar. I don't even open my eyes because I know who it is. And now I know what the look meant too. This time he's got his hands on me and my whole body is like an earthquake. Then just like that he's gone. And just like an earthquake I feel the aftershocks the whole rest of the day. I get a bunch of stares in other classes but honestly I could care less now. It's like something shifted in the universe and I've crossed a threshold in time and space and there's no going back. I've got an *I'm worth something* forcefield around me now. Until I don't.

Tara and Kaitlyn are standing against the wall across from my locker. *My* locker. It's after last class and other kids are hanging around and whispering and waving their hands in front or their faces like something stinks. I walk up in slow motion and I smell it before I see it. Shit. No actual *shit*. And it's been smeared on my locker and stuffed into the vents and all in the combination lock. There is one orange post-it that says *What Am I* on the top and one below it that says *Freak*.

Something inside me just breaks. It's like I'm climbing to the top of a mountain every day and getting shoved off. I can't take it. I look at Tara and she has such hate in her eyes. And I know why because she's not as dumb as she seems. But this is not my fault. It's *NOT MY FAULT*. I'm the opposite of a violent person but right now I want to slam Tara against my locker and rub her hair in the shit. Kaitlyn looks away like she's caught between two worlds and I get it. If I were her I'd probably stand on Tara's side too now that we all see what she's capable of. I know

Kaitlyn couldn't take this kind of hate aimed at her. Fortunately and unfortunately I'm used to it.

Instead of reacting though I turn quick so nobody sees the tears in my eyes and head to the one place I know I'll get help because even though I'm embarrassed this is something I can't ignore or fix by myself. I'm full out crying by the time I get to the janitor closet and thank god Mr. Mayfield is there.

"Show me." Is all he says. He just knows somehow. He grabs his cleaning cart and I lead him back up to my locker and point because even though there are only a couple kids left and they're leaving in a hurry I can't be near it or I'll throw up. Not even from the smell so much as from the idea that one human being could be so cruel to another.

"I'm sorry." It's all I can say because it's so horrible that Mr. Mayfield has to clean up something like this and I even say I'll come help him but he just holds up his hand.

"You stay put. I got this mess." And he actually *smiles* at me and my heart swells for this nice man. Mr. Mayfield scrubs and washes for a few minutes and then he motions for me to come over. "Can you open the lock now?" I do the combination and I'm holding my breath because I think the shit's going to be all inside my locker. But it's not really. After careful inspection it looks like it's only on the inside of the door where the vents are. I step back and he scrubs and wipes it off. "Do you know who did this?" I nod. "Wanna talk about it?" I don't really but he's so nice to me so I think *what the hell.*

"There's someone who is feeling threatened because *their* someone has taken an interest in me." Mr. Mayfield nods and says *aaah.*

"Matters of the heart ain't nothin' to play with." He smiles a crinkly-eyed wise smile.

"But it's not my fault." It's not lost on me how this theme keeps repeating itself.

"It don't matter. I had me a lady once who had eyes for another feller and when I found out I gave that guy a good left hook. It weren't his fault neither but I was mad at him for just *existing*." My head feels heavy and I realize how tired I am being a target for just *existing*. It's all got to be for something. What doesn't kill you makes you stronger or something right?

"Thanks a lot Mr. Mayfield." And I mean it.

I walk with him for a bit and then when I'm sure everyone else is gone I head outside. I don't even have my bike today to make a quick getaway because Mom dropped me off this morning. Ugh.

13

AS I WALK home I think about how I can get back at Tara. I'm not a mean person so everything I think of makes me feel bad right away. But she went way too far. I could tell Jordan to keep her away from me because why the hell does he get to be a coward in all of this? But I guess he's got more at stake and I don't know how he would even explain to her why he'd be defending me. I play the kisses over and over in my head and think about whether I'd be willing to sacrifice more of them if he won't do anything about Tara.

Then I think maybe I should ask Belinda for some advice. She seems pretty experienced. Actually she got herself into some serious trouble so maybe she's not the best advice-giver. But what choice do I have? There's no way I can trust my mom not to blow up about all this. I mean she loves me *a lot* and that can be a problem sometimes.

I see the F Mart roof and I get a pang in my heart all over again. I don't even have my friend Mr. Fadikar to talk to. But wait a minute. Maybe Arjun is my friend now. He seems pretty cool and he's younger than his father *duh* so he might be able to give me some insight.

"Hey Arjun." I'm glad it's him behind the counter and not Mrs. Fadikar.

"Hey Hy. Nice hair." He gives me a thumbs up.

Then I hear kids laughing in the back by the soda and I recognize Jorge and Pete from the neighborhood. I think they're in middle school and they're pretty much little A-holes. Pete's got on a big overcoat which looks weird and his arms are shoved deep into the pockets. *Man* the two of them just look super suspicious and as they try to leave Arjun steps in front of the door.

"Give it up Pete. And maybe I won't tell your mother." Pete's ears turn a beet red color and I'm fascinated. I've never seen *ears* blush before.

Jorge and Pete exchange a panicked look and Arjun winks at me. Wow I can't imagine Mr. Fadikar standing up to these guys the way Arjun is. I guess it's the generation thing. Then Pete hangs his head and pulls his hand out of his pocket. He's holding one of those super tall beers. So the little shit steals and not only that it's alcohol. Arjun takes it from his hand and tells them to *get lost.* They look like scolded dogs and they take off.

"Whoa. How did you know for sure?" I mean they looked suspicious but I'm impressed that he acted on it. Arjun shakes his head and puts the beer back in the cooler.

"My father said the beer inventory was always coming up short at the end of the week and he didn't have any idea why. He was very trusting. Too trusting obviously." He gives a sad kind of smile.

"They're such punks those kids." I don't know what else to say. He nods.

"Seems not everybody is brought up right." That's true.

I start browsing the candy aisle and the strawberry laces get my mouth twitching. "Arjun can I ask your opinion on something?" He settles back onto his stool behind the counter.

"Sure." There's something about him that makes me feel safe about sharing. Maybe it's because we *bonded in grief* or something.

"There's this situation at school." He raises his eyebrows like he's waiting for me to continue. "Someone's being really mean to me. Like in a bullying way. And I'm feeling like I *have* to retaliate so she won't just keep doing it." His eyes look sympathetic now and I'm so glad he's not one of those people that just talk and don't listen. I can tell he's really listening. "But I don't want to do anything mean back because that's not *me*." Arjun nods.

"So you just want to send a message." He gets it.

"Yeah. I don't need to humiliate her the way she humiliated me but it has to be effective." I realize I'm not giving him any details. I guess I have to. "The person she's seeing made a move on me in secret but I think she knows." He gives a big *Oh* like he wasn't expecting this. It's such a bold confession and he's probably trying to picture the scenario. "I didn't ask for it. It's not my fault. She shouldn't be mad at *me*." I blurt out these last sentences in a row.

"What you just said. *Not my fault.* Isn't that the mural you did for my father?" I nod and like a lightbulb in my brain I know what he's thinking. And then he says it. "You use art to express yourself. Why would this be any different?"

"Thanks Arjun." I feel lighter like a weight has been lifted. I start to leave. He calls out the door after me.

"The *Art of War* my friend. Know when to advance and when to defend." I give him the thumbs up now. He's a cool dude.

Well it's time to advance and I need to make a *not my fault* just for Tara. Something she'll seriously have to think about and understand my power in this situation. Anything I say about Jordan will reflect on Tara. I could take them both down reputation-wise in one shot if I had proof. But I don't even want to go there. I just want her to know I *can* go there so she'll back off.

Mom's not home and I'm glad because I don't want to be distracted. I grab a granola bar from the cabinet and head straight up to my room. Rufus jingle jangles up after me and I pet him for a minute. He's always glad to see me. I'm getting an idea but I need last year's yearbook. It has to be around here somewhere so I search my shelves and go through piles of stuff. I can't find it anywhere and then I go down and try the living room because my mom was probably looking at it. And *yup* there it is shoved between an old baby book and an even older cookbook.

I pull it out and start flipping through the pages. It's not hard to find Tara because she's on lots of pages. Tara in a cheerleading outfit. Tara on the yearbook committee. Tara in the Spanish club. I gag at the smiley face that's hiding the evil underneath. I go to the Cs and find Jordan's headshot and dog-ear the page. He looks so young because it's a year ago but he's still hot. I find Tara's headshot in the Ls and dog-ear that page too.

When I find mine I cringe. It's like I'm looking at someone else. It's not that I actually look that different but more like I'm now seeing through some kind of wisdom goggles. I have to laugh at myself. Like now I'm frigging Gandhi because I've had a tiny bit of experience. But I guess that's what growing up feels like. Life wouldn't make sense if we stayed the same every year.

Anyway I run back upstairs and sit at my desk with all my art supplies. Arjun got me thinking with the Art of War comment. I remember reading about these three wise monkeys which everybody knows as *see no evil* and *hear no evil* and *speak no evil*. I can use that to tell Tara that if she doesn't *see* I won't *speak* and the school won't *hear*. Pretty clever if I do say so myself.

I flip to Tara's page. I draw two cupped hands and cut them out and paste them over Tara's eyes. Next I draw two cupped hands for me and flip to my page and paste them over my mouth. Now's the hard part. I have to make *lots* more cupped hands and cut them out. This takes a good hour. Then I flip through and identify all their friends or at least most of them and paste all the little cupped hands over their ears. And saving the best for last I flip to Jordan. I make the coolest crown in gold with gems on all the spikes and cut it out. I carefully paste it onto his head and I must say he looks badass. Like he could be a real king.

I sit back and try to imagine Tara looking through the yearbook and I hope she has the good sense to look at it alone. And I *really* hope she gets it and takes it as a peace offering so we can move on. I mean forget the principal I should frigging call the police for what she did to my locker. How did she even get real shit to smear in the first place? Was it human or dog or something else? I gag thinking about it all over again and I tell myself to calm down. I try to imagine Tara's life as one of the beautiful people and what it must be like to have everyone want to be your friend and no one say no to you. I guess it must be pretty much of a shock when your friend and even your boyfriend shows interest in a different kind of person than you expect. I can't believe this but I'm actually feeling sorry for her. She must be even more insecure than I am. Whoa. Belinda is way prettier than Tara and she's got money and cool clothes but she'd never pull a stunt like that. I just know it.

I stick the yearbook in my backpack so I won't forget it tomorrow. Wait. I forgot to document the piece so I pull it back out again. I grab my phone out of my pocket and snap a picture of each page I doctored. Then I take one of the cover just for reference. I'm thinking about how I'm actually going to give the yearbook to Tara. I wonder if I could ask Kaitlyn to give it to her. *Nah* that would put her in a bad spot.

If she was thinking of maybe being my friend she wouldn't trust me after that. I guess Jordan's out of the question unless he thought it was cool but I can't take the chance of him keeping it from her if he doesn't. I wonder if he knows about the locker incident by now. It'll get back to him and everyone else by tomorrow for sure but Tara's not claiming it so I don't know if anyone's going to know who did it. I mean Jordan *should* know after that look she gave me in the hall. There are other kids who bully me for no reason like Lucas. But he stopped. Didn't he? Now I'm wondering if Lucas did it. I get a hot feeling like I'm on the wrong trail. Then I remember Tara's face. I remember the *hate* and the post-it that said the same thing Jordan put on my back once. It was definitely her. But I can't imagine her touching actual shit so maybe she got someone like Lucas to do the dirty work for her.

And now I'm sad again because Jordan must hate himself for having feelings for me and not being able to deal with it. And it must be why he went out of his way to tease me in the first place. He could've just ignored me like most other people but he *made contact* the only way that would fly under the radar I guess. God it's so obvious now. But at this point he crossed the line and we can't even have a conversation about the fact that there's a real attraction between us. Because I don't fit the mold. I don't fit into his image or his world. The cool jock with the trophy cheerleader has a desire for *me*. What? Everyone would turn on him if they knew. His comfy life at school would crumble for sure. And I get it but it makes me so sad. I finally feel what it's like to be wanted but I can't have it like a normal person. I scratch Rufus behind the ears and wonder if *I'll* ever be someone's trophy.

14

"I'M SICK." IT'S eight and I'm still in bed and Mom is standing in the doorway of my room.

"What's wrong honey?" She's not buying it because she's got that *mom-elepathy* but she's looking at me with sympathy anyway like even if I'm not physically ill she gets that I don't want to go to school for some reason.

"I just don't want to go today okay?" There's really no argument she could make because I always go to school. I can have one day off without the third degree.

She sits on the edge of my bed and I pull my covers up over my head. I feel a hand on my shoulder. "Let's talk." But I don't want to. It's all so exhausting and I just don't have the energy to deal with it.

"Mom please. Can I just stay home today? I'll make up any work tomorrow." She sighs all heavy.

"Sure. I know you're a good student honey. But can I just ask why?"

"Do I have to talk about it? I mean no offense Mom but there's just some stuff going on at school with a couple of kids and I need a break."

Truth is I'm realizing that after being a lone wolf for so long all this interaction with actual people and feelings is wearing me out. I almost want to go back to before Jordan kissed me and turned my world upside down. Almost. Mom sits there for a minute and then gets up.

"Okay. I'm trusting you to let me in when you're ready. But you *will* let me know if something bad is going on because I care about you Hy. Feed yourself and Rufus and I'll be home after my shift."

"Thanks Mom. Love you." She knows I mean it. After a minute I hear her car keys jingling in her hand and she calls upstairs.

"Why don't you use the day to go through the garage and get ready for that garage sale?"

"Good idea!" I call back because it is a good idea. Something positive to take my mind off that other crap. Ha. No pun intended.

The garage is so musty I head straight to the back and open both windows wide. *Sorry little guys* I apologize to all the inhabitants of the webs and nests I'm disturbing but it has to be done. I've never been afraid of spiders because I think they're so cool. I mean the perfect geometric architecture they build overnight is inspiring. How can anyone think these creatures are less than super intelligent? *Come on* like they're on this earth just to scare us?

Anyway I decide to make a pile of sellable stuff in the front and put the non-sellable stuff against the back wall. I'm guessing I've been at it a couple of hours because the sellable pile is pretty big already. There's a bike helmet and a scooter and a stroller and a crib and roller blades and a wooden chair and a puppet theater. The puppet theater still creeps me out because I never thought puppets were funny. Maybe Mom and I just weren't good at it. In the junk pile are three soccer balls with no air and elbow pads with too much mildew and a dented wiffle bat and a busted tire swing *really?* and some cardboard boxes.

Wait a minute. I open one of the boxes and look inside. It looks like drawings. My drawings. I sit on one of the other boxes and start going though them. I must be only five or six but the drawings are actually pretty good considering. I wonder if Mom knew that art was going to be my thing that early. Well she sure saved all these so maybe.

There are a couple of pictures of a house with the sun in the sky. I'm guessing it's our house even though it doesn't look much like it because kids always draw their own houses. In the first one there's a stick figure with a triangle skirt waving from the doorway. My mom I'm guessing. She's waving but she's got a frown and a big blue tear below her eye. There's another face in the window upstairs in the house and that must be me. I also have a frown but no tears. I don't think it takes a genius to figure out that this drawing represents my dad leaving us. The second one shows a small kiddie pool in front of the house with a head sticking out. I'm guessing it's me and this time I have a smile. There's a black dog jumping but it's not Rufus it must be Captain Hook our other mutt. He died when I was about ten. There's another picture of a rectangular red building which must be my school. It has a flagpole outside and there's a swing set with kids on it. There are also kids jumping rope and kids playing with a ball. The school has rows of windows and way at the end is a face in one of the windows. You don't have to be a genius to figure out this is me. I'm inside alone when all the other kids are outside playing. Okay this comes as no surprise but what does bother me is that in each picture I'm only a *head*. There's no body attached. Not even shoulders.

I put the boxes back against the wall and go inside for lunch. Mac and cheese or leftover meatloaf? No contest. Mac and cheese it is. I give Michael a pinch of fish flakes and watch him gobble them up at the surface. Then he swims around in circles again.

"Rufus. Bone or bone?" He barks. "Bone it is." I toss him the bone and as usual he misses it. Then he zips around in circles like something's stinging him on the butt.

As I nosh on my mac and cheese and watch Michael swim in circles I think how boring it must be to be a fish. Then I remember Mom said I have to tag the things for the sale. I have no idea how much money these old things would be worth to someone. I mean I'm just trying to make a few bucks and also clear out the garage. I think back to the garage sales Mom and I went to over the years. We went to a lot of them even in the next towns over because she said for stuff like clothes and toys that kids grow out of quick it's way cheaper than buying it all new. Which reminds me there are a couple plastic bins of my old clothes in the garage too.

I put my bowl in the sink and grab a piece of paper and tape and scissors from my room. But when I look for a marker in the junk drawer I see a package of blank *FOR SALE* stickers. Nice. Thanks Mom. This'll be way easier. On my way out to the garage I'm seeing the prices pop into my head. Maybe ten bucks each for the scooter and roller blades. Fifteen for the puppet theater and the stroller and the crib. The bike helmet's only worth a buck probably and I have to ask Mom about the chair because I don't know if it's special or anything because it's old and made of wood.

Next I open the bins of clothes. Yuck. They smell pretty musty. I wonder if we need to wash them before the sale. Well at least I can sort them so I make piles of tops and piles of bottoms and then a miscellaneous pile. I like the word *miscellaneous*. It basically covers anything. A really lazy person could just get a bunch of boxes and label them all miscellaneous and make everyone else sort through them. It wouldn't be wrong it would just be lazy.

I must've really liked stripes when I was young. There's miniature striped everything. Shorts and T-shirts and bathing suits and sweaters. I have to ask Mom later about the stripes obsession. Maybe she got it all from a prison tag sale or sailor thrift store. I crack myself up. But suddenly I feel weird. I think the problem with going through all these old clothes is the memories they're attached to.

I'm holding a stained yellow T-shirt and I'm having flashbacks like in a movie and I see myself from the outside. I remember exactly what the stain is from and it makes my skin tingle with danger all over again. My mom gave me two dollars for the ice cream truck which was a special treat and I was holding my chocolate soft serve cone when Chuck Gallagher shouted "Bee!" And all the kids in line ran in different directions. Well of course one of them knocked into me and my chocolate cone bounced from my hand to my shirt to the ground. He pointed at me and everyone laughed and he said *there was no bee* he just wanted to get to the head of the line. So I had no more ice cream and my shirt was ruined and now everyone was looking at me. Then a girl pointed at my shorts because there was another wet stain happening. For some reason I peed my pants and didn't feel it. I remember the looks on their faces and that's pretty much when I was sure I was destined be a target. Like I was born with a bullseye pinned to my back.

I toss the shirt into the throw away pile and think maybe I'll even burn it later. Nobody needs that karma. I decide that's enough of that. Memory lane isn't lined with flowers for me like it is for other people. *My* memory lane is lined with brambles and thorns and invisible bees. Funny how I thought this tag sale would take my mind off those kinds of feelings today but I guess they followed me into the garage. Or more like they were waiting for me in the garage. Anyway this sale will be good. And maybe I can even sell a few of my art pieces.

Now for the posters. I can do posters. But I don't have any poster board so I find an empty cardboard box and tear it into four pieces. I grab the brightest colored sprays I have and lay the cardboard down in the driveway. I make four *GARAGE SALE* signs in big bubble letters outlined in black. They're pretty cool. They look like the old school New York City graffiti I've seen in movies. Then I think this Saturday would be a good day so I put the date and I've mostly seen *10 to 4* on other garage sale posters so I put that as the time. I hope Belinda will want to come and hang with me because Saturday is kind of our day now. I decide to pull out my phone and ask her.

Hey garage sale at my house this Saturday?

She doesn't get back to me right away and then I remember it's a school day even though *I'm* not in school. I wonder if they let her have her phone during the day at her fancy private school.

I'm just about to call it a day with this project when I see two little matching side tables that I didn't see before. I think the bins of clothes must have been blocking them. They have ugly kiddie stickers all over so I get an idea. A blur of an hour later I've got two wicked cool looking tables painted in a purple red orange ombre down the legs. Whoa. I could charge at least fifteen bucks a piece or twenty-five for the pair. I know from those TV shows that people come from pretty far to hit up garage sales in neighborhoods like ours looking for *hidden gems* and I want them to find some here.

My heart is on fire and I look at the other stuff in the sell pile with fresh eyes. The puppet theater is plain with only *PUPPET THEATER* in black letters at the top. Oh man it's just begging for color. Why hadn't I noticed before? The scooter could be badass with flames coming from the wheels and handles. The crib could be painted like the sky with clouds passing through the bars. Less like prison and more like heaven. I'm really so full of hope and inspiration and excitement now. This garage sale is going to be amazing.

So I get to work dragging everything from the sell pile out into the driveway and going for it. I don't know how much time passes but at some point I notice little Brian Wolk is there watching me. He's hugging the big elephant I gave him and it makes me feel proud all over again. I get this strange feeling that maybe just maybe everything is going to work out.

15

SOMEWHERE A PHONE is ringing. It sounds muffled like it's underwater. I see it at the bottom of the pool and dive in head first with all my clothes on. I keep kicking and kicking but the bottom is just getting farther away. I'm starting to panic now like I'm gonna run out of air so I turn around and swim toward the surface. The phone is still ringing and I'm just about to get to the top when I see a hand come down and hold my face under the water. *I can't breathe I can't breathe I can't breathe.* I'm struggling and flailing and I see a face through the squiggly lines of the water. She looks like a big ugly clown with her red lips and black hatred dripping from her eyes and I know I'm dying.

Then all of a sudden I'm *not* dying I'm sitting upright on the couch and I'm gasping for air and Rufus is barking at me with his goofy snaggle teeth. Jesus. It was just a nightmare. My phone is ringing for real and I dig it out of the crack between the cushions.

"Shut it Rufus!" He whines and lies down.

"Hey. So a garage sale huh?" It's Belinda.

"Yeah." I hope I sound cool but I'm still pretty shaky. Besides we usually text so a call is kinda weird. I remember I asked her if she wanted to do the sale with me. Wait. Was that today or yesterday? What time is it? It's still light out and my mom's not home so I think I just fell asleep for a second after doing all the garage stuff. When I get one of those *following my inspiration* moments it really wears me out mentally. "You think you can come hang? I found some cool stuff and I even did some art projects so maybe..."

"Um yeah. I think so." She cuts me off and her voice sounds a little sad and then I remember the situation she's in. "I have an appointment in the morning but I can have Manny drop me after."

"Okay cool." I sound chill but I'm doing backflips inside. Belinda gives me confidence because she doesn't take shit from anyone and I'm gonna need that from her. I don't think I'm such a good salesperson but I bet she will be.

"Want me to go with you? To your appointment?"

I'm taking a chance here because I'm pretty sure I know what kind of appointment would make her sad but I'm not positive. A hair appointment wouldn't make you sad. A nail appointment wouldn't make you sad. Only a *doctor* appointment would make you sad and I should give her my support if I'm asking for hers.

"Nah. Thanks Hy." She sighs and does a funny voice. "But if I'm feelin' chicken I'll let you know."

"Okay good luck. See you Saturday." Then it suddenly occurs to me maybe she called me instead of texting so it wouldn't be in writing on her phone. I guess she's got to be all secretive with her dad because she'd be in serious trouble if he knew.

"Yup thanks." And she hangs up.

Mom pulls up a few minutes later and comes into the kitchen with a bag of groceries.

"Mom come see what I did." I'm actually pretty excited so I tug on her sleeve. Her eyebrows shoot up and she puts the groceries down.

"Let me just put a pot of water on to boil." I hope that's for her famous spaghetti marinara. Yum.

I take her into the garage and she stops in her tracks when she sees the painted tables and scooter and crib and for a split second I'm worried she'll be mad. But then I remember this was all junk this morning and I grin at her with some hope.

"Holy crap honey!" Now this reaction I didn't expect. Maybe a *that's nice* or *how sweet* to make me feel good. But a *holy crap?*

"Holy crap honey you like it? Or holy crap honey it's ugly?" I'm serious I don't know which it is.

"Holy crap honey you are my crazy talented angel." And something about the way she says it all quiet like she's in a church makes me want to cry. And she looks like she wants to cry too.

"How much do you think I could get for this stuff?" I'm trying to steer us both away from the crying thing.

"Um…let me think about it. Because you know people around here don't have so much money but there are people outside the neighborhood that go checking out garage sales for treasures."

I know this because I've seen those reality TV shows. My favorite one was where some guy bought a couch for twenty bucks and there was fifty thousand in cash sewn into the bottom of it. The funny thing is the guy who bought it actually *returned* the money to the seller. Who does that? Some kind of saint that's who. It was so cool because the guy could've used the money but he had such strong morals he needed to be honest. Turns out the seller's Grandpa had stashed the money in the couch without telling anyone and when he died they just cleared out his stuff. But what bummed me out a little was that the family didn't split the cash with the guy or even give him *some* of it. I think that would've made for even better TV. Oh well.

"Maybe they will love your one-of-a-kind pieces too." Mom gives me a big hug and goes back into the house to make dinner.

I love the way she says *pieces* because it makes me feel legit. So I hang out in the garage for a sec fantasizing about being discovered by a reality TV show following some perfect looking people slumming it in our hood. With my eyes closed I can see the cameraman aiming at me and the fuzzy mic boom over my head capturing the moment the perfect chick says to the perfect guy *oh my god I think we've discovered the next Salvador Dali.* She picks up my table and cradles it like a rare object and a crowd forms as the whole neighborhood comes out to see what famous person is here and it's only me. And they write me one of those big checks for ten thousand dollars and we all take pictures together. But then I watch the news the next day and they've resold my table for a *hundred thousand* dollars to a billionaire guy who has a thing for colorful tables by undiscovered outsider artists and I'm so pissed. Christ. I can't even enjoy my own fantasy.

Rufus comes over and barfs up some grass and yellow stringy stuff at my feet. Well that brings me back to reality. Do rich people have to clean up their dog's barf? I'll ask Belinda. And that makes me wonder if Belinda has a dog or cat or hamster or anything. Then I start thinking about Belinda again as I grab a roll of paper towel. "Friggin' gross Rufus!" I yell at him which isn't fair because it's not his fault *ha* but I'm mad. The paper towel is making more of a mess than soaking it up. I shove him away with my foot. Belinda has money so maybe she can tell some friends with money to come check out the sale too. From what I understand some rich people like one-of-a-kind things because they can buy anything they want so the designer stuff's not that interesting. Only *exclusive* things are interesting. Then I get an idea.

"Mom!" I'm running into the kitchen. "Do you have any old clothes you don't wear? Like shoes or T-shirts or jackets?" I know I'm loud and she stops stirring her marinara to look at me.

"Let me check." She hands me the wooden spoon and goes upstairs to her room. After an eternity she comes back with an armful of clothes.

"Cool thanks." We trade spoon and clothes and I lay the stuff out on the table. A couple of T-shirts and an ugly skirt and *yay* a denim jacket. Bingo.

"Oh wait." She bounds up the stairs again and comes back two seconds later with a pair of white cowboy boots.

"Really Mom?" I'm teasing her but she says *don't judge* like she's a teenager and it makes me cringe. "Got any Mom jeans while we're at it?" I'm actually serious because they're back in style.

She rolls her eyes and I have to tell her I mean it. She says she'll look after dinner and to clear the table. I take all the clothes up to my room and check out my own closet. I find a pair of my old jeans and the bottoms are gross but I think they'd be cool as shorts so I grab the scissors off my desk and cut across each leg mid-thigh. They're not so even but who cares. *What did I do with those fabric paints?*

After tearing through my desk drawers and bookshelves and junk bins of art supplies I find a red and a blue and a white. It's not lost on me these are the American flag colors. So I get to work on the back pockets of the denim shorts making them into big American flags. I mean where we live everyone's into all that America stuff. Then I take the denim jacket and start with a similar idea but it turns into more like one giant flag that wraps around one side and looks like it's flapping in the back. I really need a black fabric pen for creasing and shading so I just use a permanent marker because I'm pretty sure it won't come out in the wash either. Not that anyone ever washes denim jackets but just in case.

"Dinner!" Mom's calling. I admire my work and wonder how much I could charge for each one. Or as a set. I'm not really good with clothes but I'm thinking someone might want them. *Whoa* then I have another idea. I could personalize the jacket right there for whoever buys it. Put their name on it or whatever. The ideas are just sparking each other rapid fire. If I get a bunch of new T-shirts or even did whatever someone was wearing. I'm badass at canvas sneakers. I could take requests. Artist in residence at your service.

Well after dinner Mom finds one pair of Mom jeans in her closet she agrees to sacrifice for the cause.

"Ice cream?" Awesome. She's grabbing her keys which means we're driving to Crazy Cone.

"Thanks Mom. I can't wait for Saturday." I really mean it I'm so excited.

We sit in the car with our soft serve vanilla cones and it's one of those moments you just want to freeze and have forever. I feel happy. That is until I remember I have to go to school tomorrow and deal with Tara.

16

HER BACKPACK IS pink. Of course it is. And it has a big pair of red lips on it. Tara couldn't get any more princess if she tried. I'm standing behind her but far enough away that she won't see me. I know for a fact that everyone puts their bags along the wall of the gym during PE so I just have to time it right.

Five four three two one *go.* The kids are at the other end of the gym in a huddle picking teams so I make a beeline for the pink backpack with the red lips. In one stealth move I slide along the wall and drop the yearbook on top of her bag and slide out the other door. Done. I'm pretty sure nobody saw me. Even though it's gonna be obvious the yearbook came from me when she looks through it. But I don't want to risk being accused of going into someone's bag. This morning I glued a cutout of her face on the front so it would be obvious who the yearbook was meant for. Sure it looks creepy but remember this is the girl who smeared shit on my locker. If she has any good sense at all she won't show it to anyone. Not even Kaitlyn.

In chemistry Joey and some kid I don't know are talking about something that went viral. Joey pulls his phone out under the desk and aims it so the other kid can see. I can see too because I'm right behind him and I nearly fall off my chair. It's a picture of the bandshell. *What the?*

"Badass graffiti dude." The kid I don't know sounds like a surfer.

"I know right? Almost a million views. But the comments are like from India mostly. In that crazy writing." Joey says *India* in a not cool way like it's a bad thing. He's such an idiot. People like Joey are the exact reason for *not my fault*. I wonder if they know it's the bandshell in the neighborhood. Then he puts his phone away quick because the teacher's looking over at them. I'm just stunned. Who uploaded it? *Geez*. Had to be Belinda. Or Arjun. Or maybe just some random person who saw it by accident. But why was it viral? There's tons of cool graffiti out there. Joey says the comments are mostly from India so it was either because of the fact it was Hindi or Arjun had sent it to some relatives and it caught on from there. I'll ask Arjun on my way home.

I feel kind of weird today. Like I'm on one side of the universe and everyone else is on the other. I'm not really plugged in because my phone sucks and my data is limited. But more than that I go back and forth between being invisible and being a target. I just want to be normal like everyone else and have a normal group of friends I can say hi to when I come to school and hang out with at lunch or between classes. Why can't there be more Belindas here? Maybe she's the exception. It's not that there aren't other fringe kids but I guess we just haven't connected yet.

There *is* this kid Julian in my Art class who's kind of a loner I guess because I never see him hanging with anyone. I'm looking at him now and he's sort of small and skinny like he's younger than our grade but he's not. Maybe I should ask him what he's working on. I take a breath and inch closer to his desk and look over his shoulder. Whoa. He's formatting some wicked good comic book pages. The superhero is super boss with a welder-type mask and matching fists. He's fighting an insane dragon snake scorpion thing and winning. Julian looks up at me like I've just caught him cheating and I almost laugh.

"Sorry. I was just checking out the competition." I smile and he just looks suspicious. "Joke. We're not in competition. Just wanted to see some other art styles." He relaxes his shoulders so he's not hunched over the pages.

"Oh." It's all he says. He could be quite possibly more awkward than me.

"I'm Hy. Not H-I-G-H as in *wasted*. H-Y as in that's my name." He nods.

"I know. I like your art." This surprises me.

"You know my art?" He nods again. "Thanks." I don't know what to say to that. Then I get an idea. "Maybe we could work on a comic together." Or even a graphic novel if we hit it off.

"Yeah okay." He smiles sort of and rummages through his backpack and pulls out a crumpled flyer. Uh-oh. I recognize the flyer and he knows I recognize the flyer. "Like this?"

I'm distracting myself by staring at his shiny black hair that's parted in the middle like he's in a boy band. Then I look away and *duh* if that isn't obvious of me. Oh well. So what if he knows about the bully flyer. Actually it seems like he admires it and he probably never told anyone or I would've been confronted by now. I head back to my seat because that's enough stress of trying to make new friends for today.

"Hy check this out." I'm back at my desk working on a dystopian landscape complete with a red sky and Mr. Sanchez is standing over me.

He's holding out his phone for me to see and I look at the screen. It's the door of the Art room with all the figures holding hands and *not my fault* spelled across their heads. Mr. Sanchez must've put the picture up on whatever social media he's on. I don't really care about that stuff so I don't ask him.

"Look at the numbers." I try to see the tiny numbers at the bottom and he sees me squinting so he zooms in with two fingers.

"Whoa." One hundred forty-nine thousand six hundred and two. I don't know how much is considered viral really but this is *two* times in one day my art is on the internet and people are talking about it. "Is that a lot?" He looks at me like I'm an alien.

"Look at the comments." He scrolls down with his finger and I notice he has really clean fingernails. Not like an artist and not like mine covered in ink stains. I ball my hands into fists and read the comments.

What an amazing statement piece for equality.

The next Keith Haring?

That's my school! Nobody knows who did it but it was to cover up some rank hate tag against the art teacher.

This should be in The Modern. Seriously it's better than half the shit there.

Bravo.

Thanks. Just thanks.

I blink at all the compliments. Mr. Sanchez just claps a hand on my shoulder and walks over to critique Lucy's work. I can't lie it feels so good. I have to show my mom and Belinda but wonder how I'll find it again.

"Mr. Sanchez!" I blurt out and he turns around. "Sorry. How will I find that again?"

He smiles. "Just search *ArtMattersMore.*" That's a cool name.

"Okay thanks."

History class is interesting today because we're learning about spies. More specifically spy tactics. Mrs. Wyatt is talking about Morse code and my mind wanders off. Morse code could make an interesting pattern with all the dots and dashes. What if I made a T-shirt or something with *not my fault* as the pattern in Morse code. It could even become a logo for a whole line of stuff. I'm getting way too excited and I have to reel it in because Mrs. Wyatt is looking at me now and I don't want her to call on me today. I escape without being called on and head to the library.

"Greetings Mrs. Nardo DaVinci." She's stooped over and takes a second to straighten up and focus on me.

"Well hello Hy. What brings you in today?"

She's cooler than most people I know even with her old people smell and hockey teeth. I bet way before those dentures she was a nice-looking lady. It's hard to imagine now but we will all get old like Mrs. Nardo. If none of us get hit by a bus first.

"I need a book on Morse code."

"Ooh. Are we training to be a spy? She rubs her hands together and blinks her eyes fast in what I think is a flirty kind of thing and it makes me a little uncomfortable.

"*Um* not really but I'm interested in the alphabet part." She waves her claw at me like *come this way* and I follow her down an aisle of ancient books. She finally stops and pulls out a couple of faded hardcovers and hands them to me. I check out both covers and they're about World War Two mostly. I check out the shelf she took them from and right there next to the empty space is a newish paperback book that just says *Morse code*. I grab that one and put the other two back on the shelf and she *tsks* at me. Like I'm lazy or something because I don't want a whole history lesson. Whatever.

"I'll take this one thanks." I head back to the front desk and she's checking the book out when who walks in but Jordan. We both freeze. He's got a weird look on his face and I wonder if he's seen the yearbook I made for Tara.

"Here you go." I take the book from Mrs. Nardo without taking my eyes off Jordan.

Something in the way he's looking at me is almost predatory like he's a lion and I'm the gazelle. I should note that this is the first and definitely the last time I'll ever refer to myself as a gazelle. I start backing up slowly toward the reference section. Besides me there's never anyone here except this weird kid named Francis who looks like he's about thirty with his full Moses beard. I turn and start walking fast toward the other exit doors.

Jesus I almost scream when Jordan jumps out from behind one of the rows of books and blocks my path.

He covers my mouth with his hand. For a minute we just stay like that because I think the truth is we both want the contact. I can smell something on his hand like a blend of basketball and soap. Rubber meets flowers. His eyes are burning into mine like lasers. He finally drops his hand.

"Why the hell did you pull that yearbook stunt?" He's hissing like a snake so I hiss back.

"She rubbed shit on my locker. Actual *shit* Jordan. Nice girlfriend dude. A real sweetheart. She's not gonna let whatever this is go down without a fight." Jordan just looks frustrated and then something else occurs to me. "Unless it was *you*." His head snaps up.

"What? You know I didn't do that." He looks surprised now.

"How do I know that?" I'm still hissing like a snake because I'm so mad plus I'm trying to be quiet.

"Because I really like you ok?" And with that he throws both hands in the air like *duh* and slumps against the bookshelf. And the weight of it hits me like a truck. I take a step back and catch my breath.

"Then why don't you call off the dogs?" But I already know the answer. He can't. Not without everything changing for him. And for once I feel sorry for this popular kid because someone like me has no reputation to ruin. I'm like an asexual worm as far as everyone else is concerned. I'm on the bottom looking up and he's on the top reaching down and he knows I can pull him off his pedestal any second. "I had to do *something*. But I'm not gross like her. The yearbook was my only way of telling her to back off."

Jordan is quiet. He knows I'm right and he drops into a crouch position with his hands covering his face. I push my fingers through his hair and he leans into me. This is such a new amazing feeling I don't even know what to call it.

17

I RIDE MY bike home thinking about Jordan. We agreed that he'd work on Tara and I wouldn't blow his cover. For now. We also talked about maybe meeting up after school sometime and I gave him my number right before Mrs. Nosy DaVinci poked her head into the aisle and asked if we needed assistance. But she's a smart old bird and I think she was really hinting we get out before anyone sees us.

I swing into the F Mart and lean my bike against the wall. Arjun isn't behind the counter but he comes out from the back when he hears the door.

"Greetings my friend." He's smiling and I'm sad for a second because that's what Mr. Fadikar used to call me sometimes. Anyway I just have to ask him right off the bat.

"Hey Arjun. Did you post a picture of the bandshell?"

"Maybe." His smile gets bigger.

"Maybe or *yes*?" I can't help smiling too.

"Maybe yes?" I roll my eyes and he laughs.

"Why did you do that?" I was really curious.

"I wanted to show my relatives back home the friendships my father had here in America. Especially one that would honor him in such a way." He pauses for a second and I think he's going to cry but he doesn't. "Without knowing it Hy you delivered his eulogy." I'm not exactly sure what a eulogy is but I think it has something to do with dying and remembering someone.

"Well okay thanks I guess. Some kids in my class were talking about it going viral. They didn't know it was me." He nodded.

"Yes the power of the internet. But it caught on because you honored him by putting the message into his language. It is a powerful thing." I feel proud and also a little embarrassed. I decide it's a good time to ask Arjun for something.

"Hey you know those T-shirts over there? I'm pointing to the three pack on the back rack. He nods. "Can I borrow a pack and pay you after my garage sale?"

"Please. Take it. Consider it royalties from the bandshell." It takes me a second to realize what he's saying. I've heard about people monetizing their social media sites. I thank him a lot and put the T-shirt pack in my backpack next to the Morse code book.

Mom's already home when I get there and right away I can tell something's wrong. She's one of those people who can't hide what they feel because it shows on their faces. I stand in the doorway for a minute just watching her. She's sitting slumped over the kitchen table with a beer. She's just staring at it like it's gonna talk to her or something.

"Mom?" She looks up at me and smiles but it looks painful. "What's wrong?" I put my bag on the floor and sit in the chair across from her. Her eyes are kind of puffy. "You didn't lose your job did you?" It's the first thing that comes to my mind.

"No honey. I still have my job." She takes a swig of her beer.

"What then?" I wish she'd just come out with it because I'm not so good at reading people.

"I lost my man." She sighs and it sounds dramatic like one of those Country Western songs I've heard on the radio where the guy's singing about getting drunk and losing his woman and then his dog. I'm wondering if I should be concerned about Rufus.

"The butt guy?" She laughs and nearly spits out her mouthful of beer.

"That's the one." I'm confused because I don't get how she had him and lost him so quick but I'm not any kind of expert in the relationship department. Mom must see my confusion because she starts talking again. "Remember I said we were only recently together because he was with someone else before me?" I nod. "Well that someone else is a wife. And it seems she's not so ready to let him go. Even though he wants to leave."

"Oh. Sorry." I feel bad because I know Mom deserves to be happy. But I also kind of feel bad for the wife I don't even know because she must be unhappy too. *Crap* if this is what relationships are all about I'm not looking forward to any of it. And for a second I consider telling her about Jordan and Tara. For a second I want to show her I have these kinds of problems too and I'm not as much of a loser as she thinks I am because somebody wants *me* for once. But then I think it's not the right time. I think she must be wrapped up in her own disappointment about losing her man. So I decide to take her mind off it and tell her about my art pieces that've gone viral.

"So guess what?" She must hear that my voice is upbeat because her eyes widen a little.

"Chicken butt?" Now I laugh because even though it's been our joke forever I wasn't expecting it this time.

"My Art teacher..." I stop cold because I remember I haven't told my mom about either the mural or the Art room door because they were on public property and I didn't want to get in trouble. But if I didn't get in trouble at school why couldn't I tell Mom about it now?

Because then I'm confessing and I never admitted it to anyone even though Mr. Sanchez knew it was me. And now Mom is staring at me waiting for me to finish what I was saying and I'm having the conversation in my head. I make a split-second decision to trust her because *well* she's my mom.

"So the other day someone sprayed a nasty message on the Art room door."

"What kind of message?" She's sitting up straight now.

"The kind that someone who doesn't like gay people say." She makes a disgusted face because I know she gets mad about that stuff too.

"Go on."

I'm suddenly hungry so I jump up and grab a packet of crackers from the cabinet and munch them while leaning against the sink. I feel better standing somehow. Ready to run to my room if she freaks out maybe?

"So my Art teacher was scrubbing it and it wasn't coming off and I felt so bad." She's just watching me but her eyes are squinting a little now. "I really dig Mr. Sanchez and he was bummed so after school I kind of painted a better message over it?"

This last sentence I say like a question with my mouth full. As if it'll make it sound less serious. Or like I'm asking her permission after the fact. But I can't fool Mom. Public property is public property.

"Oh honey." She looks disappointed so I have to add the bright side quickly.

"Listen Mom. Mr. Sanchez liked it so much he wanted to keep it and the principal wouldn't let him. I never admitted to doing it but he knew it was me and he didn't tell anyone." She's still looking disappointed but a little less now. "And the best part is he took a picture and posted it and today he showed me all excited that it got like a hundred and fifty thousand views."

"Wow." She's impressed now so I'm happy.

"You should see the comments Mom. They're so awesome. Like my art *matters*." Then I tell her what Mr. Sanchez told me to look up online so she could see for herself. I tell her they painted over it the next day like they were going to anyway so I didn't cause any extra fuss. I tell her about Mr. Mayfield the janitor and his comments and how he's a pretty cool dude. But I stop there. I'm not getting into the shit on my locker or anything else. I'll quit while I'm ahead.

I tell Mom I'm sorry again about her *losing her man* and head upstairs with my backpack. I break into the pack of T-shirts I got from the F Mart and pull one out. I put a piece of cardboard between the front and back and grab a blue fabric pen. The book on Morse code is so cool I start reading it and get lost. My mind wanders back to the time they came up with this to communicate in secret and I'm so impressed. Just a series of dots and dashes and it's a whole other language.

not my fault

-. --- - / -- -.-- / ..-. .- ..- .-.. -

What an awesome pattern. I start at the left and go across the chest and turn it over and repeat all the way back to the start. That looks cool but kind of like a lot of other T-shirts with logos across the chest so I hold it up in front of me and decide I'll intersect it with the pattern in red starting from the left shoulder and going down the front and back.

When I'm done I try it on and I'm really proud. It's simple but I'm starting to get a sense of continuity with the clothes I'm doing. Because I'm limited in my fabric paints the red white and blue is like an America theme. Now with the *not my fault* pattern in Morse code I'm thinking being American means *anybody* who lives here and not just the people certain people *want* to live here. But the Morse code makes it a secret message. So if I sell these shirts at the garage sale do I tell people It's Morse code or do I tell them it's just a cool pattern and let them figure it out?

I've got homework so I hurry and make two more T-shirts exactly the same. Then I get a *duh* bright idea to brand myself and put my name on the bottom edge. .... -.-- I like the way my name looks in Morse code so I pull out the other clothes I painted on and find places for it. I use the white this time because it shows up better on denim.

The boots. I almost forgot them and there they are blinding me with their whiteness. They're so uncool they're cool. But I decide they'd be much cooler with the flags on the front like some cowboy superhero badass would wear. But probably more like *cowgirl* superhero badass only because the boots happen to be girl-sized.

Leather means I have to use sprays not fabric paints so I'm gonna have to make a stencil of a flag. I sketch standing at my desk all serious with the judges watching over me. Then I cut the stencil out dramatically in the air and take a bow when I'm done. Then it's kind of embarrassing because I have to excuse myself and high-tail it out to the garage with the boots and the stencil because I can't use sprays inside.

Red. Check. Blue. Check. White. Not necessary *duh*. After about a half hour I've got a very cool pair of cowboy boots with American flags waving from the pointy toes. Nice. Mom comes up behind me and gives me two thumbs up. She wraps an arm around my shoulder and we head inside for dinner.

"You rock honey." *Love you too Mom.* She's my biggest fan.

18

TODAY'S THE BIG day. The epic garage sale of the century. Well ok maybe just in my head but *still*. Yesterday I took my signs and a staple gun and some packing tape and put them up a few blocks in every direction. I stapled them to telephone poles and taped them to stop signs.

My cereal's getting mushy because I'm daydreaming about Jordan again. More like trying to extend my *night dream* into a daydream. I didn't see him yesterday at school but that didn't stop me from having an amazing dream about him. We were flying over the school holding hands and the school was crawling with ants. Not that the other kids were so small they *looked* like ants. The school was crawling with actual ants. Doesn't take a genius to figure out where that came from. The dream was G-rated but amazing.

I *did* see Tara yesterday at school. She was in the hallway outside Chemistry and it looked like she took off fast when I got close. So I don't know for sure if that's because the yearbook stunt worked and she's scared of me or it's just a coincidence. Either way I was glad not to have to deal with her.

So here it is Saturday and I got through the rest of the week without more drama. Where we live it's mostly nice weather but some days it rains so I'm really happy today's not one of those days. I'm racing around setting up and I look at the clock and it's T minus forty-five minutes to showtime. Mom switched her shift at the hospital so she could be home to help me and *thank god* because there's so much to do.

We already dragged the big pieces like the furniture out and set up them up on both sides of the driveway making a kind of path up to the small patch of grass in front of the house. For the clothes I took the curtain rod off the shower upstairs because it's one of those adjustable twisty things and put it across the double doorway of the garage. I know *brilliant* right? I grabbed pretty much all the hangers from my closet and left a big mess of clothes on the floor but who cares. My *signed* clothes are hanging from the front of the rod and all the other stuff like Mom's throwaways and old tees from the boxes is behind them.

Mom and I carry the kitchen table and two chairs outside and I find a shoebox to make a cash register. Mom stocks it with two tens and four fives and ten ones from her purse to make change. None of our prices are less than a dollar because it would be too much of a math headache and plus I don't want to deal with two hundred coins afterwards.

I take a step into the street and admire the whole scene. A car slows right by me and a lady leans out the window. "Ooh what time you open for business?" She's actually youngish and more like a girl than a lady with her pink lip gloss and sunglasses on her head.

"Ten." I'm grinning because I can't help it. "Almost ready so come back soon for sure."

My phone buzzes so I give a little wave to the girl and pull it out of my pocket. It's Belinda and my heart jumps.

On my way

Nice c u soon

"Mom!" I'm jogging up the driveway in a panic because all of a sudden I feel like we should have refreshments or something. She pokes her head out the kitchen door with a *what's up* look on her face. "Do we have anything to give people to drink or eat or anything?"

"Or sell for a buck maybe?" And just like that she comes out with a tray piled with chips and cookies and other snacks like an airline stewardess.

"Oh man. You already thought of it." She rocks.

Mom puts the tray down and I grab a sticker and write *$1* on it and put it on the table in front of the tray. Then she goes back inside and comes out two minutes later with a pitcher in one hand and stack of plastic cups in the other. She smiles at me and says *lemonade*. She says not that we have to feed anyone but it makes for a better atmosphere. Makes it more like an event or something. Yeah I'll have no problem imagining it's my art opening at a new outdoor gallery and all the people coming are interested in my pieces. I pretty much daydream about that all the time anyway.

Our first customer is a mom and a kid I'm guessing is about seven. Ten bucks he makes a bee-line for the scooter with the flames.

"Cool!" *Yup.*

"That scooter's got your name all over it." I'm just being a salesperson but then I realize I could actually put his name all over it if he wanted that. So I ask him.

Twenty minutes later my mom is dealing with other customers and I'm handing over the scooter with *Dylan* now painted on the footboard in red. Dylan's mom hands me twenty bucks and I give her back a five. We negotiated the extra five for the personalization plus the helmet which fits nice. Mom sold a bunch of the kids' clothes from the box and for a minute we have no customers so we high-five each other. This is actually fun.

"Hey Ginger." Belinda snuck up when I wasn't looking. She looks tired today and not as stylin' as usual and I remember her appointment. It's funny but with Belinda I can tell her mood by her hair. No joke. Today her hair is down and frizzy. No fun poofy mouse ears or serious slick braids. Just kinda frizzy and sad.

"Hey yourself. Glad you came." Oh I get it. Ginger as in redhead. She's staring at my hair and I forget she hasn't seen it this color. I laugh. "Is that a compliment or an insult?" At least she's smiling now.

"It's a fact. I think it looks awesome. Actually it's more burnt orange or mango."

"You showing off your big box of crayons?" We keep teasing each other and walk around watching people pick through my stuff.

"No way. These are *ripe.*" *Hmm* I've never heard this term before so I'm gonna guess it's a compliment by Belinda's tone of voice. She's holding the denim jacket with the flags and her eyes are all big.

"How. Much." She says it all dramatic like that and I'm embarrassed. I feel someone else watching from somewhere behind me. I turn around but there's only a guy and girl checking out the tables.

"For you? Twenty bucks and I'll paint your name on it too." She laughs because she knows I'm not giving her a discount. She knows *I know* she can afford it. Maybe I should even charge her more. Nah that wouldn't be cool.

"Deal. What size are the boots?" She's trying to stuff her foot into one of them and I shrug.

"Obviously not *your* size ugly step-sister."

"Hardy har har."

I hold up the denim shorts which I know for a fact are about three sizes too big for her because they were my pants before they were shorts. But she takes them anyway and says she'll cinch them with a cool belt like boyfriend jeans. Um okay. She gives me thirty bucks for both and I paint her name real small on the back of the jacket collar in white. I think when she wears her mouse poofs it'll be so rad to see *Belinda* across the back of her neck like a tattoo. But what do I know about fashion?

I *do* know I feel rich. And it's only been an hour. I feel something else too like confidence maybe. And I don't think it's coming from having Belinda here as much as I thought it would but more like from people willing to pay for my stuff. Up until the last few weeks I've never really been in a position where people want something from me and then all of a sudden the thing with Jordan and now this garage sale so I'm kind of weirded out. Plus the art thing. My work is out there in the world being viewed by hundreds of thousands of people and the comments are insane.

"Hy!" *Shoot* I must be day dreaming again because my mom is shouting my name.

"What's up?" She's pointing at the guy and girl I saw earlier looking at the tables. The girl has her hand up like she has a question so I go over to her.

"Did these tables come like this?" She's pointing to the ombre slash pixelated paint job and I shake my head. "Who's the artist? Your mom?"

"I am." Her eyebrows raise up and she points at the crib and the puppet theater which I did up graffiti style. "Yup." I answer her eyebrows. She exchanges a look with the guy and he hands me twenty-five bucks for the tables. "Thanks." I turn to go and she says *would you sign them?* Huh.

After I put my name on the tables and watch them get hauled off in the back of their SUV I turn and see a group of girls hovering around the Morse code T-shirts. *Yes.* Belinda winks at me when I walk over and she makes a big gesture with her hands.

"Girls *this* is the artist." They all look at me and I could kill Belinda if she weren't doing such a good marketing job. They look about our age and I'm wondering if she sent them here because teenagers I know don't really bother with garage sales. They look me over and I want to run but I just busy myself by pouring a cup of lemonade. Whoa. That's when I notice the snacks are almost gone. We probably could've made buckets of money with a bigger snack sale like with bottles of water and all kinds of stuff.

Anyway my mom's busy selling the crib to a pregnant lady and I'm so psyched. I also made sure it was sturdy before we sold it because I don't want to be responsible for baby accidents or anything. Mom gives me a side smile and waves me over and we help the lady put it in the back of her car. The three girls come up and each one hands me ten bucks for a shirt. I wish Morse code was a sign language so I could say *thanks* in a cool way.

I feel like a superhero. Or a super salesperson. I'm sitting on one of the chairs having some lemonade and looking around. We've sold most of the stuff and it's not even two o'clock. Amazing.

"What an awesome turnout." Belinda comes out of the kitchen and flops down next to me in the other chair. I guess she went in to use the bathroom.

"Right? I wish I had more stuff. I could do this all day." There's still the puppet theater looking all lonely but we knew it would be a hard sell because it's not the first thing people want to spend their money on. Plus it's creepy. "Hey thanks for being here." I mean it because Belinda's got other crap to deal with and she still showed up to support me.

"Sure. It was a good distraction." But her sad smile tells a different story.

"Want to talk about it?" I'm not sure what I can offer except to listen without judging. Maybe that's enough.

"It's just messed up that's all." We watch a lady with a crying toddler loading her arms up with the striped kid clothes. *Et tu Brute?* I love using random Latin phrases now just to amuse myself. Even if they're in the wrong context.

"Well did you…um.." I realize I don't have any right to ask the details of her appointment and cut myself off. She puts her hand on my knee and gives a pat like *it's ok.*

The mom with the toddler comes up to the table and *geez* she's so young. She holds up the stuff she wants.

"One two three four five six. Make it five bucks even." She's looking at me with a question on her face so I hold up five fingers. She nods and hands me a five and I hand a chocolate chip cookie to the crybaby. I can't help it. His eyes get big through his snotty face and he grabs it and gives me a little wave and his mom gives me a *Gracias.* All of a sudden I'm glad I threw out the bad karma yellow chocolate-stained T-shirt so she didn't get it. I look at Belinda and her eyes are all watery. Oh no. This time I put *my* hand on *her* knee and she leans her head on my shoulder and lets herself cry. We're done here anyway.

19

ONE HUNDRED AND seventy-three bucks. I can't believe it. Cold hard cash. Funky cold medina. All about the Benjamins baby. Or at least one Benjamin three Jacksons one Hamilton and three Washingtons. I could go blow it all on sneakers or a boatload of snacks or something stupid or I could reinvest in my future. I'll beg Mom for a ride to Artzy to get some supplies.

"Mom?" *Where is she?* Come to think of it she was really quiet last night. After we put the things that didn't sell back in the garage and cleaned up she got us a pizza. Belinda stayed for a slice but then Manny came through and got her. Mom just said *I'm tired honey* and that she had the early shift so she went to her room. Oh yeah I forgot. The early shift means she's at the hospital already.

Wait a minute. I have a bike and Artzy's not that far. I mean I wouldn't have to go on a highway and there are sidewalks the whole way so…what's my excuse? Oh maybe I need a helmet. Whatever. Nothing's gonna happen. I have to get to Artzy today. Inspiration is on full tilt from yesterday and can't wait. I throw on a pair of shorts and my favorite lion T-shirt. I don't know why but the shirt makes me feel strong like it has special powers. I grab my kicks and stuff the money into my front pocket and I'm outie.

"Serve thy master well banana bike!" I seriously hope nobody hears me say that but I look around and sure enough there's little Brian Wolk standing there at the edge of his lawn like one of those creepy ghost kids in the horror movies. *AAH!* I nearly scream but don't. "Oh hey there. Where's elephant?" And just like a creepy ghost kid he doesn't answer. He's starting to freak me out.

So I jump on my bike with my empty backpack and head off down the street. I know the route to Artzy by heart because my mom's taken me a lot. There aren't a ton of cars on the road but there *are* a lot of people on the sidewalks so I have to ride on the road most of the time. I'm getting a little nervous because a couple of times a car comes really close to me and my bike wobbles just from the vibration or whatever. I keep telling myself I'm almost there and to just chill out.

Then I'm not really sure what happens next because I'm hearing shouting but I'm not seeing anything. My eyes are closed *at least I think they are.* It's so weird. I'm just getting a feeling like I'm crowd surfing. I feel hands lifting me from all sides and then I'm on a surfboard or something and being pushed into a tunnel. But there's a loud siren screeching now and I feel the rumbling under me like I'm moving and there's no more shouting just talking. Someone puts a cup on my face and then I feel a pinch in my arm and…

"Hy? Honey?" I know that voice. Plus no one else calls me *honey.* But it sounds like she's in a big empty room like a planetarium and I have no idea why I'm even thinking that because the last time I went to a planetarium was *never.* But I always wanted to since they showed us in one of those classroom movies in science when we were studying the stars. Was it fourth grade? I don't remember but I *do* remember the feeling that I was just a speck in the big picture of things. And I remember feeling like I wanted to just blast off and float around with all the stars. Forever. Weightless and free.

And now I'm actually feeling that. At this second I know my mom wants to talk to me but I really want to float around with the stars some more. So I don't answer her. Not to be mean but it's such a cool feeling I don't want to go back to earth right now.

"Why isn't my baby answering me?" Mom sounds stressed and I realize maybe I shouldn't be selfish and make her worry. But who is she talking to?

"The sedation is enough to sustain a comfortable rest-like state. Not a deep sleep necessarily but I assure you the brain is functioning properly." I'm guessing this is a doctor. *Yup* just call me Sherlock.

"Mom." I'm not sure if I even say this out loud but I guess I do because I hear her gasp.

She's crying now and I try to open my eyes but they feel glued shut. Wait. Why won't my eyes open? *Oh god* what's happened to me. "Mom?" I'm a little panicked now. "DoIsillhaveeyes??" I'm sounding like some old drunk dude.

"Oh honey of course you have eyes!" She's laughing now but that crying slash laugh thing. "There's just a bandage over them for now." Well the relief I feel is like a tsunami because I can't imagine how I would be an artist if I didn't have eyes anymore.

But then I remember even in my weird floaty state she said *bandage* and I'm putting it all together now. Bike. Car. Sirens. Shouting. Crowd surfing. Planetarium. Doctor. Bandage. *Shit.* I'm in the hospital.

"Whahappen?" Christ I can't stop myself from sounding like an old drunk dude.

"Well you got hit by a car…" Her voice breaks like she's going to cry again.

"Ithokay Mom." But then she surprises me.

"You weren't wearing a helmet. Why honey??" She sounds mad now.

"I donhavone." Mom huffs out her breath in frustration but doesn't say anything else.

"You have a serious head injury from being thrown off your bike with no helmet protection." The doctor sounds like he's straight off the TV. "But it could've been worse. Much worse. Apparently you landed on a dirt patch and not on concrete." I'm getting really sleepy now and I just want to go back to the planetarium so that's what I do.

Beep. Hiss. Beep. Hiss. Beep. Hiss. Hey I can open my eyes! *Ow* but it's so bright. I'm looking around through slits and imagine I'm an alien from the planet Craptron looking through this cool visor thing. Or I'm a knight looking through my armor face flap thing.

Yikes this room is a color nightmare. The walls are flesh. The chairs are turd. The plastic pitcher and cup are bubblegum and the seriously ancient phone is too. Who made these hideous choices? I'm trying to picture the planning committee nodding at each other in agreement and giving the thumbs up. Maybe it was intended to be disturbing because if they made the rooms too nice nobody would want to leave. Meals brought to you in bed. TV. A lazy person's heaven. If you weren't sick that is.

Anyway I put a hand up to my head and feel a bandage pretty much all the way around. But *wait* something's missing. Like my hair. It must be under the bandage. I'll ask mom later. I try to sit up but it's not so easy so I reach over to the handrail because that's where the up down controls must be. *Whhhhrrrr.*

Now I can see around better and there's a curtain between my bed and I guess another bed. I don't hear any sounds coming from the other side though. Maybe I don't have a roommate yet. I lift my legs one at a time. Right leg *check*. Left leg *check*. Thank the gods I'm not paralyzed. I lift the sheet and see I'm naked except for a hospital gown thing that's hiked up to my waist. Ugh. I try and wrestle it back down but it hurts and I'm now seeing and feeling some big scrapes on my legs. My head's starting to pound too so I give up and lean back.

My throat feels like I swallowed a bucket of sand so I pour some water from the pink pitcher into the cup and sip it. A nurse comes in pushing a machine on wheels with all kinds of attachments. It reminds me of a book I had as a kid where these cool robots were made from old scraps of other machines like vacuum cleaners and power tools. The nurse smiles but it doesn't look genuine and tells me she has to take my vitals and I want to make some old-timey joke like *take my vitals please!* But I don't think she'd get it because she doesn't look like someone who would appreciate old-timey humor. Or any kind of humor for that matter. I know I shouldn't judge a book by its cover but we have to take some educated guesses sometimes. Her super-serious makeup and big hair tells me she's maybe the type to watch kid beauty pageants but not in a sarcastic way. I'm feeling bad for even having these judgy thoughts when my mom shows up with a bag of stuff and it looks like art supplies.

"How are you feeling honey? She looks pretty worried and then I think I should look in a mirror and see just how bad I look.

"Do you have a mirror?" I don't think I can stand up at this point without falling over because my head feels ten times its normal size. Otherwise I'd go into the bathroom. Shit. Not *shit* per se but I really do have to pee so what do I do? I can feel there's one of those baby pads under my butt so I guess I just let rip. It's not like I have a choice.

"Mom I just peed my bed." I feel five and probably sound it too. So humiliating.

"Oh baby that's okay." She's trying to smile like it's no big deal and she leaves and comes back with a nurse. A guy nurse. If I wasn't so helpless and doped up I'd make a stink about being naked and soaked in pee in front of this guy nurse. But then I think how cool it's a *guy* nurse and I just shut my eyes tight and let him change the pad thing under me and don't open my eyes until he's gone.

When I do finally open my eyes my mom is holding a mirror in front of my face and I almost choke. I look like a mummy with my head all wrapped up. There are black bruises under both eyes and the whites of my eyes are streaked red. Holy Hy-loween! I crack myself up. And then I grin to make sure I still got all my teeth. Phew. Because nobody wants to be a real-life jack-o-lantern slash mummy. But *dang it* I was just starting to get comfortable with my appearance and now this.

"Mom? Where's my hair?" I'm panicking all of a sudden because something tells me to. Mom looks like a scared rabbit.

"Well you see…" She doesn't even have to say it. But she starts to anyway. "They had to shave a big patch to fix up the cut so I thought..."

"You let them cut it all off??" I interrupt her and then my eyes are stinging and I can't stop crying because it's so unfair. I'm a bald teenage mummy with zombie eyes now and even my cool orange hair is gone. All I can think is Jordan will never kiss me again.

20

FUCK EVERYTHING. I'M using the F word because I'm that angry. My life has been so unfair having to deal with a dad that abandons me and being poor and being fat and feeling ugly. And now I'm even more ugly. I'm *fugly*. I can't stand it. I'm just done with how I take one step forward and two steps back.

I wish Mom would just get out of my hospital room. And I tell her that. I don't care anymore because everything is too messed up for me to care about her feelings. Eventually she leaves because she has to do her shift. And just my luck she actually works in the building so she'll be breathing down my neck.

I don't know how long I've been here and what they're giving me for the pain but I hate it. It was cool at first when I was floating around the planetarium but now I'm in quicksand and the meds just keep me at waist level. Like I'm stuck in a muddy hell with a dull ache that won't go away and nobody can make me feel better. I just want to cut my skin off and climb out of it.

Then I do something better. I grab the bag of art supplies Mom left on the chair and dump it out on my bed. There are colored pencils and sketch pads and *Yes!* a pack of permanent markers. And there's a red one.

I'm feeling something different as I start to write on myself. Something other than what I've *been* feeling. And it's like I'm watching someone else do this because deep down I know it's lame but the words are so powerful they're actually redirecting the pain. It's cool how the words make sense here and my own body has become part of my art project. Of course. Because I am an installment now too. And for the first time in I don't know how many hours or days my head doesn't hurt. Either physically or mentally.

I watch the red letters running into each other in some folds of skin. Round letters like the letter O are harder to draw. So the O looks more like a crown of thorns. Kinda cool. Not that I'm comparing myself to Jesus. But then I think why not compare myself to Jesus? Why was his suffering any greater than mine? I say it's all relative. I yank the sheet up over me just in time because my mom shows up in the doorway. *Christ* there's no privacy in this place.

"Hey there." She holds up a paper bag with a dark stain on the bottom. "Special jelly doughnut delivery." I turn my head because she should know I'm trying to *not* be fat anymore.

"No thanks." But now I feel bad because she's trying to make me happy in ways that used to work and I'm being an A-hole. "I'm not hungry." And it's true. I actually have no appetite and no interest in the jelly doughnut.

Mom sighs and drops the bag on the table. I turn back and look at her. She's got on her scrubs and ugly white nurse shoes. She looks more tired and older than usual. I'm not being mean I'm just noticing and it dawns on me it's probably hard to watch your kid get nearly killed.

"Sorry Mom." She plops down in the chair and sticks her hand in the paper bag and takes a big bite of the doughnut. She chews like it's a chore and sticks the rest of it back in the bag.

"You want anything else?" I want to know how long I've been here. I want to know how bad my head is. I want to know when I can get off these meds. I want to know when I can go home.

"What day is it?"

"Wednesday."

"Really? Wow." Twilight Zone much? Then I have a thought. Maybe I'm so into painting the world in color because I watched all those black and white TV shows and movies growing up. *Huh.* Definitely not one of my deepest thoughts.

"Do you want any visitors?" Mom's always interrupting my thoughts but this time I'm glad. "Belinda stopped by the house because you weren't answering her texts." Now she's talking. But wait. I can't let anyone see me like this. No way.

"Nah. When can I go home?" She shrugs and I roll my eyes and even that hurts. Then I remember I've got a phone. "Where's my phone?" Now Mom rolls *her* eyes. Am I being rude? She takes it out of the closet by the bathroom and hands it to me.

"Okay I'm going home to feed Rufus. Be back later."

"You really don't have to Mom."

"Of course I have to feed Rufus. How selfish of you honey!" She's all jokes but that's way better than tears.

She leaves and gives me a quick wave but I'm already scrolling through my one two three four five six seven messages. Whoa.

Sunday 10:06AM Mom *Morning honey. Tuna salad in the fridge for lunch. What do you want for dinner?*

Sunday 1:22PM Mom *Let me know what you want so I can stop on my way home*

Monday 1:35PM Belinda *the babes are wearing your shirts! U need to make more*

Monday 4:56PM Belinda *seriously I'm taking orders*

Monday 9:02PM Belinda *hello hylo hey Hy*

Tuesday 11:14AM Belinda *what the hell dude??? hit me back loser*

Tuesday 3:31PM Belinda *I'm coming over*

Wednesday 11:16AM No ID *Hey it's Jordan wondering if you're ok- haven't seen u in school*

My heart skips a beat and I stare at the screen. *Yes yes yes* and then *no no no.* He can't see me like this. My thigh is covered in red ink and I feel stupid. I mean I had the sense to do it high enough to be covered mostly by shorts but I'm not wearing shorts. I'm in this hospital thing that opens up all the time. *Dang it* now nobody can see me naked. As if. But seriously I have to answer Jordan because he actually cares. I can't believe it.

Yeah sorry I had a bike accident

Then I erase that. Why am I saying sorry?

Hey yeah I had a bike accident. I'm cool though. Thanks for asking

I hit send and wait. It only takes a few minutes before he answers.

No shit are you in the hospital?

Yeah

How bad

Hit my head pretty hard

Man sorry- when do you get out

Dunno

Then there's like a long pause. I think that's that and we're done talking.

Can I visit

Shit. No. I mean I want him to but just *no* he can't see me like this.

Nah I don't look so hot right now

Don't matter to me

Bullshit.

Nah seriously thanks but let me get a little better

Another long pause.

Cool

Cool

I put my phone down and get up slowly. Whoa I'm light-headed. I think because I haven't eaten much. Or could be because I have a big-ass frigging head wound. I'm giggling because I can still crack myself up but the nurse *a different nurse* catches me.

"What's so funny?" She's being playful I guess but kinda scolding too the way she *tsks* and grabs my arm and goes for the pole behind me with all the liquid bags hanging. I'm not supposed to get up without anyone helping me yet.

"I have to pee."

"And that's funny?" She's a nice older lady with a big smile. She's got a gap between her front teeth which looks good on her and an accent that makes me think of pink houses and turquoise water for some reason.

"Cool hair by the way." We're making our way to the bathroom and I'm staring at a hundred long braids with bright red yarn weaved in all piled on top of her head. This hairdo is art for sure. I'm trying to hold the sorry-ass hospital robe closed behind me but it's pointless and anyway they've all seen me naked. I know there's no privacy in a hospital but I draw the line at the bathroom.

"Please can I go by myself?" She looks at me for a second with friendly eyes and nods. A couple of the loose braids swing around her face. But then she's looking down at my legs and I follow her eyes and *oh shit* the front of my robe is caught behind the pole and *not my fault* is showing. She looks confused for a second and then looks away. Hopefully she thinks it's one of the scrapes on my legs or something because it's red. She wheels the pole into the bathroom and then steps out and closes the door behind her.

"I'll wait out here." And I'm grateful I got this nurse today because they're not all so nice. I ask her name and she tells me it's Mona.

I nearly faint seeing the bandage covering my head. Someone must've replaced the whole-head bandage with the half-head bandage when I was out cold or something. Because now I see a half inch of orange fuzz sticking out from the top and I want to scream. But I get Mom's point after I calm down a second because it would've looked worse with long hair and a big shaved patch. I so bad want to lift the bandage to see how much of a Frankenstein I am but I can't do that. My face looks different. Besides being pale and the bruises under my eyes it's like my face has more *angles*. I just focus on peeing and then try to scrub the marker off my leg with a wad of toilet paper. So stupid.

Mona knocks and says she can hand me a fresh gown. It makes me laugh because I picture her handing me a *ballgown* through the crack in the door like I'm heading to a Hollywood premiere. Like I would even wear a gown ever. I put the actual hospital gown on and feel less self-conscious immediately because this one closes around me better. Mona helps me back into bed and asks if I'm hungry. I tell her I'm not and I realize I haven't been hungry this whole time. She nods and takes all my vitals again and leaves.

My phone buzzes and it's a text from Belinda.

Your mom told me I'm so sorry

Hey I'm ok

Oh awesome can I visit?

I pause because I know I said I didn't want visitors but I really do want to see her and she would be honest with me about how I look.

Ok ask my mom for the details because I don't even know what day it is

Lol cool

Later

21

YIKES. I GOT a new roommate and he's really messed up. My mom talked with his mom this morning and then she told me. Apparently he's got this disease where his kidneys don't work well and he just had surgery because one got so infected they had to remove it or something like that. *Gag* not to be mean but that stuff freaks me out. And he's only seventeen.

I'm sitting in the chair next to my bed eating a tuna sandwich my mom had sent up special and I hear *hello?* from the other side of the curtain. Well nobody is standing around or sitting in the other chairs so it must be the new guy.

"Hey." I swallow what's in my mouth and take a sip of Ginger Ale.

A hand reaches out and pushes the curtain back and there he is lying in the bed looking at me. He's got kind of wet sand-colored hair and he looks super thin. I wonder if that's on account of what he has.

"What're you in for?" I smile because he makes it sounds like we're in prison or something which isn't far off actually. But it should be obvious by the big-ass bandage on my head.

"Bear attack." I'm trying to be funny I guess because falling off my bike sounds too lame.

"No shit."

"Yeah *bull*shit actually. Sorry." There's something about this kid that seems honest so then I'm honest. "Bike accident." I shrug and he nods. Then he points to his belly.

"Aliens stole my kidney." Guess I spoke too soon about the honesty thing. I roll my eyes and he laughs. "What's your name?" Here we go.

"Hy." He just stares at me of course.

"Um. Yeah. Hi to you too." Okay I'll let him off the hook. The guy's probably in pain.

"No Hy *is* my name." His eyebrows jump in *wtf?*

"Weird."

"Yup kinda."

"What's it short for?"

I think about all the funny answers I can choose from and take another bite of my sandwich but by the time I swallow it he's out cold. Like so I don't even get *his* name. It must be the pain meds. I know how it slams you out of nowhere and he just came back from surgery. I'm done with food for now so I push the tray table away and climb back in bed. But first I pull the curtain closed between us to give us both some privacy.

Next thing I know I hear a voice say *Hey Belinda I'm Nate.*

"Hey Nate." My eyes are open now and Belinda is sitting in my chair. Then she sees me and smiles. "Oh *there* you are Sleeping Beauty."

"Piss off." I manage to say.

"Nice. You kiss your mother with that mouth?"

"I don't kiss my mother."

"Ooh we're feeling feisty are we?" I laugh now because *well* I'm just happy to see her. I almost forget what I must look like and then I remember and turn away as if that'll help. *Ow* it hurts like something's pulling when I move my head against the pillow. "I was just getting to know your roomie over here." I turn back to look at him.

"Hey."

"Did you know aliens stole his kidney?" Belinda's cat eyes get wider and look more like tiger eyes.

"Yup I'm being monitored by the FBI as we speak." Nate *I just learned his name* is propped up against some pillows.

"Yeah he told me that nugget before he did his junkie nod." I reach down and press the button to raise the bed and scoot my back up against the pillows. He laughs and coughs.

"I'm sorry didn't you just wake up from a junkie nod too?" Now I laugh. Belinda scoots her chair closer to me and gets all up in my face.

"Take a picture it lasts longer." What am I five?

"What're you *five*?" Ha. I can't believe she said that. We are *so* on the same wavelength. I stick out my tongue and she rolls her eyes. I feel almost normal with Belinda here. Then I remember Nate is watching from the other bed and I feel self-conscious again. Belinda touches her own hair while staring at my bandage and it doesn't take a genius to know what she's thinking. "It'll grow back Hy." Yup.

"You got any candy?" Apparently I *am* five but honestly I'm just trying to switch the focus and plus I have a wicked craving for red licorice or sour gummies or *anything*. Belinda digs around in her bag and comes up with a tiny lollipop and I could kiss her. She tosses it on my bed and I unwrap it and shove it in my mouth. I close my eyes and for a second I'm back on the beach lounge chair with the unlimited towels. Must be the pineapple flavor. I open my eyes and Belinda's smiling at me kinda sad. I must look ridiculous jonesing over a lollipop.

"When do you get sprung?" I shrug and just then a guy comes in wheeling a stretcher and says *Hi I'm Ramon and I'm taking you for an MRI.* I think this is a good thing because it means they want to check and make sure my head's not messed up on the inside and maybe it means I can go home soon.

The guy says we're gonna be a while down at MRI so Belinda gets up to go and I see Nate watching her. As I get wheeled out on the stretcher I feel something weird when she smiles at him and says she'll be back to visit. Back to visit *me* or Nate? There's something in the way she's looking at him. Am I jealous? I don't know but I don't like the feeling. Someone told me once *envy* is just wanting something someone else has but *jealousy* is more the feeling of possibly losing something you already have. Well that would make sense. Not that I own Belinda or anything. She's got other friends and an ex-boyfriend even. But all of a sudden I don't want to share her with anyone.

I don't have time to feel sorry for myself because Ramon is a happy dude and he whistles some happy tune as he wheels me into the elevator. My mom is there waiting at MRI and I tell her I just saw Belinda and she says she knows. I guess she knows everything because she's in the hospital anyway. Ramon and my mom help me from the stretcher to the MRI thing and now I'm really glad I put on sweat pants. The last thing I want to worry about is anyone seeing my privates or the stupid tattoo I gave myself.

When I disappear into the tunnel I'm not feeling like the badass I thought I was earlier. Good thing I have headphones on because this shit is loud. Like standing under a jet plane loud. The thing whirs around my head with lights and grinding noises and I imagine I'm in a wood chipper. Or even better I'm the first teenage astronaut and I'm heading into deep space. My mom cheers from control center *That's my baby!* Belinda blows me kisses and even Jordan is there with his hands stuffed in his pockets all shy but *hey* he's there at least. *Aw he showed up to my space fantasy.* I don't realize I'm actually waving until Ramon says in my headphones I need to stop moving.

Mom walks alongside the stretcher as Ramon wheels me to my room. When we get back there's a doctor standing by the window. But *wait* this isn't my doctor because my doctor's a lady doctor. But I do recognize his face from…*where?* He smiles when he sees me and then at my mom but my mom's face clouds over and all of a sudden I remember.

"I didn't recognize you with your pants on." Now this must be the meds talking because I've never been so disrespectful. But memories flashed in my head of my mom crying and being so sad and it made me suddenly want to hurt this guy.

"Oh honey!" But she's laughing and he looks totally embarrassed. He opens his mouth to say something but then shuts it and squeezes out past us. Mom pats me on the shoulder and says *I love you.* But then she leans down and says it's not his fault and it's complicated so I shouldn't be sassy to him in the future.

"In the future?" I guess I've got a lot to learn about relationships because I thought anyone who made you so sad like that would be *in the past* for good. Mom waves it off like she's shooing a fly and I settle back into the chair by my bed.

"Want to watch some dumb TV?" She picks up the remote.

"Nah I'm gonna try to sketch."

I sneak a glance at Nate who's sleeping again and she hands me my sketchbook and pencils. She looks at Nate too and only then do we both see the person sitting quietly in the chair on the other side of his bed. She's knitting and my mom says *Oh! hello Delores.* Delores smiles and says *hello* and I ask her if she minds me sketching Nate while he's sleeping. She says she doesn't mind so I get to it. It feels so good to use my art brain again.

22

I'VE BEEN OUT of school a week so far. But the really nice Dr. Abrams is telling me I can go home today. She's cutting through the bandage that makes me look like the flute player in that famous Revolutionary War picture.

"Do you want to see it?"

"*Um* not really." But then I change my mind.

She holds a mirror up to the side of my head and I guess it's better than I thought because I don't faint or even cringe. It's a jagged line with stiches but it's only about an inch and a half long. I really imagined Frankenstein with it going all the way around like barbed wire. There's a bald patch the size of my fist though and Mom was right to tell them to shave it all. I mean they didn't *shave* the rest just buzzed it short but it's amazing how much hair *or no hair* changes how your face looks.

Dr. Abrams puts a square bandage just over the stitches and leaves the room so I can change into some real clothes. Mom brought some cargos and a T-shirt from home and the first thing I notice is how much weight I've lost. Crazy. The doughnut around my belly is almost completely deflated and I have actual collarbones. I see it in Mom's face too when she comes in and looks at me in my clothes. The only way I can describe the look on her face is not good or bad but more like shock.

"Ready?" She shakes out of it and I nod. I'm glad she doesn't make a big deal of it. And then I look at the empty bed where Nate was and it makes me sad. He doesn't get to go home like me. He had *complications* from his operation and had to be rushed back into surgery a second time. I feel so lucky and so bad for him at the same time. My head is going to heal. His insides will never be the same.

I tear out the sketch I did from my sketchbook and put it on the table next to his bed. I write *get better soon* on the bottom and sign my name. My mom smiles at me with that proud smile moms have and steers me out into the hallway. She saw the sketch but what she didn't see was the *not my fault* I wrote into his hair. Every tiny letter formed by strands crossing and ends curling. It'll take someone really looking for it to see it.

I get waves from all the nurses at the nurses' station especially Mona with the cool braids. I give my best *thanks* and waves but I'm feeling pretty shy. They all saw me naked and gross this week but I guess they're pretty used to seeing people at their worst. My head is hurting a little but as we start down the hall I see a really young kid maybe six or seven completely bald pushing the wheelie pole with her bags of fluids. The thing is I know she's not bald from a head wound that'll heal quick like mine and she smiles at me really big anyway. I just want to cry but I don't. I hold it back and give her a smile instead and a thumbs up and just like that my head doesn't hurt anymore.

Outside the sun is hot but feels so good on my arms and my face. For a minute I just stand in the parking lot with my face tilted up. People walk around me and head toward the hospital entrance with flowers or balloons that say *it's a boy* or *get well soon*. They check me out for a second and I wonder if I must look like a clown with my orange fuzz lit up in the sun. There's a guy on crutches with his leg in a cast and a lady pushing an old man in a wheelchair. It's so busy and it's like the hospital's a whole other planet. And this is where Mom lives half her life. Maybe even more. She's got to be one of those nice nurses like Mona who spends every day making people feel better. I can't see her being one of the A-hole nurses who act like you're bothering them when you ask for something. I give her a smile and she looks at me suspiciously because she doesn't know what I'm thinking.

"I was just thinking how you take care of me at home and then you come here and take care of all these other people." She looks surprised. "*What* I can't appreciate my mom as a person?" I say it matter-of-fact like I'm so mature but the truth is I only just realized it. She tries to give me a hug and I shrug her off because seriously we're in public.

It's Saturday so I have a couple days at home to chill before I have to jump back into school. Rufus hasn't left my side since we came home. He's acting like he hasn't seen me in a year instead of a week. But come to think of it he acts like this every day I come home from school too. Okay so maybe I'm *projecting*. I like that word. I picture an old movie projector shining my thoughts or feelings onto someone else's head in a dusty beam of light. My thoughts are in black and white so I'm picturing *Hot diggity dog I missed you!* projected onto Rufus's forehead and it makes me laugh. He barks like he gets it. "Good boy Rufus."

There's a knock at the door and I hide while Mom answers it because I'm not wearing a hat.

"Well hello there Belinda." Mom leaves the door open and goes back to making stuff I can heat up later because she has to go to work.

"Did you arrange this?" I'm accusing Mom but in a joking way because even though she didn't ask me I really am happy Belinda's here.

"Dinner's in the fridge for later. Snacks in the closet." She washes her hands and dries them on the dishtowel.

Belinda and I watch Mom pull out of the driveway sipping our sodas and I ask her what she wants to do. She walks around me and looks me up and down like I'm a coat for sale or something. Then she gets a wicked smile on her face and goes and pulls a big black thing out of her bag. *What the? Are we doing Karaoke?*

"No way!" I laugh not because it's a microphone but because it's *not* a microphone. It's actually one of those hair clipper things with no cord so it must be battery powered and at first I think she's joking. But then she turns it on and it makes a buzzing sound and while looking me right in the eye she drags it over the top of her head. I'm just stunned. Her hair is all loose and fluffy today and now she's got a row of hair missing like a tiny lawnmower went through it. "Jesus Belinda!"

She hands me the clippers and makes a nodding gesture like *go on.* Do I have a choice? I take the clippers and push it over her skull in rows from where she started. Her hair falls in big clumps right there on the kitchen floor and Rufus is whining. I guess from a dog's standpoint she's falling apart. Maybe she is. Why else would she do this? We don't talk because I'm thinking it should be understood she's doing it out of solidarity with me so I don't feel so ugly. But part of me is thinking she's staging some other personal rebellion like with her whole *ex-boyfriend pregnancy absent father* situation and this is a good opportunity to take it up a notch. Either way she and I are both buzzheads now. I sweep up the hair and dump it in the trash so Rufus can chill out and we both go stand in front of the bathroom mirror.

"Shee-ite what a motley crew." With makeup on *she* looks more like a trendy model and I'm representing post-apocalyptic youth.

"I think we look cool." To make her point she sticks her tongue out and puts two fingers up in a peace sign. Then she runs down and grabs her phone and we spend the next few minutes taking badass selfies and pics of each other in crazy poses.

We collapse on my bed laughing and exhausted and lie on our backs side by side staring up at the ceiling. I feel a little dizzy like I should take it easy so I close my eyes. Then there's a hand on my hand. *Wait what?* The hand slowly moves to my leg and rests there. I don't dare open my eyes because I have no idea if this is really happening or if I'm dreaming.

I try to breathe in and out as the fingers move up my leg. And then they move in circles. My eyes are still closed and I don't want it to stop because it feels good but it has to. Stop. The *not my fault* is right there under my cargos and it's like *she knows*. Like she's tracing the letters I drew on my flesh when I was so angry and she's telling me it's okay. But how could she know? Or she doesn't know and it's a coincidence and she's trying to tell me something else. But the *something else* is not right either because my brain is rejecting the way my body is reacting to her touch. I'm wigged out so I jump up all awkward and head downstairs.

"Want anything to eat?"

I make a big deal of opening the fridge even though I'm not hungry at all. Belinda comes down to the kitchen and I'm trying hard not to be weird but I can't look her in the eye. I put some chips into a bowl and sit down with it at the kitchen table. She seems quiet and I'm guessing I didn't react the way she wanted me to. But she's cool so she shakes it off by sitting next to me and pulling out her phone and we watch some stupid fail videos of grown men getting hit in the nuts with wiffle bats. In no time we're laughing and scrolling through martial arts fails of people falling on their butts. And then it's on to screaming goats and people being chased by geese.

I think an hour must go by because Rufus is doing that growly bark to remind me to feed him. *Geez* dogs have this wicked internal clock. It's insane because it's dead-on give or take five minutes. Back in the old days before clocks they probably used the dogs to tell time on the rainy days when they couldn't read the sundial. I grab an open can from the fridge and scoop the wet stuff into his bowl with some kibble. I still can't figure out why dog food stinks so bad if it's just chicken and rice like it says. I mean it smells like what comes out on the other end *no lie.* Now I'm wondering if maybe there's a reason for that. Like maybe they're actually recycling it because dogs will eat anything including poop. Gross.

I feel Belinda watching me and all of a sudden it makes me sad that something changed between us. I just really count on her and our friendship and now it feels different. Does it have to be? As if she hears my thoughts she gets up and stretches big and punches me in the arm.

"Ow!" It doesn't hurt but that's what you say when someone tease-punches you.

"Oh *please.*" She's joking and I'm so glad she's teasing me because it means maybe we can forget about the other thing. She texts Manny and in minutes he's outside. "Later dude."

"Later nerd."

That night I have a hot and sweaty dream. It's filled with all these faceless bodies touching and groping each other and I wake up all twisted in my sheets feeling embarrassed.

23

"BECAUSE YOU HAVE to." Mom's making me toast and I'm asking her why I have to go back to school.

"Can't I just do online school or something?"

"On what??" She's referring to our lack of computer from this century and *oh yeah* reliable internet service.

"Maybe the school has a tablet I could borrow. Don't they *have* to nowadays?" Mom just sighs.

"What's that going to solve honey? You can't stay away forever. You have to be with your peers."

"Peers are overrated." It's my best attempt at humor. It works a little because her eyes crinkle up.

I do one last check of myself in the mirror and adjust the beanie so it covers the bandage. Reality sets in. I'm going to have to ask each teacher before class if I can keep my hat on and explain why. Or I can just go to the office and get *one* pass I can show to all my teachers. I'm exhausted just thinking about it but I have to say my face looks way better than it did a few days ago. The bruises under my eyes are more like yellow smudges and I'm not looking so gray because I sat out in the sun yesterday.

"You know there were witnesses." Mom's getting into the driver's seat so she can drop me at school. "Apparently it wasn't your fault honey." *Not my fault.* "A van was speeding and cut you off." I look at her and she seems almost excited about this. "The police got the name of the delivery company and I'm going after them. They should pay for this. *They* broke the law and *we* have hospital bills."

And there it is. The silver lining. I know Mom wouldn't go after anyone unless they deserved it because she's not one of those people who pours water on the floor at a restaurant and pretends to slip just to sue them. Those people who try to game the system are A-holes.

"But I didn't have a helmet." She pulls up outside the school.

"Doesn't matter." She blows me an air kiss and says she'll see me after dinner.

The main school building looks smaller for some reason. Like it was hit by a shrink ray in the week I was gone. Or maybe it just shrank in my mind. Whoa. Deep. Either way I'm not feeling so scared today as I pass all the same kids on my way in. They look smaller too.

Stares and more stares. Doesn't anyone have anything better to do? What's weird is the stares are different this time. More like curiosity and less like disgust. I decide to stare right back. I'm looking them all in the eye one at a time and *you know what?* They all look away first. Like I've caught them doing something bad. Huh.

"Hey." I know that voice and makes my skin tingle all over.

"It's Hy actually." I turn to face Jordan with a smile because I'm teasing him and his eyes widen a little like he can't help it.

"Whoa you look…"

"Fantastic?" I finish for him. But I'm being sarcastic obviously.

"Um. Okay yeah. In a way you *do* kind of." I just stare at his lips because I want to bite them.

"Liar." But I can feel a hotness creeping up the back of my neck.

The bell rings for us to get to class and it makes me jump. I suddenly realize that Jordan and I are not alone in the Universe. We are not drifting around in our own orbit or flying over the school but are actually in a busy hallway full of kids. He jumps too and we both laugh. But then something amazing happens. We don't duck and run off in different directions like we usually do. We just start walking. In the same direction.

"What class you got?" He flips his hair out of his eyes. It makes me miss my hair. I can't flip anything out of my eyes but more important I can't hide my eyes at all. I should've worn a baseball cap instead of a beanie. Now I feel like a dumbass because I'm pretty sure my eyes give me away.

"Algebra." We're just walking side by side. Not causing anyone to notice that we're *together* or anything.

"Ugh. I'm no good at it." He's flipping his hair again. Nervous maybe?

"I'm pretty good." And it's true. "I could help you."

Jordan smiles at me and it's so nice. *Geez* I want to bottle this feeling right now and save it for when I'm feeling down so I can pour it all over me. Then I see her. And he sees me see her. And then *he* sees her too. Tara's walking toward us and she stops dead and there's a look in her eyes I don't think I've ever seen before. Fear? *No way.* But it is. Like she's on the wrong side of the rope for once.

There's this kind of standoff moment like in the movies where Jordan and Tara are locked on each other and I'm standing just outside the frame. I can almost hear the tense music swelling as I wonder which way this is gonna play out. Then this group of guys comes up behind Tara and I recognize them as part of Jordan's crew. One of the guys with blond hair puts his arm around Tara and makes a point to look right at Jordan. There's something in his cold eyes like *you snooze you lose dude.*

Tara takes the cue and makes pouty lips at the dude and tosses her ponytail. God it's so obvious what she's doing but *whatever.* Jordan looks pissed and I'm not sure but I'm guessing he's pissed because his friend is moving in on his territory and not so much because he cares about Tara. The truth is if he liked Tara so much he wouldn't be messing with me. Even on the down low.

"Later. I gotta get to Spanish." And just like that he spins a right and jogs down the Language Arts hallway with his backpack swinging.

"Yeah later." I try to sound casual but he's already gone and Tara's walking toward me with the blond dude. And she must be feeling back on the power side because she shoots me an ugly smirk on the way past. She's so gross. I wonder what her Mom's like because she must not be cool either. Or maybe she's really super nice and doesn't know her kid is so rotten.

"Hi. Are you okay?" Kaitlyn comes up next to me now and at first I think she means about the standoff and Tara but then I catch her looking at my head and I realize she means my accident.

"Totally. Thanks. But I don't have much hair left." That makes her laugh.

"It grows you know."

"For real?" I touch the back of my neck and make a fake surprise face. She laughs again but then she looks serious.

"Listen. I want to apologize." Wow. I guess I didn't expect that. "I knew Tara was a bitch but I was too afraid to stand up to her. You know... about *you.*" We reach the door to my Algebra classroom and I stop.

"I get it. Thanks."

She looks happier now like she did a good thing. Which she did. It takes guts to say sorry especially if it means risking being rejected by the Queen Bee. Queen B *as in B-yotch* is more like it.

Anyway Mr. Dobbs is at his desk taking attendance and it looks like I'm the last one so with my back to the class I ask him if I can keep my hat on. We have a *no hats in class* policy which is a joke because some of the stuff the girls wear every day is off the hook. Boobs all out and skirts barely covering butts is fine but *hats* are a distraction? Unless it's one of those giant foam hats they wear at sports arenas I beg to differ.

Mr. Dobbs asks me why and I tell him because I had an accident and I have a bandage under my hat and he says things like *oh that's why you were out* and *are you okay?* He's a nice teacher. I feel bad because he's *way* overweight and he breathes heavy just moving around the classroom and I know that's not healthy. He says I can keep my hat on as long as I need to. I tell him *thanks* and turn and head to my seat and then I hear it.

"Freak." Real low like a coward. And I know who said it.

Really? *This guy* now? I don't know what comes over me but I guess I just snap. I stop right in front of blondie's desk and pull my hat off and it's like the whole room gasps at once. I make crazy eyes and put my hands up like claws.

"RRRAAAWWRRR!" I lean over and roar in his face like a monster *or like the freak he wants me to be* and he just shrinks back in his seat.

There's a second of super quiet and then everyone breaks out into laughs. But not laughs at me. They're laughing at *him* and the scaredy-cat reaction that blew his whole cool vibe in two seconds flat. I feel victorious. The rest of class is a breeze and I even take my hat off halfway through because my head is itchy. Nobody stares. I'm just sorry Tara isn't in this class. But it should get back to her pretty quick.

Are they all gonna end up being afraid of me? It's not really what I wanted but I'm thinking of an expression I heard once as the bell rings and I head to my next class. *Poking the bear.* That's what they've all been doing. They've been poking the bear. I'm the bear and they've been poking me and poking me and finally I reacted. And it's about time.

24

"GRAM?" I GOT my hands cupped against the window but I don't see her inside. Not in the kitchen or the living room. She could be sleeping but it's four in the afternoon. I haven't seen her in a couple weeks and because of my accident neither has Mom. I don't think she ever saw my orange hair but I can't remember. And she'd probably dig it if we were twinning. But then I remember all my hair's practically gone and most of the orange went with it.

"Hey Gram?" I'm louder now and I'm knocking hard on the door. I don't know why but I've got a weird feeling which is why I'm not giving up and leaving. I text my mom.

Gram not answering door

Sleeping?

I'm being loud and nothing

I'll come

Ok

I sit on the porch swing hoping the squeaks will bring Gram to the door but they don't. Mom pulls up a few minutes later and sits next to me on the swing.

"I got a bad feeling Mom." And it's true.

"Oh honey. Let's not jump to conclusions." And she gets up and knocks on Gram's door again. "Nadine? Are you in there?"

"She could be out you know." I'm not jumping to any conclusions but we both know that's not really true. Gram never leaves her house anymore. She doesn't even drive.

Mom tries the doorknob. It's unlocked so she opens it. Even from where I'm sitting I can smell it. Even through the screen door. I don't know what the hell I'm smelling but it's rancid.

"Ugh." I cover my nose with my shirt. Mom looks like she's gonna be sick.

"Stay here." She puts her hand up to me like a crossing guard. *No problem.*

Mom pulls her shirt up over her face too and goes inside. I can't stand the smell anymore so I jump off the swing and head back toward the fence. I circle around in front to check out my handiwork. It's a little faded from the strong sun we have here but still looks pretty good. My phone buzzes.

Hey want to tutor me in Algebra?

I smile and I'm just about to answer when my mom comes rushing out of the house still holding her shirt over her face. She sees me by the fence and walks over slower now.

"Oh honey. Your Gram…" Her eyes are tearing up and she doesn't even have to say anything else. It's pretty obvious. I sit on the curb because my head feels hot all of a sudden under the beanie and it's making me dizzy. Mom sits next to me and puts her arm around my shoulder.

"What next Mom? I mean seriously can there be any more drama?" So many crazy things have been happening to me lately and this is just another one. What I really mean to say is *poor Gram.* But I guess I'm feeling a little selfish. Before I can ask her what happened she pulls out her phone and dials 911 and says things like *my mother-in-law is deceased* and *yes I'm sure* and *send the coroner* and she gives them the address.

"She just went honey. In her bed. I'm sorry." I nod and think two things. *One* it's so sad that she was alone and we didn't get to say goodbye and *two* maybe she was sleeping and that's good because she didn't have to suffer.

"What're the odds Mom? I mean first Mr. Fadikar and now Gram." It's not really a question because I don't expect her to know the actual odds of those two important people in my life dying within weeks of each other.

"Well I know it seems unfair but they were both older and had health issues." Whatever. Mom's trying to be nice but it's a pointless conversation. Mr. Fadikar and Gram didn't die just to upset me. Get a grip Hy.

An ambulance shows up while we're still sitting on the curb and Mom gets up and directs the EMT guy and girl inside the house. I notice she's not going back in but she's a nurse so I would think she's got a thick skin for this kind of thing. Maybe this is too much even for her. It's an actual corpse of someone we know that's probably been decaying for a while by the smell of it. Not a random patient that happens to die on her watch and is still *fresh*. Yuck. I'm gonna have nightmares for sure. Funny I'm not sad as much as grossed out. Maybe I'm in shock or something.

Then the stretcher wheels out onto the porch and there's a zipped-up bag lying on top of it and now I feel like I'm gonna cry. She could be a pain in the ass but she was my Gram. And now she'll never hug me with her bird arms or be crabby to me ever again. I'll never stop to see her on my way home from school or do her chores for a few bucks. My nose is itchy and then some tears come because I can't help it.

"Let's go home." Mom bends down and gives me a hug. She says they're taking Gram to the hospital morgue and try to determine how she died.

I stand up and have to brace myself against the fence because my head feels like it's filled with cotton. I get in the car and look out the window at her house. The windows are all dirty and the paint's peeling off in a hundred places and I try to imagine Gram standing in the doorway with her faded pink house dress and troll hair.

"Did Gram have anyone besides us?" In all my years growing up I never saw anyone else with her ever. Mom just shook her head all sad. Then I thought about her son. *My dad.* "What about Dad?" Mom didn't say anything. She didn't like talking about him. "Shouldn't he know his mom died?" And I sort of choked on that because it was all so real now.

It was real that he never visited Gram and that was his *mother.* And now she was gone. I'm sitting here next to my own mom and I can't even imagine that I could just leave one day and never see her again. Then it hits me. Who am I kidding? He walked away from his own kid. For sure he won't care that his *mother* bit the dust. Maybe he's got something missing. Like empathy or something. I've read about people who don't act or *feel* like normal people. They don't feel bad or responsible or anything. I think they're called sociopaths.

"Your Dad is…" But I cut her off.

"Dad's *what* Mom?" I'm angry all of a sudden. "What's wrong with him? Who the hell walks out on his family forever?" Her eyes get squinty like she's in pain or something.

I slam the car door and run inside. I go right past Rufus and slam my bedroom door too. Is this another case of *misplaced anger?*

Seriously though. Mom never talks about Dad and always changes the subject when I ask about him. But it doesn't make any sense. She chose him way back when so he couldn't have been a too much of a monster and they were even together for a while when I was little. Then he was just gone and all Mom said was that he couldn't *deal.* With what? Her? Me? Us? Being a Dad? I have so many questions still but over the years I just stopped asking because she never answered. All I know is he is alive and well and has other kids and didn't walk out on *them.*

I'm on my bed and I remember Jordan's message. My heart thumps like it's restarting and I pull out my phone.

Hey want to tutor me in Algebra?

Maybe. how much?

Joker

Not joking

I am actually but I want to see what he says. Silence. I start to panic like I've offended him and blown the whole thing.

A slice and a soda

Phew.

You're on

Rudy's @7

Everyone knows Rudy's pizza joint. I wonder why he's not worried someone will see us there. But I guess I'll be tutoring him so if anyone sees us it'll be explainable. Other kids study there after school.

Tonight?

Can you?

Yeah

Why not? I look at the time and it's six-thirty. If I ride my bike it'll take me ten minutes tops. And hell no I don't want to hang out here with Mom and be sad about my dead grandma all night. Plus I'm still feeling weird and confused about my dad. I feel like she's not telling me the whole truth or something.

"I'm going out." This time I put on a baseball cap after I changed my bandage. The hair's growing back around the cut so the doctor says I won't have to wear a bandage much longer. I have some of the garage sale cash in my pocket which feels awesome.

"Where are you going?" Mom looks at me surprised. She's sitting at the kitchen table drinking a beer and scrolling through her phone.

"Just meeting a kid from school at Rudy's." She blinks. "I'm tutoring someone in Algebra." She nods like this makes more sense. I guess I don't blame her for that.

"Home before dark if you're riding your bike." Then she jumps up like she just remembered something and runs out to her car. "Here." Mom hands me a brand-new bike helmet. And it's purple.

"Thanks Mom." And I feel bad for being mad at her. She's always looking out for me. Well I guess it would be pretty stupid to ride a bike with no helmet at this point.

25

OKAY THAT WAS something out of a rom-com for real. Just Jordan and me at a back table at Rudy's eating pizza by candle light and sort of doing Algebra. He really did need help understanding the basics and it was pretty cool for him to trust me. But sitting so close together it was hard not to lose my train of thought. I tried moving to the seat across from him but when he looked at me my whole body kind of vibrated like it was zapped with electricity so that was no easier.

I keep replaying it in my mind the last few days. Especially when I'm alone in my room at night. There's this thing between us that's *different*. I mean I'm guessing it's different because the truth is I don't really have any experience to compare it to. But I can tell by the way I've seen other people being together and making out and stuff that we're not really just about that. I don't know what our thing is yet but I know I dig it and hope that nothing messes it up for now. Like if we don't get more physical I'm okay because it's just so special. And I get that he wants to keep it quiet till he can figure it out and I don't mind.

And then I think about Belinda. And I think about how awkward it was the last time she was in my room. I mean I *really* dig Belinda and ever since I met her I've been kind of in awe of her and I've been wanting to be with her and all that. But when she touched me that way I was surprised and it was like I knew right away it was wrong. Like I didn't want *that* feeling with her. And these are things you don't know until they happen sometimes. I felt so bad though. I still feel bad and even though she blew it off I'm pretty sure she's embarrassed. She hasn't reached out in a while which is a bummer. I mean it's not like I'm *anything* like her last boyfriend so how was I supposed to see that coming?

Hey my grandma died

WTF sorry

Yeah so sad

Then a couple minutes go by so I have to say it.

You okay? We okay?

Sure

Hmm.

How's everyone liking your buzz cut

NOT. My dad flipped

Yikes

Yah

So what's up for Saturday

Dunno

Beach?

I'll hit you back

K

Oh well. I tried.

Relationships are so frigging complicated. I was better off when I only had myself to worry about. Deep down I know that's not true because I wouldn't trade this drama for the world but my head hurts both physically from the accident and mentally from the amount of navigating other people. And what's my go-to for escape? Art. But I don't have an idea this second. Escape doesn't mean there's *inspiration*. I think about Jordan again and how he could fit into *not my fault*.

But then I hear the door. Mom's home a couple hours after her shift ended which means she went out. Oh yeah I forgot she told me she was going out. I swear sometimes it feels like I'm living by myself. I have to eat by myself a lot because sometimes her day shift ends past dinnertime and sometimes her night shift ends after breakfast. I'm lying in bed and she comes upstairs and goes into the bathroom for a minute. Then like I knew she would she comes and sits on my bed.

"How was your date?" I'm guessing that's what she was doing out. She shrugs.

"Nothing special. A nice man from the administration department asked me to dinner but there was no *connection.*" She uses air quotes with that word.

"Oh." I don't know what else to say and she just smiles and shrugs again. I'm starting to understand the whole connection thing though.

"You get caught up on all your schoolwork?" I give her a look that says *duh* because I always do my schoolwork. It's pretty easy for me and I like using my brain. Plus it's satisfying to learn new things. Knowledge is power. I heard that somewhere.

"You're welcome." I'm being a smart-ass.

"For what?" She looks at me funny.

"For being such a great student. That's one thing you don't have to worry about right?" She looks at me long and hard and then ruffles my short buzzy hair.

"Right honey. And thanks." I can tell she's being sincere and I feel bad.

Mom starts to talk about how she contacted a lawyer to take our case in the bike accident thing. I asked her where she found the lawyer and don't they cost money? She says this lawyer will only charge us if he wins any money from the defendant. And *if I must know* she got his name from a billboard on her way to work. I roll my eyes and she tickles me in the armpit like I'm five which I hate.

When I finally get away from her I tell her *good luck with the ambulance chaser.* Literally! I think she's lying and she met the sad-ass lawyer at the hospital because he was actually chasing my ambulance. I tell her nicknames don't just come from thin air. She tells me since I'm so cynical she's going to get a million bucks and not give me any of it. Then she's going to run away to Tahiti by herself and drink those drinks with tiny umbrellas all day. I give her a thumbs up and tell her she'd look boss in a coconut bra.

Then Mom runs downstairs and I hear the fridge open and a clinking sound and a cabinet door. When she shows up she's got two glasses of milk and a big chocolate bar. Omg. I sit up against the pillow and she breaks the chocolate bar in half and we clink our milk glasses together. I eat the chocolate slowly and enjoy it because I'm not doing that emotional eating thing anymore. Plus I've lost a lot of the extra weight I put on from doing that and I like the way it feels and looks so there's no point in self-sabotaging.

I brush my teeth and give my mom a nice long hug. *Crap* but now I'm kind of awake and I remember there's caffeine in chocolate. I sit at my desk and stare at the ants walking all over my walls and I'm kind of impressed. Impressed leads to *inspired* and I feel the scar on my head start to itch. Think Hy think.

Jordan isn't far off in my brain nowadays and I'm realizing how ironic it is that not too long ago he was the source of my pain and now he's the source of my pleasure. I mean the pendulum couldn't have swung any farther from left to right on that one. And not only that. It's not my fault that I am the way I am and it bothers some people enough to make them bully me and at the same time it's not Jordan's fault that he was attracted to me and he didn't want to be.

So I guess he acted out in a way for me to notice him? But then he couldn't live with himself for hating me because it wasn't giving him what he wanted. So he risked everything and let himself feel the other side of hate. I guess it makes sense because they're both really strong emotions so I bet they get mixed up a lot. And feeling a connection isn't anyone's fault. It wasn't my fault and it's not Jordan's fault. So how can I work that into something?

I feel the familiar jolt of inspiration and know I have to follow it. *Right Mr. Sanchez?* I grab my sketchbook and start playing with the idea of magnets. Two things being drawn to each other with such a force that they have to be pried apart. But here's the kicker. When you flip one over it gets repelled by the other one. It's literally pushed away. But the magnet didn't change. It's just coming at the other magnet from a different angle. Interesting.

I sketch one of those horseshoe shaped magnets like in the cartoons and rotate it until it looks like the letter J. Then I draw an H that looks like steel beams with rivets and everything. *Hmm* the H would have to be a magnet also to make the point so I redraw it. Then I get a great idea. I rummage through my school supplies for a pack of index cards. *Yes* there's an unopened pack at the back of the drawer. Probably from seventh grade or something because I remember we made flip books that year. So I turn the snaky neck of my clip lamp to shine up from underneath and rig a light box out of the clear plastic top of a pencil case. *Genius* if I do say so myself.

It's like two in the morning before I finish my flipbook. I staple all the cards together and give it a try. The letter H spins in the center while the J magnet pushes it away and pulls it in with those wavy lines.

Finally the H gets pulled in and stuck to the J and at the end *not my fault* flashes on and off like a neon sign.

I flip through it again and again and I'm so proud of it. I wonder if Jordan will like it as much as I do. I hope so but the one thing I've learned as an artist is that sometimes other people don't get it the way you're feeling it when you're actually creating it. Well I hope I even get up the nerve to give it to him at all.

I fall asleep fast and hard and dream really good dreams.

26

JULIAN AND I are working on a comic strip together. I like Julian. He's pretty uncomplicated for me because we share a passion for art and we can just be art friends. We're cracking each other up with ideas for the characters like Sir Charge a superhero who leaves the mayor a bill after he captures the bad guy and Mister Ree a billionaire hermit who lives in his mom's basement.

"You two are having way too much fun in my class." Mr. Sanchez is grinning and checking out our sketches. Julian and I move on to deciding about the setting and Mr. Sanchez makes the rounds to see what the rest of the kids are working on. I wouldn't want to brag but I guess *yeah* we're his favorites. It's just that we're way more into art than the other kids and that's cool. If I were a teacher *I'd* dig the kids that were into it more than the ones who weren't. Just makes sense.

"Hey Mr. Sanchez?" I waited till all the other kids left for their next class.

"Yes?" He's cleaning some paint brushes in the sink.

"You know that website you told me about?"

"It's more of a movement but yes it's called ArtMattersMore. What about it?"

"Well there's this mural. It's pretty cool graffiti and it's got about a million views. I thought maybe you'd want to know about it for your page or whatever." He dries the paint brushes on a paper towel and is looking at me with that kind of smile like he knows something. I look at him like *what?* Then I know what he's thinking but I can't back out now. "This friend of mine says it was a tribute to a guy from India. He came here to start a business and people weren't always so cool to him." Mr. Sanchez sits at his computer. He searches India + graffiti + mural and there it is. It's right at the top. And he says *is this it?* and I say *yeah.*

"Hy this has five million six hundred and twenty-four thousand nine hundred and seven views." He looks at me with his eyebrows way up.

"Oh." I'm surprised too because that does sound like a lot. He looks at it again and scrolls down the comments till I guess he finds what he's looking for.

"It's Hindi. The translation is *not my fault.*" I don't know why but I look away.

Maybe because it just hit me that I'm basically confessing to vandalism. It's graffiti on public property so I could really get in trouble if he told anyone. But he didn't tell anyone that I know of that the door of the Art room was me. And the bully flyer also said *not my fault* so he's now tagging it all to me if he hasn't already.

But all he says is *very cool.* And he says he's gonna link it to his page. Mr. Sanchez turns his computer and shows me some other work on ArtMattersMore and some of it looks amateur-hour to me but some of it is really great. The thing that ties all the pieces together is the message. Each one has a positive message of some kind either in the picture or in the words inside the picture. There's a lot of people doing this stuff out there and for the first time instead of feeling alone in what I'm doing I actually feel a part of something.

"I gotta run Mr. Sanchez." And before he can say anything else I take off. Partly because I'm late for my next class and partly because I'm a little overwhelmed.

On my way home from school I stop in at F Mart to pay Arjun back for the pack of T-shirts. I make a mental note my tires need air when I'm leaning the bike against the wall. I also make a mental note that I'm riding a bike meant for a middle schooler and I should really use the garage sale money I earned towards a new bike instead of art supplies.

Mrs. Fadikar is behind the counter doing something with her hands. When I get closer It looks like she's knitting.

"Hello dear." She has a nice smile and I realize I haven't seen her since Mr. Fadikar died.

"I'm sorry for your loss."

I think that's what Mom told me to say. It does seem a little formal because I kinda lost him too but for her it was a bigger loss and I don't really know her that well.

"Thank you my dear." She stops knitting and looks at me closer like she's trying to figure out who I am.

"Is Arjun around?" Now she smiles with her whole face and holds up the thing she's knitting and it looks like a tiny hat.

"No he is in hospital." But she's smiling now and I'm confused. Why would she be happy he's in the hospital? And then I get it. But I don't know how to ask what I'm thinking. Good thing she fills in the blanks. "I am a grandmother. I am rich!" I think she means it figuratively and not like they're two different statements.

"Congratulations." I didn't even know Arjun had a wife or family or whatever. But I guess I never asked and he never offered. "Does he have other kids?"

"No it is our first grandchild!" But then her whole face drops and I'm sorry I asked. It obviously made her think about Mr. Fadikar because she said *our* instead of *my*.

"Do you have a picture?" I'm trying to distract her. She shakes her head.

"Not yet."

I nod and make my way back to the chips aisle. It's just out of habit because I haven't really been jonesing for snacks the way I used to. I hear the door open and then a couple of kid voices. There's an aisle between us but I recognize one of the voices. It's that little shit Pete who's been stealing beer from the cooler. And now I hear them whispering because I'm sure they noticed it's Mrs. Fadikar and not Arjun behind the counter.

Suddenly I feel a big responsibility to Arjun and I get this sense of empowerment being in his store. I wait until I've seen Pete open the cooler and take out the beer and before he can stash it in his pocket I take off my cap and step in front of him with the craziest eyes I can make. He kind of wobbles backward.

"What the fuck?" Oh yeah he's a real badass dropping an F-bomb to impress his new little friend.

"Put it back." I'm trying my best to look mean with my buzz cut and head scar.

"Says who?" *Omg* what are we five?

"Says this side of crazy. Wanna try me?" Pete looks at my scar and his friend doesn't even wait for an explanation. He just takes off. I'm trying not to laugh which makes me flare my nose like a bull and Pete looks scared now. He tries to recover with a *whatever freak* I can barely hear and puts the can back in the cooler. "If I see you in here again I'm calling the cops *and* your mom. In that order."

Well I'm sure I sound like a bad movie actor but it worked anyway. He leaves and now I get to let out the laugh I was holding in. Mrs. Fadikar looks at me with a question and I warn her about *that Pete kid.* I tell her that Arjun's on it but he's not here so I jumped in. I grab a pack of cinnamon gum and hand her the money for it. She says *thank you* again and I tell her to give Arjun my congratulations.

I'm all proud of myself and feeling so puffed up like a peacock from telling off that kid Pete that I don't even notice the tires. I put on my new helmet and jump on my bike and try to ride out of the parking lot but it's like riding through broken glass. The rims grind on the pavement and I look down. That little shit-tard. Both tires are slashed and I just want to cry because now the rims are all bent up.

So without thinking I just throw my frigging banana-mobile against the garbage cans and leave it there. So much for being the cool one. I hear laughing and see Pete and the other kid give me the finger before Pete shouts *you're welcome!* and they take off on their own bikes in the other direction. I know he means the bike is a piece of crap so he put it down like a sick dog. And right at that moment because the Universe hates me for some reason it starts to rain. It almost never rains but when it does it's like walking through a door and a bucket dumping water on your head as a joke.

By the time I get home the rain's stopped. Mom is in the kitchen and she looks at me and looks around me and then looks *at* me again with her eyebrows up. I know I must look like a soaking wet apocalyptic black lagoon creature in a helmet.

"Where's your bike?" She finally asks me and I just start to cry.

I'm so tired of all this unfairness and I just want to be normal and have normal friends and live normal days. I just push past her and drop the helmet on a chair and go upstairs to change into dry clothes.

Instead I turn on a hot shower and stay in there for as long as I can stand it. I soap up and feel all the parts of my body with my hands. It feels good not to have so much bulk and rolls of flesh that I have to soap in between. It feels good to have hands on my body even if they're my own. But I'm still trying to get comfortable with all the parts of my body. Like when will it feel like it belongs to me? That's the most frustrating thing because I don't want to talk to anyone about it because I don't know if it's normal or not. I don't know if everyone feels this way at my age or it's something weird that only *I'm* feeling.

I'm all dry and dressed and sitting on my bed when Mom knocks.

"Yeah." I know I sound sad and she opens the door but stays in the doorway.

"What happened now honey?" See this is what I hate. What happened *now?* As in something's always happening to me.

"My bike was stolen." It just comes out because it's easier than going into the whole thing.

But she makes a weird face like she feels sorry for me and doesn't really buy it. I don't blame her because *seriously* no one would steal that rusted out banana on wheels. So when she doesn't say anything else I get the hint and confess about the little A-hole Pete and how I tried to help The Fadikars by defending the store. She comes over and gives me a big hug and that's that. We have some not too terrible frozen dinners and then check out some antiques show together on TV. I almost feel normal again. My normal.

21

"**I NEED YOUR** help with Gram." We haven't talked about Gram in a few days and it's now Saturday.

"Today? But today's my usual day with Belinda." I'm being a brat because Belinda never got back to me about hanging today. I thought maybe I'd see Jordan on the weekends now but he's got tons of sports and family stuff.

"I really need your help honey." Mom looks serious. "We've got to clear out her house." Well she could've said *we've got to swim in a pond with leeches* and I'd be less disgusted.

"No Mom. Yuck." Then she takes that deep breath that moms take before they tell you they're not asking you they're telling you.

"I'm not asking you I'm telling you." Bingo.

I start to head to her car and she says *no I'll meet you there.* And I ask how I'm supposed to get there. And she says *take your bike.* And I say *very funny.* And then she points to the garage. My skin feels all tingly and I go over and open the garage door slowly like it's a trick.

"Mom!"

And right inside is the most beautiful thing I've ever seen. For a bike that is. All blue metallic with big wheels and *whoa* ten gears? And it's my size. I can tell it's not exactly new but I could care less. It's new to me and it's in great shape from what I can see. I pinch the tires and swing my leg over the seat and walk it out to the driveway.

"You like it?" I just roll my eyes because she knows I love it.

She knows she's the best mom right now. Now I definitely can't get out of cleaning Gram's house with her. I grab my helmet from inside and do a few donuts in the driveway to get used to my new bike. I feel like a million bucks. Or at least however much this bike cost. Actually I'm independent again and that's priceless.

"Last one there's a rotten egg!" I take off down the street and have a little trouble changing gears so Mom passes me in her car. She sticks out her tongue and I shake my fist at her like they do in the old movies. I don't try and keep up with her car because the last thing I need right now is another bike accident. But I do take off like the wind after a few minutes and it feels so good.

Speaking of rotten eggs the really bad smell is gone because *ugh* that must've been Gram. But it still smells in the house and I figure the bad smells like cigarettes and mold are just in the walls. There's also some rotting garbage and cat turds in the kitchen but judging by the mounds of newspapers and boxes in the living room she was no stranger to hoarding either. Wait. Where *is* the cat?

Mom opens all the windows and doors and hands me some big garbage bags.

"All clothes in one bag. Sheets and towels and blankets in another. Leave stuff that looks like trash and if you're not sure about something just ask me."

I start opening closets and grab the towels and sheets *gag* even the sheets off her bed and any other stuff like that I find. When I've got a big bag of stuff I tie it off. There is a closet full of heinous polyester pantsuits and shapeless house dress thingies. Hard to believe this stuff was probably fashionable at one point. I grab everything off the hangers in one big hug and dump it on the bed. I'm gonna need another trash bag for all this.

Mom's in the living room looking through some books. "What's gonna happen to this house?" Mom sighs big and shrugs. "The bank owns it now." I'm not really sure what that means but I guess she wasn't paying what she owed to the bank or something like that. Then something else occurs to me.

"So why do we have to clean it?"

"We're not *cleaning* it we're taking her things out. Maybe we can donate some of it or even get some cash." I bust out a laugh.

"Have you seen Gram's clothes? I think we're going to have to *pay* someone to take them. Or we could make a big bonfire and roast marshmallows."

"One man's trash is another man's treasure." Good one. She says she was more thinking about some of the really old books and the grandfather clock. Stuff that she knows came from Gram's parents.

So now that I know that I'm looking for valuables I head back to her bedroom and check out the dresser. There's just some dusty glass perfume bottles and other random junk on top but when I open the drawer there's a couple of smallish boxes inside. The boxes look really old and made of maybe leather?

I open the first box and there's a gold ring with a diamond on it like one of those engagement rings in the ads for jewelry stores. The diamond is round and pretty small but it's nice and simple. I remember Gram saying her husband *my grandpa* was a sailor in the US Navy and they were married when she was nineteen. I can't imagine getting married at nineteen. But I guess if you were going off to live on a military base in another country or something you'd want someone waiting for you at home. I never knew my grandpa because I was told he died before I was born.

The second box is bigger and has a long chain and one of those lockets in silver. I open the locket and there's two pictures. One is an old picture of a young man in a Navy uniform *that must be Grandpa* and the other tiny picture is a baby boy. But the picture is in color and looks newer so this must be their son. My dad. I stare at the picture and wonder what happened that he just went away and never came back. I think Gram must've been pretty sad about it. Her only kid. Sad enough to have that locket still in her top drawer for sure. After I look around and don't really find anything else I take both boxes to Mom.

I'm staring at the back of Mom's head because she didn't hear me walk up and watch as she looks through a photo album. Over her shoulder I can see pictures from maybe the eighties because the clothes people are wearing are all primary colors like red and blue and yellow. There's a kid in one of the photos with one of those mullets and I must've laughed because Mom turns around.

"Come sit." She pats the couch next to her. I sit down and point to the photo of the kid. She looks at me and kind of sighs. "That's your father." I knew that because even I can see he looks like me. I mean *I* look like *him*. That's probably why I laughed. Because it's so weird how much I look like him. Mom flips back to the beginning of the album and there's a picture of Gram. I mean I think it's Gram.

"*Whoa* she looks so different." From what I've seen in movies this photo looks like it was from the sixties. She had big poufy hair and red lips and rad white boots. Mom nods. "What happened to her? Why'd she get old so fast?"

"Oh I guess hard luck happened to her." Mom's quiet for a minute. "Her husband died when your dad was young and she never really recovered from that." I suddenly feel so sad for Gram sitting here in her house going through her things and talking about her in the past tense.

"How did Gram actually die?" I just realized we never talked about this.

"Well the official report was a pulmonary embolism." Mom takes a deep breath and after she explains what that means feels sad but true. "It means she basically died from smoking." I knew it. Gram was always smoking.

"Where is she now?" I don't know how else to ask this.

"You mean is she in heaven?" Actually I meant where is she as in what happened to her body but I don't want to sound disrespectful so I just nod. "Oh that depends on what you believe honey. I'll leave that for you to think about." And then when I don't say anything she answers me anyway by saying Gram was cremated a few days ago and her ashes are at the funeral home. Now I'm thinking about the boy in the picture. Shouldn't he know his mother died? "I told your dad." Wait. Did I say that out loud? "And he's coming next week so we can all say goodbye to Gram together."

"But he hasn't seen her in years right?" I'm pissed now that my dad who not only doesn't give a crap about me but doesn't give a crap about his own mom has the balls to show up now.

"Well we do have to go over her will." What? I'm confused now. The Gram I know barely had enough money for cigarettes.

"Gram made a will?"

Mom nods. "I got a call from a lawyer."

"Does Dad know?" She laughs but it doesn't sound like a funny *ha ha* laugh.

"I'm guessing that's why I got a call from a lawyer." I don't know about all this inheritance stuff but if the bank owns Gram's house then she must not have had much to leave to anyone. "It's a *formality*." Mom makes finger quotes but then I look down at the boxes I'm still holding and wonder then why we're taking stuff.

Mom reaches for the boxes in my hands and opens each one. She *oohs* at the ring and smiles at the pictures in the locket. She sees me watching her and I think she knows what I'm thinking because she sighs. "Listen. Your father hasn't been a part of her life for a long time and he knows that." She stands up and gets ready to go. "He's not here to deal with her body or her funeral arrangements or especially her stuff." She makes a big sweep around the room with her arm. "If any of these things are listed in her will and it's supposed to go to him then it goes to him. But if he doesn't know or ask or *care* about her things then he won't miss anything." She grabs a couple of the garbage bags. "Deal?"

"Deal." I don't know what else to say. She's my mom and what she says goes. Plus it's not my dad who just got me a bike.

28

YO YOU AROUND today?

I stare at my phone. Belinda. I know it's Sunday but what time is it? My phone says 8:25AM. Isn't she with her Dad on Sunday? Oh well his loss.

Yup

Cool- be there in an hour. Be ready for beach

Roger that

Nice! We're going to the beach today. So I'm on my hands and knees looking under my bed for the shoebox with the garage sale cash. I panic for a second and then I remember I put it in my closet thinking it would be safer. Safer from *what* I don't know. It's not like our house is gonna get robbed any time soon. Any robbers would win the dumbass criminal award if they chose our house. All they'd make off with is a computer from the stone age and some of my mom's costume jewelry. I picture two guys with striped shirts and black burglar masks like in the old cartoons tiptoeing into our house and stuffing plastic tumblers and an old toaster into a big sack until Rufus latches onto one of their legs with his crazy underbite. I crack myself up.

"Mom?" No answer. Then I remember she traded her Saturday shift for a Sunday one.

In my closet I find the shoe box and stuff forty bucks into the pocket of my shorts. These shorts will have to serve as a bathing suit too if I even go in the water. Okay maybe I'll bring a suit. I am more confident these days. Hoodie and flip-flops *check*. Teeth brushed *check*. Baseball cap *check*.

I sit and have a bowl of corn flakes and scratch Rufus behind the ears. I watch Michael swim in figure eights and wonder if he'd consider swimming backwards. The fish equivalent to moonwalking maybe. Now *that* would be entertaining. I feel bad he doesn't have any fish buddies to impress. Maybe I'll ask Belinda if I can try and win him a friend at that carnival where we got him.

Manny beeps and I head out to the car. Well the first thing I notice is Belinda's smile through the window. Whoa. She looks five years older without the silver bar. Not that it really covered that much teeth but it might as well have spelled out *teenager*. Now she could pass for twenty-one easy.

"Hey Manny." He gives me a wave and I climb in.

Belinda's buzz cut is growing in cool of course. More like little waves. She must've put some gel stuff in it. She looks so glamorous like in the old movies. We don't say anything for a while and I hope it's not because things are now weird with us. That would really suck.

"So remember that thing I told you about?" She puts her hand on her belly. I know it's because she doesn't want Manny to overhear.

"Yeah."

"I couldn't do it." I look at her like *huh?* She rolls her eyes. "I couldn't go through with it."

"Oh shit. Really?" I get it now. "But what are you gonna do?" My eyes go right to her belly to see if there's anything there. Not really. She just shrugs and sighs and I'm thinking this is one messed up situation for her. I want to ask her more but don't want to risk Manny hearing so I clam up. Then I remember my plan to win a fish friend for Michael. "Hey can we go back to that carnival?" She looks at me like *really?*

"Nah. I got something else planned." There it is again that wicked smile. The one that's like if the Joker was a supermodel.

We spend the car ride playing Would You Rather and she's throwing out really disturbing ones like would you rather dive into a pool of spit or bloodworms. And I say *whose spit* but my stomach is turning by the time we pull up at the Blue Horizon gate.

We don't head to the beach chairs this time. There's a dock a ways up the beach and she points and says *c'mon*. Uh oh. I'm not really a boat person and last time I checked docks mean boats. When we get close I see a white motor boat and I get even more nervous because that means speed. On the ocean. With big sea creatures right under the surface. Now I wish I never read Moby Dick.

"Here." Belinda's holding a life jacket out to me. "Put it on."

But it's not just a life jacket it's more like a harness and she says *trust me* so I put it around me and some dude comes out of nowhere and adjusts the straps so they're tight and then does the same for hers. And before I can ask her *wtf?* he attaches the loops on the front to *wait* is that a parachute? Holy crapola.

"No Belinda!" She just laughs.

"What's wrong scaredy cat? You do the Tilt-o-Wheel and the Drop Down so what's the problem?" Before I can answer the boat revs and takes off for the deep ocean and with a big gust of wind the chute fills up and we get lifted off our feet. *Omigod omigod omigod I'm gonna die.* "Whoohoo! Fucking righteous!" And it's apparent Belinda's having a totally different experience than me.

My eyes are shut so tight I'm trying to imagine I'm only three feet off the water. And it's a swimming pool not an ocean with sharks and octopi *or is it octopuses?* I believe the word octopus is from Greek and not Latin which would mean octopi would be the wrong plural…"Hy! Open your eyes!" She's yelling either because of the wind or because I was in my own head so I hold my breath and open one eye. Then the other. And you know what? I'm not dead. And not only am I not dead I'm *flying*. Like an eagle. I put my arms out like I've got wings and I'm looking all around me three-sixty and it's awesome.

"Oh my god Belinda." She puts her head back now and closes her eyes. She looks so peaceful. It's definitely not her first time doing this and all of a sudden I'm jealous. I mean envious. It seems like she gets to try anything she wants and have any cool adventure because money doesn't matter. But I know I shouldn't be envious because she's so generous with me and we're true friends. At least I think we are. And then as if she's hearing my thoughts she takes my hand just for a second to confirm it. I let her because it's cool that we're flying together way up high in the clouds. Okay maybe not *in* the clouds but pretty friggin' close.

We fly like this for a while then something tells me to look down and there are these shapes in the water. Three four five of them swimming fast right underneath us. The ocean seems bottomless with the thick blue and green strokes of a Monet. The ripples turn into little white dots near the shore. And then like one of those old hand crank movies the dark shapes start leaping out of the water one after the other. But when they break the surface I can see they're more of a silver gray.

"Look! Dolphins!" I'm shouting at Belinda and she laughs and says *you don't have to shout.*

She's right because it's pretty quiet up here but I guess I'm excited and then I notice we're slowly falling. The boat is now making a big u-turn and I'm imagining being lowered down onto the back of one of the dolphins. I ride it into shore and jump off and it talks to me in dolphin squeaks and gives me a wave of its flipper before heading back out to sea. I swear I could just entertain myself in my own head all day if I was the only one left on the planet.

The dude on the motorboat is reeling us in like big fish. Only it's from the sky with a big white puff sail behind us so it probably looks more like reeling in a big *jelly*fish. Our feet are touching down on the back of the boat and I give a last look around to see if the dolphins are still nearby. Nope. But I'll have that magical image of them stuck in my head forever.

Once we get back to the beach club the parade of people bending over backwards to give us whatever we want starts up and I look for Gerard but don't see him. We sit at a table and a nice middle-aged lady with glasses brings me a Shirley Temple and a chocolate milkshake for Belinda. We split a big plate of nachos and some enchiladas and I feel like I'm in heaven even though I know later it'll probably feel more like hell because I'm stuffing myself like a pig now.

I'm noticing from what I've seen so far the people here at the beach house are all basically vanilla like me and not caramel like Belinda. And they're either old people *minus the old people smell* or families with little kids. And they're staring at us because they apparently have nothing better to do. To be fair I'm trying to picture Belinda and me from the outside. Two really different looking teenagers with matching buzz cuts. We're here on our own without parents but obviously one of us comes from money because we're getting served with big smiles. Feels almost like we're crashing their party but then again

Belinda doesn't seem to notice so maybe she feels like she belongs here and it's just my own insecurity. It's probably stamped on my forehead. *I don't belong here.*

"Sorry about the other day." She says out of nowhere and I blush but luckily the sun has made my face red already.

"Nah. Don't stress. Are we cool though? Because your friendship means a lot to me." *Whoa* I can't believe I just said that out loud. Must be the Shirley Temple talking. She rolls her eyes and snorts. Then she punches me in the arm.

"Yes knucklehead. Just had to trip over my own ego for a sec. That and I'm feeling like an ass."

"Ok good." Not that she's feeling like an ass but that we're cool.

I think hard on the way home in the car. We're both kinda quiet and I think about what my life was like before I met Belinda and how she changed me in so many ways. I get cynical for a second and wonder if I would feel the same about her if she were poor like me. I wonder if without all the adventures whether we'd have enough to do or talk about or laugh at.

And then I look over at her and remember how I felt at the bandshell when I first met her. Before I saw the shiny car or Manny or the beach or the carnival or anything I just dug her. So that's that and I can let myself off the hook. But I didn't know till the other day in my room how she was feeling about me and I was caught off guard. And maybe it's because I didn't even know myself how I was feeling about her until just then.

"Hey listen." My voice cracks a little and Belinda turns from the window and looks at me like she was just somewhere else. "Thanks for today. It was…well it was friggin' off the hook is all."

She gives me the saddest but truest smile and the way the light from outside the car is falling on her face I want to paint her just like that. I whip out my phone and snap a pic before she can say anything. I look down at the picture on my phone and when I look back up her eyes are shiny. *Ugh* this stuff is so complicated.

29

WELL THE WEEK flew by. Tara hasn't been bothering with me or Jordan lately. She seems wrapped up in her new dude *thank god.* But it almost feels too quiet so Jordan and I are still careful not to be obvious about hanging out. We mostly meet up in the library and there's something kind of exciting about it like half the fun is trying not to get caught.

I'll tell you who *is* noticing us though. Mrs. Nardo that's who. But she's cool and even helps by steering some kids to tables farther away from us. I think she's been around long enough to know who the potential troublemakers are. She thinks Jordan and I are doing homework or I'm tutoring him in Algebra. And I am basically. But nobody can see the other stuff under the table. I don't think Mrs. Nardo would be so cool if she knew that either.

"My dad's coming tomorrow." I'm kinda loud and Jordan looks at me with his eyebrows up. He knows I haven't seen him since I was really little.

"Why now?" The library's busy so we don't have to whisper so much.

"Remember I told you my grandma died? That was his mom so we have to have a memorial and read her will."

"Heavy."

"Yeah. I don't really want to see him."

"They can't make you." I smile at him because something in his voice sounds protective.

"I guess so but I'm kind of curious. I didn't pick him but he's still the only dad I have." He shrugs and I know why. Jordan confessed to me last week that even though his own dad lives at home he's this overly macho meathead and he has more and more trouble relating to him as he grows up. He said his dad watches a lot of sports and forces him to be on a team every season. Jordan says he used to like playing sports when he was little but now he's hating it and his dad is all against him quitting. He says he wants time to try other stuff like maybe screenwriting. I totally get it because I can't imagine what I'd do if I didn't have time for my art. "So what about *your* dad? When are you gonna tell him you want to quit sports?" Now he looks really pissed. But not at me.

"I tried. He called me a *pussy*." Jordan looks me right in the eye like he's trying to make a point. Uh-oh. This isn't good. I'm getting the picture. I'm also starting to understand why maybe Jordan made fun of me before. He was just continuing the tradition. All of a sudden I feel so bad for him. His dad's probably never gonna let him be himself. At least my dad *left* so all I had at home was the support of my mom and no potentially scarring criticism.

"What's that supposed to mean?" I'm not actually asking because I know. He just snorts.

"It means his idea of a son is the stereotype sports knucklehead with the cheerleader girlfriend and anything *um else* is not cool."

I wonder where I fit into the *um else* category but my guess is probably somewhere between *wtf* and *not MY son*. It makes me smile just a smidge how the tables turned so quickly and somehow I'm the one now in the more desirable position.

"So I made you something." I blurt it out because I'm feeling brave.

I dig into my bag and just when I'm panicking because I think I lost it I remember putting it in the side pocket to keep it safe. I take a deep breath and pull out the flipbook and slide it across to Jordan. He tosses his hair *I love when he does that* and looks at the flipbook but doesn't touch it. He blinks a few times and then looks around. When he's sure nobody's watching he picks it up and fumbles with it trying to open the pages. I don't think he's ever seen a flipbook before.

"What is it?"

"Let me show you."

I take it and flip the pages so he can see. I do it a couple more times and his eyes follow the magnets. Then I put it on the table and he says *thanks* and takes it and stuffs it in his backpack without looking at me.

I have absolutely no frigging idea what he's thinking. He could be thinking *how cool* this person was inspired to make something for me or *oh shit* this person was inspired to make something for me and I should bolt now. Or he could even be feeling bad because he used to spend his time torturing me and here I am giving him presents. Is he *good* embarrassed or *bad* embarrassed? Maybe this was a bad idea because I could just die right now.

But if I died then I wouldn't have Mom's amazing mac and cheese which I can smell the second I open the door. She uses these three kinds of cheese and bakes it till the top is crispy brown and we fight over the corner pieces. Since Jordan and I did homework at the library after school it's already five-thirty. I asked him if he wanted to come for dinner but he said he had a lacrosse game. I think it's sexy he's a jock but since now I know it's making him unhappy I guess it's not so sexy. I'm also scared that the flipbook made him feel weird. I'm scared it made whatever this is too real for him because he didn't say much after that and then I just came home.

I notice there are already a couple empty beer cans on the table and now sitting down with Mom to eat she takes out another one. Her eyes are glazed over a little and what's weirder is she's not fighting me for the corner piece.

"Okay Mom." I've got a mouthful of cheesy heaven. "What gives?"

"*What* I can't have a few beers?" She says beers like *beersss*. I just raise my eyebrows at her.

"Um okay. We celebrating?" Now she laughs a weird choke sounding laugh. I didn't think it was that funny.

"Why yes honey! We're celebrating your deadbeat dad coming to bless us with his presence tomorrow!" Ah. I get it now.

I get that she's stressed. *Me too* I want to tell her but I don't. She's not in the right frame of mind. After she sucks down another beer I tell her to go watch some bad TV and I'll clean up the dishes. She doesn't argue. Mom falls asleep on the couch watching some stupid reality show about alligator hunters and I go take a shower.

I'm looking at myself in the bathroom mirror and thinking if I were my dad what would my reaction be to my kid I haven't seen in ten years with this face and this body and this haircut. Would I feel guilty I'd missed all these years or *relieved* like I dodged a bullet? My hair's growing in and I can gel it up in a cool way a little now and the scar is pretty covered up. In other words I'm looking less like Frankenstein and more like a Frankie.

I go through my closet trying to figure out what's appropriate to wear to the lawyer's office tomorrow. As if I have any idea. I'm guessing shorts are out of the question but I don't want to look all dressed up like a tool either. Plus since I lost weight some things don't exactly fit anymore. And I'm seeing my dad for the first time since forever.

In the way back of my closet is some old Halloween stuff. There's a cowboy hat and Hawaiian shirt and *yup* a white blazer I got at a thrift store. I think it was for an eighties costume. It still fits because it was meant to be oversized anyway but it needs something. I scan the room.

Bingo. Staring *right* at me is the Morse code alphabet I pinned up over my desk. All kinds of bells are going off in my head like I could say anything I wanted and wear it without people knowing what it says because it's in code. Seriously like anybody even knowing it was Morse code would corner me trying to decipher it.

So what to say? I consider the occasion. Gram is dead and Mom and Dad and I have to reunite in front of a lawyer just to see who gets her filthy ashtrays and polyester suits. Because seriously she was dirt poor so I can't see why this is necessary. I wish I could just write him a letter and not have to see him. And just like that I'm *following my inspiration* again.

No black fabric pen still so I'll use a permanent marker. Down the front lapel I write *Dear Dad* in Morse code. Then I just write whatever comes into my head. All in Morse code.

You left us

Please explain

Did you love Mom

You took our memories

I am an artist

Where are my sister and brother

Am I real to you

I write and I write and it's all in dashes and dots. And before I know it the whole jacket is filled. The clock says it's been hours. I put the jacket on and turn around in the mirror to see it from all angles. *Geez* it's so unique. I can wear it with my black joggers. So retro. I take out my phone and take a few selfies. *Whoa* I really am changing. I never ever took selfies before. I shoot one off to Belinda because I think she'll dig it.

Mom's still passed out on the couch so I just put the blanket on her. The TV is showing some garbage reality show about a nail salon. *Seriously?* I shut it off and head up to bed.

30

"LET'S GO HONEY!" *Um yeah chill.* I'm not the one who spent two hours getting ready this morning but I'm not gonna say that. Actually if you count the time I spent on the jacket last night I shouldn't talk. Mom is looking really nice. If I didn't know better I'd say she were trying to impress the A-hole. But I'm not gonna say that either.

"You look nice Mom." She smiles her *thanks* and then stares at my jacket for a long time. I start to get nervous. "Do you know the code?"

"The what?" But then she winks and pats my shoulder. Whatever. I can't figure people out sometimes.

We drive about fifteen minutes. The lawyer's office is in a strip mall between a sandwich place and a dollar store.

"Ooh fancy." I can't help myself and Mom bursts out laughing. She must be nervous because it isn't *that* funny. But it is actually because suddenly I feel overdressed. We walk through a bunch of people in dirty sweatpants and house slippers standing in front of a sign that says *Robert Cartucci Attorney at Law*. The coolness of my outfit is definitely wasted on them but oh well.

So here's the thing about seeing your dad for the first time since you can pretty much remember. There's no big swell of music or anything. You don't do a big slow-motion hug and spin in a circle. Actually it's the opposite. I look at this guy and I mean physically there's a resemblance but there's nothing in his eyes that make me feel anything but sorry for him. He's got this big belly and a red face that looks unhealthy. Not red from too much sun but more like red from the *inside*. And he's got big sweat stains under his arms.

"Hi." He sticks out his hand to me and I don't even want to take it but I look at my mom and she nods so I do. *Yuck* it's sweaty and I wipe my hand on my pants after. I'm not trying to be rude but I can't help it.

"Alan." The way my mom says his name sounds more like an accusation.

"Mary Beth." He says with this business-like voice.

And that's it.

Mr. Cartucci comes out of the inside office and shakes all our hands and we follow him into another tiny room with a rectangle folding table and one two three four five plastic chairs. Classy. I sit closest to the door in case I need to escape. Because right now I really want to.

But I like Mr. Cartucci. He's got those kind eyes like a nice grandpa or even Santa. I can picture sitting on his lap as a kid and him reading me a story. Then I think just my luck of all the parents and grandparents in the world I ended up with mine. But that's not fair of me 'cause Mom's kind of a rock star.

I cringe when he reads my full name out loud. But I guess he has to. He's reading Gram's will now. Blah blah blah and blah blah blah *wait what?* What'd I miss? Mom's smiling at me but with tears now and Dad *ugh I don't want to call him that* well he just looks confused.

"Do you understand what this means?" Mr. Cartucci is looking right at me. I shake my head because actually I wasn't even listening.

"Could you please repeat it?" I hope I'm being polite.

"It means your grandmother left you a tidy sum. The account is in *your name only* and will mature when you turn eighteen. Then you can either remove the money or reinvest it to earn more. It's up to you." He stops and smiles and his smile is so warm I want to wrap it around me like a blanket.

"Excuse me how much is a *tidy sum* again?" I don't want him to think I wasn't listening but I really wasn't.

"Roughly one hundred thousand dollars." Mom makes a *fwuh* sound like she was holding her breath all this time.

I reflexively look at the Dad dude and he's shaking his head now. I want to ask him what he's shaking his head for but I look back at Mom. We don't say anything but just widen our eyes at each other because we can communicate without words. Then Mom laughs and that makes me laugh and she says *crazy old bird* and we hug like we're the only two people in the room.

"My first art patron Mom!" Meaning the fence and we laugh at our inside joke.

Mr. Cartucci pretty much confirms the rest of it though. Gram owed more on the house than it is worth so the bank owns it now. Like Mom had figured the Dad dude says he doesn't want any of her other stuff so he says Mom could keep anything else left in the house. Mr. Cartucci says *just to be thorough* we had to wait while he drew up a document that says exactly that for the Dad dude to sign.

So we wait and while we wait I daydream about what I would do with one hundred thousand dollars. *Ka-ching!* That's a lifetime of art supplies or a brand-new car or even part of a house for Mom and me *I think*. I don't really know how much things cost. And I do have to wait over two years but still. I'm rich! Or at least I'm not dirt poor anymore. I've seen those stories on TV about lottery winners and how they blow it all in no time and then the friends and family who were the first to put their hands out don't talk to them anymore. I gotta be careful who I tell about this.

The Dad dude goes outside to make a call. My guess is he's telling his other wife that it turns out his mother wasn't dirt-poor after all but his own kids won't get that Hawaiian vacation or pool or whatever because the kid he tossed away got Gram's money. But even more than that according to Mr. Cartucci Gram went out of her way to make a special account just for me so nobody else could touch it. Wow. I say a silent *thanks* to Gram in my head. I know she's watching this play out and laughing. The red-faced dude she raised who never ever came to see her is outside probably rewinding his actions over the last decade in his head and kicking himself.

So speak of the devil he comes back into the room and signs the paper Mr. Cartucci puts in front of him. Mr. Cartucci then calls the lady from the front room in to *notarize* it whatever that means.

"I guess we're done here." Mr. Cartucci shakes all our hands again and gives a pile of papers to both Mom and the Dad dude. We say our *thanks* and *nice to meet you* again and head out into the sunshine.

The pajama squad is mostly gone. Probably somebody complained. They were bringing down the vibe *if that's even possible*. But who cares I just remembered I'm loaded. Or I will be in a few years anyway. Gives me time to work out a plan for the money. I need to be smart about this so I don't end up on one of those TV shows. But *nah* those people blew millions. Even I know the money coming my way isn't the lifetime kind.

"So. Want to grab a coffee or a soda before we head to the funeral home?" The red-faced Dad dude is sweating more now out in the sun and I swear he looks like he's melting.

I actually feel bad for the guy. Mom looks at me and shrugs and so I shrug too and I guess we both feel like *why not* he came all this way. Plus the good guys came out the winners here so I guess we're feeling pretty vindicated.

We walk over to the Sunshine Diner without saying a word. We grab a booth by the front just in case it gets weird and a tall kid with crazy bad acne hands us some menus. Not being mean but I don't think they should let him work out front when his acne is so bad because it's a real appetite suppressant. But maybe that's a good thing for the Dad dude because he apparently hasn't skipped a meal lately. Then I feel something like fear. Could it be genetic?

I'm sort of aware that somebody like me shouldn't be having these mean thoughts about other people and I feel kinda sad it was so easy for me to switch sides. I think maybe I'm just noticing other people more now from the outside.

The Dad dude doesn't seem to notice the kid with acne though. He's too busy staring at my blazer. I watch his eyes and *uh oh* is he reading it for real? He's pretty much following the groups of dots and dashes in the right order and direction. I cross my arms over my chest and move around and put up the menu to block him. Too late.

"I was in the Navy. We learned Morse code." He *was* reading it. Oh shit. And I thought I was being so clever. Mom looks at me and then at my blazer and then back at me and my face is on fire. I'm so embarrassed I don't even know what to say. The kid comes back and we manage to order some food and then the Dad dude speaks again. "You have every right to feel hurt." *Blah blah.* "But in my defense you never responded to any of the birthday or Christmas cards so I thought you didn't want to have anything to do with me." *Wait what?*

"What cards?" And now I look at Mom and she's clenching her hands into fists and looking out the window. "Mom? What cards?" She's not saying a word and my world feels like it's crumbling.

"You never gave *our* kid the cards I sent?" The Dad dude is raising his voice at Mom and some people are starting to stare. I'm looking at him now. I'm looking in his eyes for the truth but he slumps down like he's exhausted all of a sudden. Like the weight of whatever he realized just hit him over the head. "What have you done Mary Beth?"

The food and drinks come and nobody moves. Nobody drinks or eats and we all just sit there like zombies. I think it's pretty obvious we're all trying to digest this new information. Except Mom. Apparently she's *had* this information all along. She's not denying it so I'm trying to wrap my head around why she would let me think my dad didn't care about me all these years. Didn't she know how much that could mess someone up? Didn't she think I'd ever find out?

And just like that my mom loses her halo. I'm actually picturing myself crumpling up the *not my fault* sketches I made for her and lighting them on fire. I'm watching them flame up and turn into ashes. But I'm mesmerized by the patterns of reds and blues and oranges and so as I stand there my anger burns up too. Then I blast the fire with ice water from my fingertips and it sputters out. What's left is a black soggy puddle of mush and that pretty much sums up my mood.

In the funeral home we sit in the front row of about four rows facing a black urn with a framed picture of Gram when she was young. I look around and there are only about five or six people behind us. One or two I recognize as her neighbors but the others I don't know. There's some guy who looks about a hundred years old playing one of those electric keyboards. It sounds like we're at the skating rink. I haven't been to any other funerals to compare it to but this feels pretty pathetic. Aren't people supposed to get up and say nice stuff about Gram? Well my mom and the Dad dude have barely spoken since we left the diner so they're probably not gonna start now.

I can't take it anymore so I stand up and turn around. I don't know what to do with my hands so I shove them in my pockets. *Don't think Hy just speak.*

"Gram was alright you know? She wasn't perfect. She wasn't always happy or even friendly but that made it so special when she was. Her random smiles and laughs were like little diamonds in a dark mine." I hear sniffles now. I think I nailed the metaphor. "We had a *connection* Gram and me. And I for one am gonna miss her." I honestly wasn't even thinking about the fact that she left me money and how that really took planning and sacrifice on her part. But that's nobody's business. "Thanks Gram. Love you lots."

"Amen." My mom pats my shoulder as I sit down. It would've made me laugh if I didn't just find out she's been lying to me.

31

ARJUN BROUGHT HIS baby to the F Mart. The thing is so tiny it looks like a doll. He's got it in one of those carrier things strapped to his chest. I get this flash of Belinda for a second. Anyway Mrs. Fadikar is behind the counter so I ask Arjun if I can get some advice. He's so good at it.

"Want to take a walk?" I nod and we start heading in the direction of the bandshell. It must be somehow pulling us both in that direction.

"So my Gram died and my dad came to pay his respects or whatever you call showing up and not saying much." Arjun knew Gram died but not about my dad.

"How was it seeing him?" I shake my head.

"So here's the thing. He says *I didn't think you wanted anything to do with me because you didn't answer any of my letters.* Or cards or whatever. And I said *what cards?*" Arjun stops walking and so I stop too.

"Oh no. Your mom?" I nod and his eyes get big.

"She won't talk about it. She didn't deny it so I guess she hid that my dad was trying to connect with me for years after he left." He shakes his head slowly. His eyes are sad.

"I'm sorry Hy. That's unfortunate. But I understand your mother's a good person so there must be more to the story. You know *what* she did but did you ask her *why* she did it?" I think about this. Arjun has a way of making me see things from a different angle. "Ask her in a way that shows her you'll understand and not judge. Maybe you'll get an honest answer. Keep in mind parents are only human."

"Ok. I'm gonna ask her." He's got a point about the *only human* thing. We walk until we get to the bandshell. Someone's tagged over one corner of it. What an A-hole. It's disrespectful to tag over someone's piece and now I have to fix it. But I guess it could use a fresh coat anyway. "I wish I had your dad." I say it without even thinking. But it's a compliment and Arjun nods.

"That's really nice. And I know I'm lucky but don't fool yourself. He was strict when I was growing up. I felt pretty suffocated by him *knowing what was best for me.*" He uses air quotes. "I didn't have much freedom to be what I wanted to be. I actually really wanted to be a musician." This surprises me. I know he does some job with computers now.

"What do you play?"

"Guitar." Then the baby starts to cry and Arjun does some bouncing up and down.

"Cool." I want to ask him more about his music but the baby's not getting quiet so he says *I have to feed him his bottle* and we start walking back to the F Mart.

I grab a big bag of chocolate minis and bring it to the counter which must mean I'm upset and Arjun remembers something. "Oh by the way the mural exploded on the internet. It's in the millions."

"Yeah I know. My art teacher put it up on this thing called ArtMattersMore." Arjun gives me a thumbs up.

"Keep up the artwork. I mean it Hy. You've got talent. Don't let anyone or anything discourage you."

"Thanks Arjun. And thanks for talking to me."

"Anytime my friend." And the way he says *my friend* reminds me of Mr. Fadikar.

On the way home I think about what Arjun said. There must be a good reason Mom would do what she did. I seriously want to hash it out with her but she's at the hospital today. I'm really trying to be all cool about it but I'm pissed off. I feel robbed. She actually took things that *belonged* to me. Maybe that's what Arjun meant about his dad knowing what's best for him. Maybe Mom thought she knew what was best for me too.

I'm sitting on my bed plowing through the bag of chocolate minis with Rufus watching me and drooling. "No Rufus. Chocolate is bad for dogs." Technically chocolate is bad for humans too in such a huge amount. *Crap* I hate that I'm doing this. I thought I was over the emotional eating thing. But I can't seem to stop until I feel sick to my stomach. I hate that I'm glad to finally feel sick to my stomach.

I go into the bathroom to pee and on my way out I pull a left into Mom's bedroom for some reason. I never go into my mom's room especially when she's not here. But something is telling me to. I feel like I know her well enough to know that she wouldn't have just thrown out all those cards. She doesn't throw anything out. It's like she has an *I'll deal with it later* attitude. And later turns into *much later* and then that turns into never. Good thing though or I wouldn't have had any stuff for the garage sale. Ha. Silver lining.

I'm looking around her room I'm thinking about how when Mom was busy talking to neighbors outside the funeral home the Dad dude gave me a business card with his name on it and said I could reach out anytime. I stood there thinking about this guy and how my life might've been different if I knew him. I never told my mom about the business card.

I get on my hands and knees and look under her bed. Nothing but a lot of dust. Gross. Then I dig around in the back of her closet. Only old boots and shoes on the floor. I'm about to leave because I feel like a total chump for snooping and then I see an old shoebox on the very top of the bookcase in the corner. It stands out because it's the only thing on the bookcase that's not an actual book. I hold my breath. *Aw man.* Inside is stack of card sized envelopes. Until this very second I thought I wanted to find the cards and now that it looks like I *have* I wish I hadn't. I take the box into my room and put it on my bed.

"Do I really want to do this?" I'm asking my fans watching me carefully from their positions. I mean I can just put the box back and forget about it. But the cards are right in front of me. Mom didn't throw them out so a tiny part of her must've known this day would come.

Ugh. I scrunch all the chocolate wrappers into one big ball and make a jump shot into the trash. Then I give the big wad of wrappers the finger. My phone buzzes. *Not now Belinda.* But I don't say this to her. I'll just answer her later. I pick up the envelope on the top of the pile. The postmark says it's from years ago and there's an address with a P.O. box in the left corner. I open it and the card's in the shape of a snowman.

Merry Christmas
I hope Santa gives you what you want this year.
Love Dad

I put it back in the box and take out another envelope. Same year. A dog holding balloons.

Have a pawsome birthday!

Love Dad

And another and another and another. Well it's just surreal. I feel like I just got punched in the stomach. But honestly that could also be the big lump of chocolate sitting in there.

All the Christmases and birthdays I waited to hear from my dad and he *had* actually thought of me. I sit for a long time opening all the cards and reading them over and over. I check the postmarks and put them in order from first to last. Seven years. Seven *friggin'* years of Christmas cards and birthday cards. The last one was four years ago and I don't blame him for giving up. I would've gotten the message too. But unfortunately it was the wrong message.

"It was *your* fucking message Mom!" I scream and throw the box against the wall and it feels good. The cards go everywhere and I leave them all where they are. There's no point hiding the fact I snooped but I don't care because what she did is *way* worse.

I'm not hungry for dinner because of the chocolate binge so I grab some sprays and get on my bike and ride around the neighborhood while it's still light out. I ride and ride trying to clear my head. I ride past Gram's fence and smile just thinking about her. I want to tell her that her son was trying to see his kid after all. I want her to be happy about that.

I ride to the top of the park and stop at the bandshell. I ditch my helmet and spend the next hour fixing the part where the dumbass tagged over it. It's not even good. Then I just give it an all-over refresh and stand back. It looks really nice again and I'm happy. Wait a second. *Not my fault.* What about the Dad dude? *Holy crap* all this time I'm thinking it's his fault. And now...and now? I grab my helmet and jump on my bike and take off. I pedal as fast as I can and get home before Mom does.

In my room the cards are still all over the floor. There's something about the randomness that gets me thinking about them being suspended in time all these years. I hear the front door open and I ignore it because I'm busy *following my inspiration* and also because Mom and I haven't even talked to each other since yesterday. She finally comes up and knocks on my door. I'm sitting at my desk doing some Spanish homework.

"Yeah?" It's not polite but I'm in battle mode because I know she's gonna freak.

"Oh no." That's all she says when she opens the door and then she backs out. That's it? That's all she's gonna say to seeing the years and years' worth of her lies dangling from the ceiling? The Dad dude's business card is suspended in the middle of them all.

After a minute I hear some crying I think. Well it serves her right. I mean I love her but this is kind of unforgivable isn't it? But then it gets late and I'm about to go to bed and I can't stand it. I have to do what Arjun said and give her a chance to explain. So I knock on her door and there's no answer. And I'm a little worried and I'm thinking about how Arjun says parents are just people too or something like that. So I knock louder and she says *come in* this time in a quiet voice. I sit on the end of her bed because she's all tucked into a ball like she's sleeping.

"Mom." It's not a question.

"Oh honey."

"No Mom. *Oh honey* isn't gonna work this time." She actually laughs and sniffles. Then she sits up against the headboard.

"Your father. He left me. He left *us* when you were so little. He's not a nice man." I'm just staring at her waiting for some big revelation like *he molested you* or *he beat me.* Nope. "I was so hurt I just didn't want to share you after that. You understand?" She sighs. "Not with him. Not with another family. Not when *he* decided."

I let this sink in. Huh. Turns out *Mom* is the A-hole.

32

I GOT A better dad story than you
No shit what?
Trust me. Can u hang after school n grab pizza?
Lemme ask. hit u back
Right on
I want to see Belinda. Somehow she makes me feel normal. Mom and I are on shaky ground for a couple days now. I keep trying to remind myself she's only human. That works out because in my eyes she's lost her halo big time. And I'm not even religious but I always thought of her as this saint of a single mother and now I find out I could've had two parents? But *nooo* because her ego got in the way. She didn't want to *share* me. So she says. But I think it's because she was trying to get back at the Dad dude by taking away his kid. And that makes me really mad because *I'm* that kid. And how could she not think of what that might do to my head?

It just occurs to me that maybe I should call him *Dad* for real now that I know he was trying to be my dad all this time. Maybe I owe him that respect. I still haven't called the number on the card he gave me though. I can't just flip a switch and everything's okay and we're sharing ice cream in the park. Also there was something about the way he looked me over. Like the way my mom's boyfriends look me over sometimes. Like I'm a riddle and they're trying to break the code. Ha that's funny because he actually did break the code. The one I wrote on my blazer like I was all clever. And that was embarrassing but maybe a good thing after all because it got him explaining and that's when I found out everything.

Manny can bring me after school

Awesome

Hey I could get Manny to get you from school too

Seriously?

What time

3:45 main door

"Hy?" Oh snap. I'm busted.

"Sorry Mrs. Wyatt. My mom was telling me she has to work at the hospital tonight." She nods and says *please pay attention* and I feel bad for lying but it sounds like a better excuse than *I'm making plans to hang out with my friend later.* I don't want to disrespect Mrs. Wyatt because she tries hard to be a good teacher. In back of me someone coughs and it sounds more like *bullshit* and this actually makes me happy because it has nothing to do with my name.

The shiny black car pulls up in front of the main entrance and Manny gets out. He's all slick looking with his suit and tie and he walks around and opens the back door. Kids are stopping and whispering and craning their necks to see what celebrity could be in the back. Belinda leans out and she looks like a frigging movie star with big sunglasses and a cool purple cowboy hat.

She sees me and waves and it's hilarious to watch all the kids on the steps look at her and then back at me like *wtf?* I want to laugh because their pea brains can't compute the connection. I wave back like it's normal for someone like me to get picked up in a shiny black car with a driver and hot movie star in the back. Inside the car I high-five her.

"That was awesome. Thanks." She laughs and takes the hat and puts it on my head. Manny pulls away and out the window I see Jordan walking up the block. "Manny can you stop over there?" I can't help myself. I'm pointing to the right and he pulls over. I roll down the window. "Hey."

Jordan stops and looks at me with a big question mark over his head like in the comics. Then I remember the purple cowboy hat is down over my eyes and take it off.

"Uh hi." This time he's the magnet and I can't resist the pull.

I turn to Belinda. "This is my friend Jordan. Can he hang with us?" She looks at him all curious and then says *sure*. I turn back to Jordan. "Hey wanna hang with me and my friend Belinda?" Belinda pokes her head out and waves.

"I got Lacrosse." But his smile tells me I should ask him to ditch. So I do.

"Ditch." He screws up his face like he's really weighing his options.

"Ok twist my arm." The high I feel when he slides in next to me is like I'm inside a helium balloon. But it pops a second later when I see the way Belinda's looking at him. *Oh come on.*

"Belinda Jordan. Jordan Belinda." I'm already regretting this. She's looking at him with those eyes and it changes her from being her chill self to some predator. I give her my best *back off* look and she laughs.

"What's so funny?" Jordan wants in on the joke and we both say *nothing* at the same time. And then we say *jinx* at the same time because apparently we're five.

"Gino's?" I say changing the subject.

"Yeah. Manny you know Gino's?"

"Best pizza around." I'm thinking he could be right. Not that I'm an expert or anything. It's better than Rudy's but Rudy's is closer to my house so that's usually where we go.

"My Dad's gonna kill me." Jordan's eyeballing me and I'm not sure if he means about ditching practice or about *me* in general and I feel the heat creep up my neck. Then Jordan remembers Belinda. "What school you go to?" And she comes to life like a wind-up doll.

"Abingdon Hall." Jordan nods like he knows it.

"I think we beat them a couple weeks ago." Belinda just shrugs. "It's all girls."

"Oh right. I meant the girls' team." I knew he probably didn't know the school but I guess he was trying to look cool.

"We met over at the bandshell." I'm trying to steer us away from the private school thing but it's kinda pointless when you're being driven around by a driver in a suit. Jordan looks at me funny.

"The one in East Park?"

"Yeah."

"What were you doing there?" His eyes get squinty and I think he must know what kids usually do out there and he's trying to picture me doing those things.

"Oh it's just near my house. I walk through the park sometimes to get to the F Mart."

"And I was slumming." Belinda chimes in and we both crack up. But Jordan thinks she's joking so he cracks up too. He doesn't know she actually *was* slumming but with some loser who got her preggo and not with me.

The car pulls into Gino's parking lot and we all get out. Manny tells Belinda he'll wait for us on the other side of the lot. Belinda and I head to a table at the back and Jordan heads to the counter. That's cool of him. A few minutes later he comes back with three slices.

"Can you grab some sodas?" He says to no one in particular and sits. Belinda starts to get up but I block her.

"I got it." I know she expects to pay all the time but I still got some garage sale money. Plus I almost forgot that in a couple of years I'll be rich too. Holy crap. I wonder if I should tell anyone. Like these guys for instance. Or Arjun maybe.

I'm getting three sodas when *no way* Tara pushes through Gino's doors with Jordan's replacement like they're Lord and Lady of the manor with two of his minions following behind. They grab a table right up front. Tara's just so fake I can't even look at her. Lord and Lady Jackass. But I have to pass them on the way back to our table and I can tell they notice me because they get all quiet.

Jordan and Lord Jackass are already having this intense stare-down. Belinda and I are just eating our slices and then suddenly the dude gets up and starts walking to our table with his minions behind him. *Wait* is he going to challenge Jordan to a duel? That would be awesome. Still cracking myself up.

"Leave it Lance." Did Jordan just call him *Lance?* No way. Sir Lance-or-not. It's a funny coincidence but maybe I prefer Lord Jackass. He might too. I make a mental note to ask him later which medieval stage name he prefers.

"This freak show is what you gave up Tara for? Ha. Your loss is my gain asswipe." He looks at me and Belinda like we smell bad. *Yup* he's all class. Sir Lance-o-*naught*. Lord Zero. Senor Nada.

"You can have her man. Sloppy seconds and all that." Go Jordan.

It happened so fast I'm not sure who threw the first punch but all I know is there's three of them on Jordan and Gino the owner is running to the back yelling at us to *take it outside*. Belinda and I run out and she's motioning at the car for Manny. He starts the car and pulls up in front and rolls down the window.

"Hy's friend's getting the shit beat out of him inside. Can you help Manny?" I have such gratitude for Belinda right now.

Manny jumps out and runs inside and elbows his way through the crowd. Tara's all fake whining like a damsel in distress like they're actually fighting over her. *Geez* if she only knew what Jordan said. Gino's managed to pull the two brainless minions off of Jordan and is shoving them out the door. You don't mess with Gino's business. Manny's grabbing Sir Thanks-a-lot by the shoulders and *whoa* tossing him like a rag doll. He puts his hand out to Jordan and pulls him to his feet.

Yuck. There's blood on Jordan's face. I'm rushing to the counter. "Sorry Gino. And thanks. You got some ice for his nose?" Gino hands me a towel filled up with some ice cubes and winks at me.

"I know it's not you guys. Now get outta here before I make you clean up the mess." I give him the thumbs up. Manny shakes his hand.

We're sitting in the car and Jordan's holding the ice pack on his nose. "My fault. I knew that would set him off." He laughs.

"But what else were you supposed to do? He was begging for a reason to overcompensate for his small penis." Now I laugh. Sir Lance-o-*little*. Belinda's so dead-on sometimes.

Jordan insists we drop him off a couple blocks from his house so he can make up an excuse about falling or something. He said it actually worked out for him this way because it could explain skipping practice. But I never get to tell them about my dad or Gram's money. Lord and Lady Jackass ruined the vibe. What else is new.

Mom's in the kitchen putting groceries away when Manny drops me off and I go right past her and up to my room. A half hour later I'm doing my homework when I hear her coming up. The cards are all still dangling and they start spinning when someone comes in and stirs up the air.

"Honey we need to talk about this." I roll my eyes.

"You messed up Mom. What else is there to say?" *I'm* even surprised at my tone but my feelings have changed towards her for a minute.

"I'm so sorry it turned out this way. But you have to believe me I was thinking of what was best for you too." *What?* Now I'm really mad. Revisionist history much?

"Are you kidding me Mom?" I get up and cross the room because I don't want to be so close to her right now.

"What *might* have been best for me was to have a dad!" I'm raising my voice now. "What *might* have been best for me would be to NOT grow up thinking my dad just walked away from me like I was nothing. Like I was unwanted." I can feel my eyes stinging but I can't help it.

There's this weird charge in the air like a shift or something. Mom's face is slowly melting from stock parental defiance into what must be shame or something. She's full out crying now. "I loved you enough for both of us honey. Didn't I? Didn't I love you and protect you and make you feel special?" She's got snot running out of her nose and she looks pathetic. *Gross.* I've never seen her like this.

"Yeah you did. You've always been great Mom." And I mean it. "But maybe because you were trying to be both Mom and *Dad.*" I think about this some more. "Without caring about what *I* would've wanted."

"He could've been a part of your life. But he left." *Wow.* Grudge much?

"No. You can't do that. He left *you* Mom." I think about how she called him an A-hole all my life and I just accepted it. "He was an A-hole to *you*. I didn't get a chance to decide if he was an *A-hole*." I put my fingers up for quotes because that's the only way she ever talked about him.

There's silence for a long time. Or it feels like a long time anyway. Then Mom moves to the door and stops. "I love you honey. So very much. I can't take back what I did but I hope you can forgive me. I kept the cards because I *was* going to give them to you one day."

I'm just so confused. I know she's feeling bad but for once I don't feel like trying to make her feel better. I guess this is *not* a case of misplaced anger. I'm pretty sure my anger is directed at her. Looking up at all the cards I decide I've made my point so this installation can come down. But before I pull them down I take a few pics with my phone from different angles. The pic I take lying on my back is my favorite. Then I snatch the twirling business card and turn it over in my hand. Before I talk myself out of it I type in the number and attach the photo. I hold my breath while my ancient phone struggles to send. Finally a ding and I breathe. Next.

33

"HY MURPHY PLEASE report the principal's office. Hy Murphy to the principal's office please."

Oh no. I feel like Zeus just summoned me and is going to toss a thunderbolt and the whole world is going to watch me go up in flames. What could they want? It can't be good because if it was some kind of academic honor or something they'd give it to my teacher or mail it home. I can barely move but I have to or Zeus will keep shouting from the speaker for the whole school to hear. My only saving grace is that classes just let out and I'm face deep in my locker getting the books I need for home.

I hear some whispering and I just know it's about me because why wouldn't it be? It's not every day the teacher's pet slash freak gets called into the principal's office. I take a deep breath and shove everything into my backpack. Then I head to administration on the other side of the building. Could there be a longer walk of shame? The whole time I'm ignoring the stares and wracking my brain because it could be about any of the hundred frigging things that have been happening to me lately.

I come around the corner into the admin hallway and there's names and titles on all the doors so I keep walking till I find the principal and *yup* it's Mr. Lockheed. The same Mr. Lockheed who told

Mr. Sanchez to erase the *not my fault* from the art room door and the *vandal* wouldn't be punished. Oh god. I'm the vandal.

The door is open and the only way I can describe the feeling I have when I look inside is that it's like I'm in a horror movie. All the monsters from my nightmares are sitting in chairs waiting for me to come in so they can literally jump up and scare me to death and then hack me into pieces. But when I blink I see it's actually Mr. Sanchez and Mrs. Nardo and *my mom* in the chairs across from Principal Lockheed.

"Please come in." Mr. Lockheed doesn't look or sound friendly and all of a sudden I want to run. Just haul ass and never come back.

"Come sit honey." Mom's patting an empty chair next to her. She doesn't sound friendly either but that's no surprise considering how chilly I've been to her lately.

I sit down in the chair without looking at either Mr. Sanchez or Mrs. Nardo. Suddenly I know what I'm doing here. They say right before you die your life flashes in front of your eyes like a movie reel. Well my *life* isn't on the movie reel but every *not my fault* installation is. One after the other. Bandshell. Fence. Door. Library. *Library.* Shit.

"Hy do you have any idea why you're here?" Well I want to say *not till two seconds ago* but I don't. I just shake my head because what if I'm wrong? "Mrs. Nardo has brought to our attention there has been some vandalism in the library." And there it is. I don't move a muscle because Principal Lockheed sounds like he's enjoying this. I think he'd love for me to freak out or something. "Mrs. Nardo will you please describe the nature of the vandalism?" *Stop saying that word.*

I looked it up and vandalism is the malicious destruction of property. My *non mea culpa* is an artistic installment done with inspiration. I sneak a side-eye at Mrs. Nardo and she looks back at me with sad old eyes. I can't tell if she's sad because I disappointed her or she's sad because she didn't know it was me until now.

"Yes well I suppose you would call it a carving. Three Latin words are carved into one of the work tables." Everyone waits because she's struggling to speak clearly but her teeth are slipping so she sticks her fingers in her mouth and jams them back in with a suction noise. "It reads *non mea culpa*. And for those of you who aren't familiar with Latin it translates to *not my fault*."

Well I'm pretty sure the air just got sucked out of the room because both Mom and Mr. Sanchez know this is my work. No question. Even Mrs. Nardo senses the hammer that's about to fall on my head because she makes this gesture with her claws.

"It's quite beautifully done. The carving. I know it's not *ahem* appropriate but I just wanted to add that." Then she drops her claws into her lap and kinda folds in half.

Part of me is wondering why it took so damn long for someone to notice it. Or report it. I mean I know the reference section is no big draw anymore because kids have computers but *still*. Doesn't anyone clean the tables? Oh right. Mr. Mayfield does.

"Are you going to deny this vandalism?" *Shut up with the vandalism already.* "Because I have enough evidence this... this *phrase* is a common theme in your art work." I sneak a side-eye at Mr. Sanchez but he's not looking at me. "And this would *not* be your first offense." I guess Mr. Sanchez would have to rat me out if Principal Lockheed made him because the school pays his salary.

So I just shake my head. First *offense* like I'm a criminal. Whatever. This is BS.

"Do you have anything you want to say?" I shake my head again.

I want to say *sorry not sorry* and *where were you when I was being bullied every single day* and *go after the real vandal who wrote FAG on the art room door.* But I don't say any of that.

"Honey apologize please." Mom sounds desperate. I shake my head again and she sighs.

"Well. You leave me no choice." Principal Lockheed stands up. "Mrs. Murphy your child is suspended from school indefinitely until responsibility is taken in the form of a formal apology in writing and restitution is made to replace the damaged item." *Wait* what? I think I just got kicked out of school.

I'm coming out of the principal's office with my mom and I see Tara in the hallway. Kaitlyn is with her and her eyes get big for a second when she sees me and then she looks away. Is Tara smiling at me? I get closer and *yup* Tara's smiling but it's not friendly. It's more like a *gotcha.*

And that's when I know. She was the one. She told Mrs. Nardo about the carving. Not because she's a good Samaritan and cares about the school but because she knew it was me. Somehow she knew I did it. *Man* I guess she really got me good. Bottom of the ninth and she hit it out of the park. And then I do something that I honestly didn't expect to do. I nod at her like *well-played Tara.* And her smile drops.

Mr. Sanchez catches up with Mom and me by my locker. I'm filling a tote bag with as much stuff as I can.

"It's not fair Hy." I nod because really what else is there to say? "But if you just apologize I'm sure Principal Lockheed will take it into consideration…"

"But that's just *it* Mr. Sanchez." It's the first thing I've said and I feel like I'm going to explode. "That's all he wants. He's such a tool. I'm sorry but he could care less about me or why I did it or what it means or anything. He just cares about his own image. I don't think he should be a school principal." Now Mr. Sanchez nods. I know he's not a fan either.

"But I don't want to lose you as a student Hy." I don't know why but I look at my mom. maybe because I'm proud for a second that I'm important to a teacher and I want to see her reaction or maybe I'm just looking at her for help. I don't want to lose Mr. Sanchez either. Or any of my other classes because I actually *dig* school. Minus the kids. Well *most* of the kids. Ugh. I really didn't think this through.

Mom and I head out through the double doors. She's being cool enough to hold some of the stuff from my locker but I'm sure later she'll be different. I see Jordan sitting on the low wall at the bottom of the steps. Is he waiting for me? Half of me is thrilled and the other half says this is the wrong time to introduce him to my mom.

"Hey." He jumps off the wall when we get close. I want to say *not now I'm being suspended* but I don't.

"Mom this is Jordan." I never forget my manners.

"Nice to meet you Jordan." Mom's face is going through all kinds of expressions. They're subtle but I know her. And right now she's thinking *what a nice-looking boy* and *how well does he know my Hy* and *why haven't I heard about him yet?*

"I'm tutoring him in Algebra. Remember I told you?" *Please don't push for details.*

"Right." She smiles at Jordan too long.

"Nice to meet you too." I can tell he's uncomfortable. "So what gives? Why'd you get called to the principal's and why are you taking all your stuff?" He's so concerned and I just have to say it.

"I got suspended." His eyes go big and his head snaps back. I could've said *I'm a shape-shifting alien* and he probably would've had the same reaction.

"For what?"

"For art." He looks at me like *wtf?* "Okay maybe for *vandalism of school property.*" I use air quotes.

"No way."

"Yes way."

"Why'd you do that?" Good question. Why *did* I think I could just do that?

Then I have this kind of flashback. I went into the library that day feeling pretty bad about myself. And you know what? It was after being harassed by Jordan. No kidding it's easy to forget he was one of the reasons I had to *act out* or whatever you'd call it by doing the only thing I'm good at. And it made me feel better about myself. I'm in the library carving and I'm feeling better. Should I tell him that now? I mean we never really talked about it and he never apologized. Part of me doesn't want to ruin whatever we got going on by making him feel bad at this point but a bigger part of me is mad at him now. I mean he *is* the reason I'm in this position isn't he?

"I gotta go." I turn away because I don't want to stand here and talk to him in front of my mom anymore. It's embarrassing enough to be holding all my stuff and getting escorted out like in the movies when someone does something bad and gets fired on the spot.

"Okay." And that was it. He said *nice meeting you* again to Mom and took off.

34

THREE DAYS. SEVENTY-TWO hours. Four thousand three hundred and twenty minutes. That's enough time for a pity-party. I haven't been out of my room except to watch TV or eat. And when she's home which isn't a lot lately Mom keeps looking at me funny and asking if I'm okay. What am I supposed to say? *I'm fine? No biggie being suspended from school and finding out I could've had a dad. Oh and now that I do have a dad he hasn't responded to me.* Crap. I just want everything to go back to the way it was before. Even though it sucked before. That's what a mess this is.

Jordan hasn't reached out either and I don't care. I was pretty cold to him when I left so I don't blame him. But Belinda's been calling *thank the almighty gods* so finally I call her back.

"Hey."

"What gives loser?"

"I got suspended from school." She's quiet.

"Seriously?"

"Seriously."

"What kind of Hy-jinx could possibly get *your* ass kicked out of school?"

"Hardy har." I'm lying on my bed thinking maybe I should get out of PJs for the first time in days. She's kinda right calling me a loser.

"For real though. What happened?"

"You know how I've been doing my art project all over the place? The *not my fault* thing?"

"Yeeaah?" Belinda knows about mostly all of them. I tell her because that's how we met and I trust her. She didn't tell anyone about the bandshell *that I know of.*

"Well I sorta carved one into one of the big tables at the library."

"Yikes. Carved huh? That's hard to undo. But how long are you suspended? A week?"

"Nah. Indefinitely which means permanently if I don't apologize and replace the table."

"So apologize. What's the big deal? You need money for the table?" I feel myself getting mad but I have to be careful it's not misplaced anger.

"First of all *no* I don't want your money. But thanks. Second of all I'm not gonna apologize because I can't explain it but this principal doesn't deserve an apology. He's such a dick and I just can't."

Something's happening to me. I'm using harsh words out loud and I never would've walked out on the principal a few months ago. I guess I'm just so sick of being bullied and nobody from administration ever helping me or asking me about it. And they knew. They all knew because it was obvious and everyone just got used to me being target practice for the popular kids. And if I didn't complain why step in right? Because then they would be admitting to knowing and having the bullshit *no bullying* campaign blow up in their faces. I'm guessing this is what it feels like to stand up for myself but it doesn't solve the problem of being kicked out of school with two years left.

"Well okay sorry. But what're you gonna do?" Like she just read my mind.

"Dunno." And it's true. I'm really stuck. I mean I got Gram's money coming to me in a few years but even I know it won't last if I don't finish high school and make a plan for the future.

Three more days go by *I think* and I'm not even motivated to get out of my room anymore. Mom's been leaving some food by my bed but I have no appetite. I'm just sleeping or staring into space most of the day and tracing the *not my fault* on my leg with my finger. It's pretty much faded now and I get the urge to redraw it and bring it back to life.

Because really *I* am the walking billboard for this project. And more than ever I want to make Principal Lockheed *feel* what I feel every day walking through the hallways of his precious school. I want to make him understand why I can't apologize. But how do I do that because he doesn't give a rat's ass if I come back to school or not.

And then something un*frigging*believable happens. The home phone rings and for a second I think it could be my dad because I haven't heard back from him yet and maybe Mom gave him the land line number. Mom answers from her room and after I hear a *what?* and *really?* she tells me to hurry up and pick up the extension downstairs. I jump up and hustle downstairs hoping I'm right but it's not my dad's voice. It's a girl's voice.

"Can you please repeat what you just told me?" My mom's talking to the girl who says she's a reporter and she's doing a story and *what?* the story is about me and my art and my situation at school *blah blah*.

"How did you get all this information?" And more important I'm wondering why would she care? She says *an anonymous source.* Half of me believes this is just part of a long dream and I'm about to wake up any second. I *am* in fact still in my PJs.

"Can I come and get the story in your words?"

"Sure." Have at me because I'm all in on this weird fairytale at this point. Got nothing to lose.

For the first time in a while I'm actually glad Mom is around because I wouldn't have known what to say to this person or whether I *could* even say anything being I'm a minor and all. We're sitting at the kitchen table and this reporter named Andrea put a little tape recorder between us. No wait it's a cellphone. That makes more sense because she's super young like maybe just out of college so she'd have the latest tech not some dinosaur recording device from my mom's era.

So she asks me questions and I answer them. Until she asks me about the bandshell. Shite. I side-eye mom for a second because I don't know whether to cop to this. Could I get in more trouble for vandalism? At this point I don't know if it's Belinda or Arjun or the fact that it went viral that tipped her off.

"Okay then tell me about what the project means to you? Why *not my fault?*" I guess she took the hint to move on.

"Well I saw a pattern in people getting blamed or bullied for being different or acting or feeling a certain way and I wanted to create a pattern to offset that." This is the first time I'm realizing exactly what I've been doing.

"The pattern is to defend the targets that can't defend themselves." She's nodding and smiling. I've decided I trust this girl in her wire-rimmed glasses and cool spaceman T-shirt.

"Is anything *your* fault?"

"Um yeah sure." This takes me by surprise. But she's not done.

"So why isn't the *non mea culpa* carving *your fault?*"

"Um. Well I guess the actual carving is my fault because it was someone else's property..."

"Exactly. And you had to have known it would be discovered." Actually maybe I don't like her after all. Then I think *really mature Hy.*

But I go into how I feel about Principal Lockheed and maybe I was subconsciously making a statement about the school not getting involved in my bullying. I point out the fact I made it in Latin for the Lady Justice or *Justitia* holding the scales. I'm getting so deep about it I'm worried I sound like a joke all of a sudden. So I stop explaining.

"Well I think it's a compelling story. And very relatable. So I'll do my best to represent you in a way you'd find appropriate." Andrea the reporter sounds so formal being only a few years older than me. But I guess that's what being *professional* is all about.

She stands up and asks if she can get a couple pictures maybe in front of some of my artwork and I think about what piece I have lying around the house. *Duh. My marching ants.* But they're in my bedroom of all places. After a minute I think at this stage there's no point in being shy so I motion for her to follow me upstairs.

"Oh wow." I can't help but smile because that's a reaction an artist craves. Andrea turns in a circle taking in every wall from top to bottom until she points at the section next to my desk. "There."

"I agree." The ants look really busy in that section but the words are still clear. So I stand in front and then say *wait* and run check my hair in the mirror. It's growing out and not looking half bad actually but I take a little water and spike it up some in front.

Finally I lean up against the busiest wall of ants and kick everything out of the way so the picture won't show a crazy messy room. Andrea laughs and says she'll show me the pic after to *okay* it. There are no camera sounds because it's a phone and at first I just stare like a dumbass but then in my head I hear the *snap snap snap* shutter sounds like the paparazzi are fighting over me and I strike a pose. I make my best duck face and this makes Andrea laugh and that makes me laugh and then I'm being stupid and making my fingers into a gun like James Bond.

We sit on my bed and she scrolls through the pics and as funny as they are the one we both agree on is one of the first serious ones because it has the right *tone* for the article. This whole time my mom has been cool about keeping her distance and not interfering and I think maybe we can start getting back on track with each other because I kinda miss her.

Downstairs Andrea gives Mom a business card and says *nice meeting you both* and heads out to her car. She has a beat-up car like my mom's and I'm thinking newbie reporters must not make so much money.

"I'm trying for this Sunday's Gazette." She's getting in the driver's seat. "So I better hustle." Mom and I wave and turn to go back inside.

"Oh! What name should I use? Your full name?" She's poking her head above the roof. I guess she must know my name from the school. Or Mom probably. *Geez.*

"No just Hy please. H-Y."

35

OK I MISS Jordan. Does that make me a loser? Or what's that word for someone who likes to get hurt? Masochist. They say relationships are complicated and this one *if that's what I can call it* might take the cake. The guy tortures me and I fall for him. But to be fair I know how conflicted he was and he risked a lot to do a one-eighty. Somehow I don't think I was meant to have normal relationships anyway. It was pretty obvious way back which is why I spent so much time on my own.

Mom slams the kitchen door and it scares the crap out of me.

"Wha da?" I've got a mouthful of cereal so I sound like a baby.

"I went to see that lawyer." She sounds really pissed off and I shrug because I don't know which one she means. "The lawyer about your bike accident." Oh that lawyer.

"The ambulance chaser." I'm being a smartass but she's trying not to laugh now so it's worth it.

"The personal injury lawyer yes." She pulls open the fridge and just stands there staring into it.

"Did he tell you to make him a sandwich?" I'm not sure she'll even get this one. She slams that door too. Yikes.

"He said we don't have a case." Mom plops down into the kitchen chair with the bad leg and it snaps. I knew it was only a matter of time. She crashes to the floor and lands on her butt.

"Oh my god Mom." I've got my hand over my mouth because with her legs sticking out in front of her she looks like a doll propped up for a kid's tea party and I lose it.

"Stop it!" Nope. There's no way I can hold back this tidal wave. I'm laughing so hard I can hardly breathe and she's got both hands covering her face so I can't tell if she's laughing or crying. Rufus helps out by charging at her and trying to lick her face with his smelly tongue. She's trying to push him off and I can see she was laughing not crying. I knew it.

"Mom that was brilliant." I draw a 9.0 in my sketch book and hold it above my head. She fumbles to her feet and air kicks the broken chair over and over like a circus clown. Then she takes a big bow in my direction and one in Rufus's direction. He's panting because he's so excited. Man that dog is *fugly*. No offense Rufus. This feels like the right time to let go of all the hard feelings. The embarrassing fall on her butt reminds me she's just a person. "Love you Mom." I'm serious now and she looks like she's going to cry. "Oh please don't. No drama okay?" She *has* to know I'm all out of drama.

"Okay you got it." Phew.

So she pulls up another chair after tossing the broken one out into the yard which I wanna tell her will do nothing for our house's curb appeal and tells me what the lawyer said. To be honest I forgot she was trying to get money from the company whose van ran me off the road. I was thinking the money from Gram took the place of her having to do that. But now that I think about it I guess the money from Gram is meant for me. It makes sense if she sues the van company the money would go to her because I'm a minor. I'm just wondering how much of the money thing is medical bills like she says or maybe she's just looking for a payday. Because I'm pretty sure our insurance is good being she works at the hospital and all. I mean I can't blame her if it's a money grab because we don't have much.

"He says that by law you should've been wearing a helmet because you're under sixteen and as yours was a head injury it falls under that safety responsibility."

I knew it. Stupid me thinking I could go on the big roads like it was my dinky neighborhood. If I could take that day back I would in a heartbeat. Then she says it turns out *she's* actually legally responsible for *me* not wearing a helmet. So if we try to sue them they might countersue us for emotional distress or lost wages blah blah blah.

"What about the witnesses?" I just remembered she said some people saw the van cut me off.

"Well just our luck! One was an old drunk so he's *unreliable* and the other witness wouldn't make a formal statement because she was *undocumented.*" I don't know why but I laugh. And keep laughing. Maybe because I'm already in the mood for laughing and maybe because it's just so crazy. I mean what are the friggin' odds? Mom laughs too probably for the same reasons as me. *Man* you can't make this stuff up. As far as being interesting my life went from zero to sixty in a matter of weeks. Speaking of which *uh-oh* Belinda's now at the screen door looking kinda busted *again.*

"What happened?" I open the door wide and my mom comes and puts her arm around her. She's totally been crying and I'm starting to notice this happens a lot. She's also got a big tote bag over her shoulder.

"My dad kicked me out." I knew it.

"Why?" My mom has no clue what's up with Belinda and what a mess she's in.

Belinda looks at me sort of nervous. Probably because if she's got a bag with her and her dad kicked her out that means she wants to stay here. And that means she has to tell my mom what's up. But I don't even know all of it. I guess her dad must've found out. She sits at the table and wipes her nose with her sleeve. Ick.

"I'm sorry Mrs. Murphy. I…" But she doesn't finish.

"She's preggo Mom." Wait for the disappointment.

"Oh Belinda." And there it is. "Well you can certainly stay with us tonight." Mom's just being nice but I roll my eyes but then pretend I've got something in my eye in case anyone saw it. I'm not trying to be mean because Belinda is so cool with me. But I can't help feeling what I feel. This is *my* mom who's got her arm around Belinda and telling her *we'll figure this out* and *I'll talk to your dad*. But now all the attention is gonna be on Belinda. In my house. Then I remember Belinda has no mom and how selfish of me not to share mine for a second.

"I'm heading upstairs." Mom smiles at me and I'm actually glad to leave them alone because talking about this stuff makes me uncomfortable.

They talk for a long time and I sketch with my headphones on. Nothing like *Punk Immortal* to make me feel included. The energy is awesome and it's like they speak to everybody. I'm sketching a dolphin with angel wings and I realize it's so weird not to have homework. I actually miss it. I guess I like learning and getting smarter and having more things to think about. Mom always says she admires my curiosity. So what the hell am I gonna do?

And what is it with dads anyway. My dad and Jordan's dad and Belinda's dad. All different types but same stress. My door opens and I'm about to yell *knock please* but then I realize there's no way I would've heard anyone knocking anyway.

"Hey." Belinda drops her bag and shuts the door behind her and sits on my bed. I pull my headphones down.

"So um your mom is on the phone with my dad right now." My eyebrows go up.

"Whoa. That was quick." I don't know whether to feel glad or jealous. *I've* never even met her dad yet.

"Yeah. I guess maybe it's the whole *Daddy's little girl* thing. I mean he's not a bad guy but I can't talk to my dad about stuff because he just doesn't know how to deal with me getting older. So we avoid each other lately. Except he found out about the *appointment*." I think about this.

"Hey do you think you might've gotten preggo subconsciously? Like to get his attention or something?" *What am I a psychologist?*

"What are you a psychologist?" Jinx. But she's smiling so she can't be that offended. Ok cool. Good to know I'm not that off the mark. Mom knocks on my door.

"ENTER!" I use my best stage voice. She opens the door and leans against the frame with her arms crossed.

"So he's coming to get you." She's smiling what looks like an *I did it* smile. I look at Belinda because I'm not sure this is the outcome she wanted. Her eyes get watery again. "He sounds like he really loves you Belinda. He says he didn't throw you out. He admits he was angry but that you just left when he asked you about the call from the clinic." Belinda's head is down now.

"He said he didn't want a baby to ruin my life."

"At *sixteen* sweetheart. I understand that. He wants you to grow up and live your dreams first." Mom comes in and sits on the bed. "It's a huge responsibility bringing up a baby." She winks at me. I stick my tongue out at her.

It's way too serious in here so I jump up and grab my hairbrush and sing a song everyone knows. "Oh no baby baby oh no."

"Baby oh no baby oh no…" They join in and we all laugh and sing along in a huddle until we hear a knock and Rufus barks like a rabid dog. I look out my window and see the most awesome silver sportscar. "Calvin Briggs." His hand is about twice the size of mine.

I don't know what I imagined but he's kind of older with a square jaw and gray stripes of hair on the sides of his head like a comic book commissioner or something. His skin is chocolate milkshake and now I see Belinda has his goldish eyes.

"Hy. Sir." Belinda laughs out loud at me. Either because I'm going to have to explain *Hy* so it doesn't sound like I just said a casual *Hi* or because I added *Sir* for the same reason.

We all do our awkward introductions and stand there just as awkwardly for a few more minutes and then Belinda gets in the car and goes home with her dad. I can't help but notice again that her belly looks pretty flat for someone who's supposed to be preggo. But what do *I* know.

36

"**WELL WELL WELL.** I just had a very interesting conversation with your teacher Mr. Sanchez." Mom's in the doorway of the garage.

I'm picking through my art supplies and school feels like another lifetime. Even though it's only been about a week. I'm just a full-time artist-in-residence now. Except this is my actual residence.

"You mean my *former* teacher? I have fond memories of him." Mom rolls her eyes.

"No I mean your *current* teacher because you're going back to school sooner than later." She's smiling wicked now.

"What gives?"

"Turns out somebody called the school and bought the table."

"What table?"

"Stop it honey. *The* table. The one you vandalized. The one that got you suspended."

"Expelled."

"No Hy. Suspended. Enough of this nonsense." She's not having fun with me.

"Who would buy a big vandalized library table?" I'm serious now just to get the rest of the story.

"Apparently an Outsider Art fan." Now I'm really paying attention. I know what Outsider Art is. I've daydreamed *and* actually dreamed about being discovered in my sad-ass neighborhood as the next self-taught sensation.

"How did this person find out about me and the library?" I'm truly stumped. Then it dawns on me. The reporter. As if reading my mind, Mom pulls out her phone and comes over to where I'm sitting on an overturned bucket. I suddenly feel ridiculous in my overalls. One week out of school and I'm busking for change in my own garage. She shows me the article from the online version of the Gazette. *Whose fault is it anyway?* By Andrea Larsen. Hey that's a pretty clever title. And right at the top is the picture of me in front of my marching ants. I grin at Mom because I'm *yikes* famous.

We read the thing together with her scrolling the tiny print too quick and me yelling at her to go back and then I'm grabbing her phone and she's slapping my hand away. We're like The Marx Brothers and *yes* I watch them because one of our TV channels shows them a lot and it's so much better than the other depressing crap. If I want to see regular people hoarding too much stuff or complaining about men I'll just grab a bowl of popcorn and sit at my kitchen table.

The article talks about a sophomore at West Glade High *blah blah blah* suspended for vandalism but *vandalism* is in quotes so that's good. Bullied *blah blah* no support from administration *blah blah blah* expressing frustration through art and on and on. Wow she did a pretty good job representing the truth so far.

"Hey there's a quote from Mr. Sanchez." I'm pointing like my mom's not reading the same thing I am. Duh. *"…by far one of the most talented and inspired students I've had in recent memory…"* I'm blushing and I know it. Mom puts her arm around me. Mr. Sanchez goes on to say that my statement is reaching beyond the walls of the school and is much more important than the so-called damage to an old desk. *Whoa*

I wonder if he's not nervous about his job talking like this. "*There's no self-promotion here. Hy's web of individual pieces is organically woven and connects with an audience through the pure message of inclusion. That's what art is all about.*" I have to read this a few times to absorb it. He goes on to give the link to ArtMattersMore and I send a silent thumbs up to Mr. Sanchez. Awesome. Then there's a picture of the Art room door with the restroom heads spelling out *not my fault*. Well the cat's definitely out of the frigging bag. If Principal Lockheed didn't have proof who did *that* vandalism he does now.

Apparently Andrea also interviewed some random students and teachers who knew me and they all backed up the bullying thing. That doesn't surprise me because you had to be blind not to see it. Plus they were probably hoping to get their names in the paper because everyone wants to be famous.

I think the last paragraph shows Principal Lockheed for the A-hole he really is. He's like *there are no exceptions for vandalism* and *that oak table will cost several thousand dollars of tax payer money to replace* blah blah blah. Nothing about me or why I did it. Whatever. So that brings me back to the fact someone actually bought the table. And it must've been for enough money that they can replace it without using tax payer dollars. Ha.

"So wait does that mean I can go back to school?" Although at this point I'm not sure I even want to. I mean I've been discovered haven't I? Who needs Algebra?

"Well they've got the money to replace the table now." But she doesn't sound so convinced. "We'll go in the morning."

So I take my lazy butt into the shower and stand there for a while. I hope they're not still expecting me to apologize because I really don't know if I can at this point. I mean like Mr. Sanchez says the whole project has taken on a life of its own and is actually speaking for itself. Like it was always meant to be. If I were to say sorry for any of it then that could change the whole trajectory. *Trajectory.* I love that word. What's it called when a word sounds like what it is?

Anyway I'm turning into a prune so I get out. It's just nuts this whole thing. I'm in the Art and Style section of the actual newspaper today and I still don't know who tipped off the reporter. *Ha* listen to me. Tipped off the reporter. Ping.

You're famous can I be your friend?

If I'm famous I don't need you to be my friend

Hardy har so Andrea did you right

Wait what

Belinda knows Andrea the reporter?

Please how else would a newspaper know about your sitch

Shut up

I'm mad because I don't want to owe Belinda for this but grateful at the same time because she seems to really do nice things for me.

She's my cuz

Oh

And like she read my mind…

She was into your story for real

I let this sink in for a second. I'm trying to be objective and I guess it is kind of interesting for an Art and Style section to report on how art *finds an audience in our digital generation.* The joke is it went viral or whatever anyway without input from me because my tech situation is tragic.

k cool thanks

And then I remember.

what about yur sitch

I'm okay ttyl

Which means she doesn't want to talk about it over text.

k later

And it's funny I remember the article also mentioning the *rebellious nature* and I wasn't meaning to be rebellious at the time I don't think. Not for me but I guess it could be seen as rebellious like I'm an outsider. Outside of the trained art scene or outside of society in general. Speaking of which I definitely want to meet the person who bought the table from the school. That's crazy. And does that mean I've got a collector? Whoa. And what's it gonna be like going back to school? I mean I'm kind of a local celebrity now. I wonder if I'll get some respect or be more of a freak than ever.

Well I guess I'll never know. Not according to Mr. Lockheed and his nasty mean face telling my mom that *unless I apologize for my actions* in a written letter to be posted on the bulletin board in the main hallway I will never be allowed to come back to school. Mom's not having it.

"With all due respect Principal Lockheed the school has been reimbursed for the desk. Don't you think this letter will again single out and make my kid vulnerable to the same bullying that started this whole thing?"

"With all due respect to *you* Mrs. Murphy this is actually the second offense and your child does not seem to have any respect for school property."

"It's my understanding that the *first* offense was actually to neutralize another kid's vandalism. What happened with that investigation incidentally?" Principal Lockheed's face gets this dark shade of pink. I wonder what's going on there because Mom seems to know something.

"What if I sue the school for negligent supervision? Would you like to open *that* can of worms?"

Mom's on a roll. She's definitely done her homework. Principal Lockheed stands up and motions to the door with his hand all dramatic like he's in a play.

"If there's nothing further…" In other words *get the fuck out.* Mom raises her eyebrows at him in a *you wanna try me?* I know this one pretty well. Like two animals in a stand-off they glare at each other for a minute.

"Let's go honey." We pass the secretaries on the way out and I can't help but notice they look sort of embarrassed.

37

"IT'S YOUR DAD." Mom's holding out the phone to me. She's smiling? She doesn't usually smile about the A-hole. "Go on honey. He's calling to speak to you not me." I put the phone to my ear.

"Um hi." I really don't know what else to say. I'm kind of mad because he didn't respond to the picture I sent. Why's he even calling?

"Hi there Hy. So your mom emailed me the article." Oh so that's it.

"Oh." Kill me now I have no idea what to say to this Dad dude. Huh. I'm back to that.

"Well first of all let me say what a talented artist you are." Um okay. So why didn't he respond to the picture I sent?

"Why didn't you respond to the picture I sent?"

"What picture?" Seriously is he gonna tell me he didn't get it? "I didn't get a picture. Did you mail it?" No dummy. Nobody mails anything anymore.

"No I texted it."

"To what number?" Uh oh. My face is getting hot because it dawns on me.

"The number on the business card you gave me."

"The *office* number? Because that number wouldn't accept a text message. It's a land line." Arrgh. What an idiot I am. I try to come up with some other explanation that won't make me look like an idiot but there's no use. I'm just not slick like that.

"Oh." That's it. That's all I can get out.

"Well I'd like to see it whatever it is so can you send it to my email address on the card?" Mom's watching me like a hawk. I mouth *go away.* She mouths *make me.* I almost lose it.

"Okay."

"Anyway I'm sorry to hear that you were having a hard time with some kids at school. You didn't tell your mom? She could've helped." I want to tell him that it would've made it worse because then you're hiding behind your parents and kids see you as even more pathetic but I don't have the energy.

"Whatever. I dealt with it."

"Yes I heard. But now I understand you're in a pickle." Who even says that? I guess this guy does. My dad. It feels okay to call him that again because now I know it was just a misunderstanding.

"The principal won't let me come back to school."

"Well that's not entirely true."

"But someone bought the desk Dad. Paid the school to replace it. Can you believe it? Did Mom tell you?" *Wtf Hy.* I just called him Dad to his face. Well technically not to his face but whatever. I think he realizes it too because he's quiet for a couple seconds.

"I know and I'm impressed." His voice sounds a little shaky.

"And Principal Lockheed can't let it go. His ego or something needs me to make this formal apology to the whole school and...and after all this I just can't."

I wonder if Dad knows what a good student I am and respectful to my teachers and everything. I feel this sudden urge to impress him more and explain why it doesn't feel right to do the letter thing for Principal Lockheed. But it seems like he gets it anyway.

"I'm going to try and help. You know I grew up around there right?" I guess I did because Gram still lives here. *Lived* here.

"How come you never visited Gram?" It just comes out. Part of me wants to take it back but another part wants to make him answer. I hear a big sigh.

"Well that's a whole 'nother story for another day." Fair enough but I'm going to hold him to it. "Anyway I went to school with a kid who stuck around there and eventually became the mayor. And we still keep in touch some." I think I see where this is going.

"So how can this guy help me go back to school?"

"The article is a great start. It made it public and to anyone with half a brain it shows it's not a run-of-the-mill vandalism story." Huh. I may even like my dad one day.

So we talk a little more and then he says *let me talk to your mother* and she takes the phone into the living room. I head upstairs and dump my text books onto my bed because if there's a chance I'm going back to school soon I don't want to fall behind. I mean it's been less than a couple weeks and I'm pretty sure I can jump ahead some pages in each class to catch up.

"Crazy. Right Zeus?" He's not smiling but he's never smiling. I know he approves. Then I'm kind of absorbed in the Shang Dynasty when *ping.*

So whats up?

Jordan. My heart trips over itself. How long since I've seen him or talked to him?

With what?

Okay maybe I don't have to be such a tool.

I'm still suspended

I know. I mean with you and me

Oh. And then I just say it because why not?

All the shit you did to me before

Crickets. So then I go for it because I'm pissed.

You never even said sorry

Now I really don't expect an answer because I put him on the spot. I put my phone away and open my Algebra notebook. Ha. Algebra. Bet he's missing me now. But who am hurting really? I probably miss him just as much if not more. And maybe when all this drama dies down I should thank him for inspiring me to react in the way I did. It seems *non mea culpa* either ultimately brings me down or shoots me out of a cannon. But I know for sure my life changed either way. And I don't want to go back to being that scaredy sad-sack I was before. So I guess change is necessary for growth. Whoa. Who is this enlightened soul?

Mom sticks her head into my room. "You doing okay?" I nod and actually mean it this time. "Interesting the way your…*dad* is back in the picture at this point." It sounds like she's still having a hard time calling him that too.

"Wasn't it random? I mean wasn't it Gram dying that brought him back after so much time?"

"Yes. But here's the funny thing…" She sits down in my desk chair and faces me. "He just got divorced."

Mom's eyebrows are arched in a comical *isn't that interesting.* And I'm thinking the only way that could be interesting is if she's still *interested* in him after all this time.

"Mom."

"What?" She does a mock surprise thing.

"*Mom.*" I say it with more warning and she laughs.

"What are you implying honey bee?" *Oh crap* she's got that fake flirty tone in her voice. Please no.

"You can't be serious. What did you or should I say *do you* see in him?" I want out of this nut show.

But then I think back on all the things she said about him and all the names she called him and by all that I guess she was really hurt. And you only get really hurt if you *really* care about someone and they reject you. And it's not fair of me to judge the guy by how fat or sweaty he is because I only saw him the once and I don't *or didn't* like people judging me by how fat or sweaty I am or *was*.

"What happened back then Mom?" I'm trying to think if she ever told me.

"Oh honey I was so young and stupid." She seems to be considering telling me some something. Then she shakes her head and stands up.

She leaves the room and I just get this urge to find the business card my dad gave me and look at it again. I stare at it and *duh* now I can see the number I sent the picture to says *office* and the email is right below it. But that's not the weird part. The weird part is his name. Alan D. Ball. *Come on* seriously? My brain goes into overdrive.

Not only am I realizing that I must have my mom's last name instead of his but also I'm so dang thankful I do. Hy Ball. Isn't that some old-fashioned cocktail or something? And even worse my middle initial is also a *D* so it could've been Hy D. Ball. *Hey guys! I can't find the ball. Did someone Hy D. Ball?* Yup. Dodged a bullet. If my mom and dad ever hook up *said no one ever* I'm not taking his name. I guess mom thought of that when I was born. Or did she?

"Mom!" She comes back into my room with a foamy toothbrush hanging out of her mouth.

"Wha?"

"How come my last name is different from Dad's?" I'm eyeballing her and I can tell she's thinking about what to say. Convenient she's got a mouth full of toothpaste and she sticks a finger in the air and then goes back to the bathroom to spit.

"Well honey." I'm thinking *now the frick what*? "We were never exactly married…" Oh great. I'm a what do you call that? An orphan? No a *bastard*. That's it. But I don't say that 'cause even I know that's dramatic. I just slap my hand over my face.

"Why weren't you *exactly* married? What does that even mean?" She just stands there for a minute looking out the window. "What else don't I know about who I am Mom?" But she's not giving me any more today. I'll just have to figure it out and blackmail her later for something I want.

38

PING.

Sorry

I can't help smiling because it's such an amazing word. I open my other eye and *yup* it's still there.

Thanks

Do I smell bacon? I'm tracing the crack on the screen with my finger and I'm wondering if maybe I can ask my new dad for a new phone. Or at least a loan until I get my Gram money. I'm trying to remember what he does for work. *Something* technologies. Yeah that means he probably gets deals on technology. Duh.

"Honey you dressed? We've got to go in fifteen!" *Wait what?*

"Where are we going?" I'm rolling to the edge of my bed.

"To meet the mayor!" Oh my god. Dad did it. *Thump.*

"I'm okay!" I yell before she asks me because my butt shook the whole house when it hit the floor.

I've seriously got to get a better wardrobe with all these important things coming up all the time now. The whole T-shirt look doesn't express how serious I feel sometimes. But I have this button-down shirt that looks cool buttoned all the way up and if I wear cargo shorts it keeps it from looking too churchy. I wish I had a cool haircut or glasses or black nail polish or anything that made me feel more like an artist but it's okay.

The mayor's office is in one of those giant glass buildings downtown with sub-zero AC that makes the hair stand up on the back of your arms. There's got to be at least twenty floors and the lobby is the size of my school cafeteria. Mom shows her license to the lady at the desk who checks it out and hands a name tag back to her. We have to go through a metal detector like ones I've seen in the movies and I get nervous for no reason. Like the thing's gonna go off and they'll find a gun in my underwear I didn't know about or something. *How'd that get there?*

I'm starring in a crime drama in my head when Mom pokes me in the shoulder.

"Press twelve honey." Right. We're in the elevator and there's a man in a dark suit staring at me for too many floors. So I fart. And it's loud. "Honey!" Mom's trying to sound mad but she's covering her mouth because she's cracking up.

"Consider yourself crop-dusted." I stick my tongue out at the FBI wannabe and he makes a disgusted face as we get off on twelve. Maybe next time he'll know that staring is impolite.

Mayor Sloane is really friendly. He comes out to meet us in his waiting room and puts his hand out to me and says *so you're Alan's kid.* I say *so you're the mayor* and that makes him laugh. He has all his hair and it's dark brown which is the opposite of what I pictured in my head. We follow him into his office and I stop in my tracks. Mom bangs into me from behind and *tsks* in my ear. Until she sees what I'm seeing.

Principal Lockheed is sitting in a chair facing the Mayor's big desk. He looks busted and miserable. Like *he's* the one who got in trouble this time. This is huge.

"I believe you know Principal Lockheed." The mayor is motioning to him and Mom and I both just nod in his direction without saying hello. I mean the guy was *not* cool to us last time we saw him. Plus he only nods too. "Please take a seat." I take the one farther from the principal and Mom sits between us. "So thank you all for coming here as I see there's a situation that needs fixing." He smiles when he looks me in the eyes and I've already decided he's my new best friend.

"If I may…Mayor Sloane." *Lockheed takes the ball.*

"Just a minute." *Oh! Sloane intercepts.* "I've read the article by a junior reporter at our very own Gazette and found it truly enlightening." He smiles that winning smile again. "And it's come to my attention that since the article was published an art patron has come forward and purchased the table in question for substantially *more* than the replacement value. Is that correct Principal Lockheed?" Mom and I look at him.

"*Ahem* that's correct. But…" The mayor cuts him off.

"So the damage to the school was negligible. Or safe to say even profitable?" Lockheed says nothing so he continues. "What is the basis then for the public apology?" Now he's on the edge of his seat all animated. Lockheed sits up taller.

"The message that vandalism is an acceptable form of protest goes against school policy. The student should have come to us about the alleged bullying that was taking place." Mayor Sloan gives him a *seriously?* look.

Alleged bullying. It's so hard for me but I sit here and keep my mouth shut. My mom can't though.

"These are *kids*. My kid doesn't tell me half the things going on because tattling can backfire. The adults should know better and intervene. I know for a fact they knew Hy was a target from what the teachers said. Where is the investigation and discipline for these bullies?" Mom sighs all frustrated.

"What about you Hy? I want to hear from you." My face burns. He must notice. "This is a safe place to speak your mind."

"Um." Here goes nothing. "I hated it but I got used to being made fun of. Like it was never going to change. So my art project was a way to…talk back I guess." I'm getting better at this.

"Principal Lockheed." Mayor Sloan is leaning back in his chair with his hands together. "With all due respect I know West Glade has its challenges. Are you able to see the big picture here?" Lockheed looks down at his shoes and for a second I feel bad for him. But the mayor's not finished. "This student is a bright spot in the murky abyss that is too often public high school. Given the circumstances I personally think the *school* owes the *student* an apology." Oh my god he's on a roll. "And regardless of what your strict definitions and opinions are of vandalism I believe the positive energy generated by this student using *art* as a personal protest to be a shared strength with others in similar situations is in *itself* the only form of apology which should be upheld for all to see." Whoa. Mind blown.

I feel all tingly. I hear the Star-Spangled Banner all loud in my head and see the room painted in stars and stripes and feel like I should stand and salute someone or something. My mom's eyes are watery and Principal Lockheed looks stunned and for a solid minute nobody says anything.

"Well." Principal Lockheed stands up and I think he's going to storm out. But he doesn't. He turns to me and takes a big breath. "It would seem I owe you an apology on behalf of West Glade High. If we failed you by not managing to protect your personal safety well then I'm…personally sorry." Mind blown twice in one day.

"And I'm sorry for breaking the rules." *Wait what?* Did that just come out of my mouth?

It must have because I look around and *I'm* standing now too. But it's true. I've always been sorry for carving into the table instead of using something that could get washed off or whatever. *Wait is* that a smile coming from his crinkly old eyes? I've never seen him do anything but frown before.

Then the next few minutes is a blur. Mom stands and Principal Lockheed thrusts his hand out to shake both of ours and Mayor Sloan comes around the desk. Then the two of them shake hands and say *thank you.* It feels literally like someone takes a big vacuum and sucks the stormy gray vibe out of the room and replaces it with a rainbow. I almost expect to see Principal Lockheed mount a unicorn and ride off into the sunset. But he doesn't because that would be absurd.

"Well Hy. May I call you Hy?" I nod. "We'll expect to see you back in school on Monday." Again with the crinkly-eyed smile. I need time to adjust to this new and improved version of Mr. Lockheed. "And in the future I'll expect you to bring to my attention anyone who bothers you so we can put an end to it." The fireworks grand finale.

"Yes. Thanks sir." My mom puts her arm around me because that's what moms do when they're proud. They embarrass you at just the right moments.

In the car on the way home Mom and I talk about what just went down and how my dad is pretty cool to hook this up. So we're back talking about Dad. And we're both in pretty good moods so I try again to find out more.

"Why did you and Dad never get married?" The smile she had on her face a second ago drops off and she's quiet. Cue the dramatic music because something's coming.

"When we met I was young and your dad was…"

"Older?" I'm a genius.

"Well yes. But also… he was already married." Oh. I didn't think of that. "And he already had kids." Double *oh*. I do the math in my head. "Wait so my half-brother and sister are *older* than me?"

"Yes." This takes a second to comprehend because I always thought he left my mom and me for someone else and had a new family but it turns out *my mom* was the someone else?

"So let me get this straight. You had an affair with a married man and got preggo?" She just cringes. I guess it sounds harsh.

"I didn't know he was married at first honey. He wasn't honest with me." At a stop sign she sneaks a look at me. *Does she think I'll jump out?* "Yes I got pregnant with you. Then he told me he had a family. I was devastated."

"Sorry Mom." I don't know why I said it. I'm full of apologies today. I guess feel sorry for her. She smiles and musses my hair.

"Anyway for a while he said he'd leave his wife and kids for me and I believed him. But he didn't. And then he just moved his family away." *Geez* talk about a soap opera.

"Did they know about you? Or me?"

"Not at first I don't think." She just shrugs. "But maybe his wife knew when they moved or maybe that's *why* they moved. I don't really know."

I still have so many questions like for one why did he leave Gram behind too? But I'm tired. "Was I a mistake Mom?" She shoots a look at me with her eyes wide.

"Not for one goddamned second honey."

39

"SAY WHAT?" SPEAKING of mistakes I'm sitting on the porch step watching Belinda. She's pumping her feet back and forth and the swing is creaking like crazy.

There's a big *Foreclosure* sign on Gram's lawn right in front of the fence. Actually it was hiding the cat I painted so I moved it a little. Like anyone cares. What happened to Gram's cat?

"I said I'm not preggo." Well that makes sense because her stomach is as flat as a board. Her hair's growing back and she's looking like the old Belinda.

"Why not?" I don't really need to know why not but don't know what else I'm supposed to say. She shrugs.

"Dunno. I thought I was but the clinic told me I'm not anymore."

"Well that's good right?" I'm sure this is great news but she shrugs again.

Huh. The fact that she's not jumping up and down because her life is back to normal is weird to me. Maybe there was something about it that she was into. Like she doesn't *want* her life back to normal. She also could've made it all up but of course you can't fake something like that at a doctor's appointment so I guess maybe she was at one point even if it didn't last. What would Gram say? I can kinda feel her presence because this is her porch after all. Maybe she's up there somewhere watching us. And maybe she's pissed because the shells of the sunflower seeds I'm eating are making a mess.

"My dad threatened to send me to an all girls' *boarding* school." Oh man. Even I know that's such a cliche. Right out of the movies. And like this solution ever works. Usually the girl gets even more rebellious and something worse happens before she and Daddy make up.

"I thought your dad seemed pretty nice and not so much like the MIA monster I'd imagined. Seems like he really cares about you." Belinda rolls her eyes. My lips are so puckered from the salt and I'm dying of thirst all of a sudden. "I need a soda."

I jump off the porch and the seeds go flying from my lap. Sorry Gram. Belinda and I walk to the F Mart because where else would we get a soda? I stop in my tracks when we hit the parking lot because I can't believe it. There's a *For Lease* sign in the window. No way. I run inside and Arjun is filling the back case with sodas. At least he's still here for now and I'm glad.

"Arjun what's up with the sign?" I've screwed up my manners but he'll get over it.

"And hello to you Hy." I can't remember whether he's met Belinda so I introduce them again just in case.

"You're leaving?" Arjun nods and hands us each a can of orange soda. We say *thanks* at the same time. *Jinx.* This is getting silly.

"My mother is too lonely here without my father. This store was *his* dream." Arjun closes the coolers and heads back to the counter with the empty boxes. We follow him. "She's heading back to India to be with family."

"But *you're* family." I'm confused.

"Yes but I cannot run the store. My wife and I both have careers and my own family is growing." By *growing* he means the addition of the baby and not that they're all actually getting bigger and stomping on buildings like a Godzilla family. I crack myself up but sometimes my funny thoughts are so random.

Arjun tosses the boxes out the front door and nearly clocks someone coming in.

"Oh! Sorry my friend." In a second I see the *someone* is Jordan and I immediately get tingly arms. Amazing it still happens. But he doesn't seem surprised to see me so I'm thinking he knew I was here.

"Stalk much?" I'm an ace at sarcasm especially when I'm nervous. He just grins and Belinda looks at me then at him then back at me. I can't tell what's on her face but it looks almost territorial. For who though? I can't take any more of this triangle drama.

"You got somethin' against stalkers?" What's with the cowboy accent? But *dang* it works for him.

"*I* do." Belinda's trying to be funny I think. But it sounds kinda mean. Whatever.

"Arjun this is … my friend Jordan." Arjun smiles.

"Nice to meet you *my friend Jordan.*" Then I realize how much I'm gonna miss Arjun.

I need older wise folks to turn to. Like Confucius. I need my own personal Confucius. First I lost Mr. Fadikar then Gram and now Arjun. I do still have my mom *does she count?* and Mr. Sanchez once I go back to school. I feel like I have to repair some trust with Mrs. Nardo but I think it'll be okay because she'll probably forget all this. Then there's Mr. Mayfield the janitor. He seems like a cool dude. Oh and maybe just maybe I have a dad now. What a trip. So I guess it'll even out eventually.

"Seriously how'd you find me?" I'm wondering if Jordan is actually a stalker.

"Actually I ran into your mom and she says you come here."
Right. Nobody needs to stalk me when my mom will tell them anything
they want to know. She's a straight-up information booth. "She said
you're coming back to school Monday." Case and point.

"Yup. Did you get all the details like what I was wearing and
whether I brushed my teeth?" Jordan looks confused but then laughs.

"Nah. Just that you'd tell me about it." Oh well I stand corrected.

"My dad hooked up a meeting with the *mayor*." Now I've got
everyone's attention.

"No way." Jordan leans against the magazine rack.

"Yeah I guess they were friends back in high school and when
mom and I showed up Principal Lockheed was there too." Jordan's
all into it but Belinda's quiet. Maybe because I didn't tell her first? Or
maybe just because she doesn't know Principal Lockheed.

Arjun sits behind the counter and Belinda's sitting on the ice
cream freezer. I'm standing in the middle holding court now. And
the F Mart is my palace. For now at least. I'm telling everyone about
what happened and a couple people come in and buy snacks and
leave again. I tell them how Mayor Sloan made the speech about *kids
like me* being bright spots in the abyss and shouldn't be punished. Or
something like that.

"I know I'm not doing it any justice but it was powerful. And
you know what? When Principal Lockheed said *sorry* to me I said
sorry too. Not because anyone made me. But because I wanted to. It
just felt right." *Whoa* then it hits me and I look at Jordan and he gives
me that shy smile that we're both thinking the same thing. That it was
him feeling that exact way with me the other day.

Belinda buys a big bag of licorice laces and hands a couple out
to me and Jordan as we head over to the bandshell. I still haven't told

anyone about my money from Gram and I wonder if I even should. It's not like I get it for two years and who knows if these friends will even be my friends at that point. I surprise myself with this one. I just got these friends and I'm already writing them off. I know what Mom would say. She'd say I'm just protecting myself. So that if I lose them for some reason I'm not crushed. Whatever. She's probably right because she talks like a therapist sometimes. Not that I've ever been to one but I've seen them in movies. Maybe that's what I should do with my Gram money. Go to a therapist and get some good advice if I can't find my own Confucius by then.

"What the frick?" Belinda stops walking and I must've been daydreaming because I run smack into her. Only now I see the police tape and whole crew of people around the bandshell.

The yellow tape and blue uniforms get me shaking because I feel like I'm finally gonna be busted for the mural. Shit. And I only just climbed out of the other sack of trouble with the school.

"I'm going." I spin around and start speed walking in the other direction. Jordan grabs me by the arm.

"Wait. You got to own this now. They know it's you." He's pointing at the crew of people because one of them is pointing right at us. *Double* shit.

"Hy Murphy?" There's a tall lady not in a uniform rushing over to us and Jordan drops my arm.

"Just be cool." Belinda whispers like she's done this before.

"Are you Hy Murphy?" But all of a sudden I'm not afraid because she's smiling and she's got an accent. So I just nod. "My name eez Stephanie Gireaux and I represent zee Gireaux Art Gallery downtown." *Wait what?* I think the accent is French. I do this shake my head back and forth thing like in the cartoons because I can't believe this is real. Plus even her accent is cartoony.

"You know that spells GAG right?" It's the first thing that comes to my mind and she laughs out loud. Even her laugh has a French accent.

"Oui. I love it. And so fitting because we do *zee* Outside Art." I think she means *Outsider* Art but I'm not going to correct her. "So I see *ziss* article online about *not my fault* movement and I ask where to find *ziss* mural." For once it's not my mom blabbing. Or is it?

"But why is there a cop here?" Because that's what I'm really concerned about.

"Ah oui! *Ziss* park is property of *zee* city no? So I have been given permission from Mayor Sloan to include *zee* mural as a remote *ee*nstallation in a new show at my gallery." She waves a hand with all this serious bling on it. "And police have to make *zee* barrier around to protect." I want to tell her in this part of town she more likely needs a barrier around that bling on her hand.

But wait. Two things strike me at once. One. My piece is being included in a show at an actual art gallery *yikes*. And two I don't own it. It's like I'm getting a crack lesson in who actually owns street art.

"That is badass. So people are gonna come here just to see it?" Belinda is puffed up like a peacock. "Bonjour. Je m'appelle Belinda. I'm Hy's agent." What is she doing? I just glare at her.

"Bonjour Belinda." This Stephanie woman isn't buying it for a second.

"Hy has a whole body of work you need to see." *Jesus Belinda.*

"Agreed." She hands Belinda her business card and winks at me. So that happened.

40

I MAKE A beeline for the art room. "Mr. Sanchez!" I'm all out of breath and he jumps in his chair. I guess I surprised him.

"Hy!" He comes over and gives me a big bearhug. It feels more like two months not two weeks since I've been in his class. Probably because I've missed him and his class the most. I've got about fifteen till the first bell so I try to tell him everything really fast. I guess he hadn't heard anything because he's saying a lot of *what?* and *excellent* and *victory*. With *victory* he throws his arms up in a V like we're on the same team and I just made the game winning goal. *God* it feels so good to be back in his classroom I want to cry. He told me to follow my inspiration and it led me all the way to this point.

"I just can't thank you enough Mr. Sanchez." Uh oh. My voice just cracked for sure and he just pulls me into another bearhug.

"I just saw the diamond in the rough Hy." Ha. I'm a diamond.

"Can you do me a favor?" I pull the business card out of my pocket from the gallery and hand it to him. He looks at it for a minute and then looks at me with a question I'm about to answer. "So the last part of the story is that this lady Stephanie was roping off the bandshell Saturday with the police and a whole crew and everything. And she says she got permission from the mayor which makes sense on account of our whole meeting with him…"

"Permission for what?" Mr. Sanchez's eyebrows are way up.

"To include the mural as an installation in her show at the gallery. I guess like an Outsider Art show or something." Mr. Sanchez just shakes his head kind of like how I did when she told *me*. "And my friend Belinda said *I'm Hy's manager and you need to see the whole body of work blah blah*." He's got a smile that's starting in his eyes and spreading like wildfire across his face. "And I was embarrassed but then I thought I do need someone to help me. Like represent me. And you know my art so well and all…"

I'm babbling and kids are starting to come in for class and take their seats. He gets it.

"We'll talk. Come see me after last period." I nod and sit too. Julian looks happy to see me and says he's glad I'm back and Mr. Sanchez lets us work on our comic strip.

The next couple of classes go pretty well. Maybe I'm imagining it but it seems like people are leaving me alone. Leaving me alone in a good way and not in a mean way like purposely ignoring me. But *whoa* could it be out of some kind of respect? What a concept that little old me would ever earn something like respect from the popular kids? And just in time for me to not give a rat's ass. Still cracking myself up. Anyway now that I'm freed up from that shite maybe I can focus on what's important like catching up in my classes and not blowing this opportunity with the gallery.

Then I'm walking to Algebra and there's that girl with the pink hair I saw digging the *not my fault* door stencil I did and she raises her hand way up when she's just about to pass me. I don't know why but some anti-gravitational force lifts my hand too and as pink hair passes me she slaps it with a loud "*Hy-five!*"

She smiles and I smile too because I can't help it and what it means is that everyone at school must've connected the dots and they now know that all of it was me. The door and the library table and the flyers at the antibullying assembly. Maybe from the article they know about the mural and the fence…wait *the fence!* I gotta somehow get that before the bank knows about it don't I? I wonder if that Stephanie gallery person knows about it. I'm thinking about this when I hear someone call my name. Or at least I think I do because again my name sounds like a common salutation. Ha. I like that word *salutation*. It sounds so formal.

"Hy!" Kaitlyn is jogging up behind me and I stop.

"Hey." She looks different. Better. Less make-up I think. Yeah that's it. Huh.

"I just want to say…" She's looking around like a nervous chihuahua. "That I think you're really cool with everything you did and well I'm just sorry I let someone like Tara decide who I got to be friends with." *Whoa* ok. That took guts.

"Oh thanks Kaitlyn. I get it." And I really do. Kaitlyn looks like I just told her she isn't going to the gallows or something. I'm thinking that maybe she gives other people too much power over her. Including now me. I mean I'm flattered but maybe she's just trading one kind of popular for another. Like I'm the flavor of the month. But she was nice to me *before* I was cool so I could be wrong. Anyway she gives a little wave and kind of bounces off down the hall like a rabbit. *Geez* that girl is peppy. I'm thinking of all the names people would use to describe me and peppy wouldn't even make the list. More like *schleppy*.

Speaking of *not* peppy people I stopped in at the library and Mrs. Nardo is hugging me with her birdie arms. I never noticed before how much her birdie arms are like Grams' and it makes me miss Gram all over again. I sort of hug her back but I don't want to break her and plus the old people smell is too strong at this close range.

"Oh I am just so happy you're back!" Her fake teeth make a suction noise on the word *back* and I'm afraid they're gonna pop out and land on me. I'm not trying to be mean but it's a real fear. I wonder if the technical term would be denturophobia? Ha. I'm smiling now but probably not why she thinks. But seriously I owe her. Even though she had to tattle she stood up for me in the lion's den when it mattered. I'm probably one of the only kids who even talk to her or see her as a real person.

"Thanks Mrs. Nardo DaVinci. I'm actually glad to *be* back." She gives me another little squeeze and slumps back into her stooping posture.

"They came with a big trolly thingie and took the table." Her eyes are all lit up and she's pointing a crooked finger sort of in the direction of the reference section.

"My biggest commission so far." I'm being funny but it *is* kinda true. Even though I don't get the money.

She chuckles and waves me off because a kid is waiting to check out some books. I've never seen him before. *Geez* he looks twelve. He must be one of those geniuses who skipped a couple grades or something.

"Later Mrs. N-D!" Okay what was *that?* I know what that is. That's me on a whole new level of cool. That's right. Uh-huh. You know it.

"Lunch?" Whoa. It's like rapid fire today. I've never been pulled out of my head by so many people so much *ever.* Jordan isn't just anybody though.

"Like in the cafeteria?"

"You know somewhere else they serve food?" He's being a wise-ass but it suits him.

"Well I'm just used to eating outside now." Do I really need to say why? I mean he's been there when I've been ganged up on. Hell he's even been the instigator but I try and push that from my mind.

"Yeah but it's raining and I don't bring lunch from home." Oh. I'm about to tell him I'll catch him after lunch but it's no fun eating in the rain.

"Okay."

My heart's pumping hard like we're going into the *belly of the beast.* Jordan doesn't seem fazed at all. He gets on the food line and I look around for an empty table. I guess I'm haunted by this place because nothing ever good happens to me in here.

And then I see her. The star of my nightmares. Tara's with her usual group of bobble-heads over at a table in the far-left corner. Except Kaitlyn's not with them. But then I see her too and she's at a table by herself on the opposite side of the cafeteria with her head down. I watch as Tara and her crew look over at Kaitlyn all obvious and then laugh. I elbow Jordan and nod in Kaitlyn's direction. He sees what's going on and he nods back at me.

"Hey is anyone sitting here?" Kaitlyn looks up startled and I can tell she's been crying.

That bitch Tara. I hate using that word but if the shoe fits and all that. What a waste of space. I wonder how insecure someone's got to be to make other people so miserable all the time just so they can feel superior. Kaitlyn shakes her head *no* and so I sit down and take out my sandwich. Egg salad. Ugh. May as well be a *fart* sandwich. From now on I probably should think about what my lunch smells like if I'm gonna eat with people. Jordan sits next to me and wrinkles up his nose. I elbow him in the ribs and Kaitlyn laughs. She looks happier now.

"Hey Hy." Then Julian's standing there with his tray.

"Julian! Sit with us." He looks glad and I introduce him to Jordan and Kaitlyn when he sits. I notice he gives her a shy smile. Uh oh. *Wow* lunch is so fun I don't want to go to class. I notice Tara looking over at us a couple times but she's not making jokes anymore.

The bell rings and as we head out Jordan goes to return his tray and I stand right next to Tara's table for a second. I'm feeling strangely bold and I just stand over her and she knows I'm there but she won't look up. Jordan comes back and Kaitlyn and Julian stand behind me. My whole body is vibrating.

"We done here Tara? We done with all this crap?" And I almost laugh out loud because I don't mean to sound like the hero finally standing up to the villain but I probably do.

Anyway she knows exactly what I mean. Her friends are quiet and the whole lunchroom seems suspended in time. She's picking at a hot dog bun I'm sure she has no intention of eating and after a few seconds she snorts without looking up at me.

"Yeah. We're done." And the crowd goes wild. *In my head at least.*

41

"DO I LOOK ok?" I can't believe it's finally here.

Actually it's only been three weeks but it feels more like three years. Seriously it's not every day you get your own curated show. As a teenager. What? Somebody pinch me. Mom circles me like she's my fairy godmother and I feel like Cinderella. Or Cinder*fella* maybe. Ha. I'm wearing these rad shiny fake snakeskin pants she got me at Manic Fashionz. The blue-black color changes in the light and my white button down is a nice contrast. I thought about wearing one of my own creations like the Morse code jacket but I think it would've looked awkward like I'm trying too hard. Plus it was a personal message for my dad and that's nobody's business. Mom looks kinda dorky next to me in her flowery dress but it's okay. Moms aren't supposed to look cooler than their kids.

A horn beeps outside because Belinda insisted on Manny picking us up and I guess it definitely feels more like going to the ball in a carriage instead of in a pumpkin.

"Hey Manny. Thanks." Manny gets out and touches his driver's cap at me in a half salute thing. Did he always wear that cap? I don't think so because I probably would've remembered. Maybe he saves it for special occasions.

"No. Thank *you* Hy." I just stare at him a second. He smiles at me with his eyes and it seems sincere. I'm wondering if it's about my friendship with Belinda because I don't know why else he'd be thanking *me*. So when he opens the back door for us I smile back at him big and Mom and I scoot in next to Belinda.

"Whoa." Belinda is rocking a gold sparkle tube top and shredded jeans that set off her caramel milkshake skin and some bad-ass vintage high-tops.

"Dy-no-mite Belinda. And you've got enough hair again for some *mini*-puffs." She smiles at the compliment and then laughs because she knows I'm making a joke about her desperate attempt at the big mouse ears she had before. I bet she regrets shaving her head in solidarity with me but it's all good now. We've been through a lot in the not-so-long time we've known each other. I think about what my life was like before I just happened to meet her at the bandshell that day. I mean it's hard to even remember because it's like I stepped through a portal. And the Universe better zip that sucker up because I'm not going back through it *ever*.

We pull up outside the gallery. It's on the bottom floor of a two-story building with big glass windows in front. *No way* there's a crowd. An actual frigging crowd in front of the building with more people crammed inside the big glass windows. I just stand there blinking for a second. But I know I'm not in the desert and this is no mirage.

The next hour is a complete blur. The first thing I see when we go inside is *not my fault* painted in huge black letters on the wall. There's a bunch of writing below it like in a real art gallery describing me and my project.

"Hy!" Stephanie floats out of the crowd and wraps her arms around me before I can step back. She reeks of some really strong perfume. I mean it's an okay smell but it seems all the fancy people here are trying to out-reek each other with designer smelliness and it's giving me a headache. But I'm not complaining.

I get swept around the big white space and introduced to all kinds of people who grab selfies with me in front of huge posters of my installments like the mural. There are pieces of Gram's actual fence cutting across the room *how'd they get those?* and they made a replica of the door.

Then I see it. The library table is at the very back of the room and I walk over to it and even though it says *don't touch* I touch the carving because *well* it's mine. But wait it's actually not mine because the little plaque says *'non mea culpa' on loan from Allison Ball.* A girl with blond hair walks up and I look at her and I know right away where I know her from. My yard sale. I also recognize the guy standing next to her.

Wait a frigging minute. And just like that my brain is a slot machine and the name Allison Ball lights up like I've hit the jackpot.

"*You?*" She's smiling at me guilty-like.

"Yup." She shrugs with her hands out. "What can I say? I'm a collector." But she's so much more than that. I'm seeing double. I just shake my head because it's crazy how this is all coming together like a big puzzle. Like my life was all jumbled a few months ago and the *not my fault* project helped me put together the borders and the little clusters of middle pieces and today they're all fitting together. I feel like crying now but I can't do that so I excuse myself and hide in the bathroom.

I don't know how long I'm in there because after I splash cold water on my face I open the door and they're all standing there. Together. They see me and the room gets so quiet like a giant vacuum just sucked all the air out of it. I expected to see Mr. Sanchez and Arjun and Belinda and Mom and Jordan and even Mrs. Nardo. But Principal

Lockheed and the mayor and Mr. Mayfield and *Dad?* Shit. *Don't cry don't cry.*

Mom holds what I'm guessing is champagne and comes over and hands me a soda in a fancy glass. Then I notice everybody else is holding a glass of something too.

"To Hy! An art*eest* extraordinaire and social commentator for *zee* next generation!" Stephanie's accent makes the toast sound even cooler *if that's possible.*

"To Hy!" All the glasses are being thrust into the air and I feel like my head's going to pop like a balloon. *Too high* is right. I close my eyes and think about my fan club back in my room and then I open my eyes and see the flesh and blood faces of a *real* fan club here in this room and seriously I want to scream and laugh and cry all at once. But I don't do any of that because there's a dude with a camera who gets down on one knee and starts snapping pics like the paparazzi.

Someone yells "Speech!" and it sounds suspiciously like Belinda disguising her voice. So I take a deep breath and try to get a hold of my nerves.

"*Um* I'm kinda overwhelmed by all this. But I want to thank everyone for everything." There are some laughs and I realize that was pretty lame and generic so I keep going. "And I hope the message is clear." *Come on Hy give your fans what they're waiting for.* "Stay true to yours-elf." My voice cracks. "And if someone can't accept that *well* too frigging bad. It's Not. Your. Fault."

Mic drop. The place erupts in applause. But for real this time.